INTERCEPTIONS

A NOVEL

STACI ROBINSON

Cold Tree Press
Nashville, Tennessee

A note to the reader:

The author of this book has encountered many people through the years in both her personal and professional life, and this story was inspired by some of the things that she has learned and experienced. However, Interceptions is a work of fiction, and none of those people are portrayed in this book. Names, characters, places, and incidents are either the product of the author's imagination or used fictitiously. Any resemblance to actual persons, living or dead, business establishments, events, or locales is entirely coincidental and is used with the intention to give the novel a sense of reality. Although some real New York and Los Angeles institutions, stores, restaurants and the like are mentioned, all are used fictitiously.

Published by Cold Tree Press
Nashville, Tennessee
www.coldtreepress.com

Printed in the United States of America
ISBN 978-1-58385-149-4

ACKNOWLEDGMENTS

Thank you Mom... for *everything*.

Thanks to my husband, J. Peterson and my baby boys for being so patient this past
year and giving me time to edit this book that I've written so many years
ago and decided to finally publish.

Thanks M. Monjauze for making me quit my job to pursue my writing.

Thanks S. Neal for saying to me once long ago, "You know what, Stace, you
should write a book." And thank you for giving me that confidence
to actually do it.

Thanks D. Walker for your opinion, an opinion that has always been golden to me.

Thanks L. Lenherr for telling me, "Don't wait any longer, just do it."

Thanks E. McCarden for sharing this publishing journey with me, a journey
we've laughed through, been frustrated through, but one that we've
learned so much from.

Thanks X. Robinson for all of your edits and words of encouragement.

Thanks T. Occomy for playing a key role in the whole equation.

Thanks A. Chow for your expert eyes.

Thanks H. Gottfried, C. Harris, Wiggle, L. Sechser, Stacey J., Denbro, G. Quinn,
Marcus and Big Curty for your support through the years.

Thanks Amanda Metcalf for your intelligence, Peter Honsberger for your
acceptance and creativity, Dan Flora for your objectivity, Marie Brown
for your faith and Marvin for this original idea over a decade ago.

To Dad… for all of your wisdom and warnings,
even though I didn't listen most of the time growing up.

INTERCEPTIONS

A NOVEL

STACI ROBINSON

CHAPTER ONE

Although the smog was hiding in the crisp Los Angeles night, you could still smell the stale air as the Santa Ana winds whisked through my sunroof. Babyface's "Whip Appeal" rattled the cheap radio speakers in the back of my ragged Toyota Camry as my best friend Marie and I flew up the freeway, passing the LAX International airport, northbound on the 405. Both of us, consumed by our own thoughts, sat in a comfortable silence. The speedometer pushed 85 mph, but I ignored the possibility of getting nabbed by the Highway Patrol. The faster I went, the faster I'd get home to my fiancé.

We were returning home from a "girl's weekend" in Palm Springs. Marie and our other roommate Jana had planned the weekend soiree to lure me away from Ricky, the man who she and the others believed I was "too wrapped up in." They spent the weekend warning me of the consequences I would face if I didn't get a hold of my life and start to do "my own thing." But after two nights of champagne and gossip and a morning of pedicures, manicures, facials and massages, I was more than ready to head back to L.A. one night early. Now, only two and a half miles to our exit, a feeling of anticipation and relief engulfed me.

Reaching to turn down the radio, Marie asked, "Did you call Ricky to let him know that you were coming home a night early?"

"No, I'm going to surprise him."

Marie raised her eyebrows and shot me a look of uncertainty. I avoided her stare and glanced upward through the open sunroof. A 747 jumbo jet soared directly over us, seemingly almost scraping the roof of my car. She turned the radio volume up to blast the sounds of Prince's "Erotic City." "Aww, shoot! This is my jam," Marie announced as she started dancing in her seat, wiggling her butt as if she were gliding down a Soul Train line.

With only a couple exits to go, I grew anxious thinking how good it felt to be struck by the Love Bug.

Ricky and I met during our junior year at UCLA. I had admired him for most of the quarter during a Historiography of Colonialism in Africa class we'd both taken, when one day he finally noticed me checking him out from across the lecture hall. I got butterflies in my stomach when I saw him lurking by the exit door after class ended.

"How ya' doin'?" he asked as I brushed by him without looking in his direction.

"I'm good. How you doin'?" I slowed my step, glancing up at his deep brown eyes.

"I'm alright," he said. His grin was much more confident than the one I was wearing. He walked along with me out of the school auditorium and into the fresh but gloomy morning air. Ignoring the thick stream of students as they moved in and out of our shared space, he tried desperately to catch my eyes. He grew frustrated as I deliberately looked every which way but his. When he turned his body and walked backwards, still never falling short of the beat of my stroll, I couldn't help but laugh. Face to face now, our eyes were forced to meet. I wondered which he would stumble over first, his words or the backward path of his big feet.

His smile was innocent as he tried to make the kind of small talk a seventh grader would make at his very first dance. The tiny gap between his two center teeth added character to his handsome and warm personality. "Are you going to the review session tomorrow?"

I nodded my head. "Yeah, are you?" I said, knowing that I'd had no intention of going before he asked.

"No, but do you think we could hook up before the exam so I could get the notes. I can't go because we have a late practice," he explained. I thought to myself, *Oh no, a football player.* Bad news. Most of the athletes around the campus were fairly decent guys, but the girls who entered their world were often cut out of the story before it got to the "good" part. But he was so tall and handsome that I didn't care if I only got a small part in this one.

"Sure," I said. "What's your name?" I asked.

"Ricky." His hand was calloused, but warm.

"Stefanie Pointer. Nice to meet you."

"You too," he said.

After seven sweet months of spending every possible moment together, he moved into the townhouse apartment that I shared with Jana and Marie. It didn't make sense for him to renew the lease on his apartment, especially since he was spending every night at mine. Between my school loan and his football scholarship, we were scrimpin' and scrapin' to eat two full meals a day. We decided that if we shared rent, we would be able to afford a few of the luxuries that most college students couldn't. Three months after Ricky moved in, on my twenty-first birthday, he sold his stereo and his television, borrowed some money from his older brother and bought me a diamond ring.

"Will you be my wife?" he asked as he pushed the ring across the table sliding it by the plates of the hot, steaming breakfast I'd cooked for him.

I sipped the tall glass of pulpy orange juice savoring the moment. I peeked at him over the rim. Even though I'd drunk every bit of juice that was in the glass, I still held it to my mouth, almost as if I were hiding. I was speechless.

Reaching across the table and taking the glass away so that he could see my bewildered expression, he asked earnestly, "Well?"

It was only for a moment that I relaxed the muscles in my face staring at the blue velvet box that sat aside the Aunt Jemima maple syrup bottle. "Yeah, I want to be your wife. But…"

"No 'buts'…now sit down and open it." Ricky was proud of whatever was hidden inside the tiny box. I peeked inside and discovered a tiny solitaire diamond sitting on a simple gold posting. My eyes welled up and I glanced at him. His smile was vibrant.

"Gimme that." He grabbed the ring and placed it on my finger and announced, "Mrs. Stefanie Powers."

I stared at the ring.

Mixed with emotions of excitement and anxiety, my mind raced into the future. Ricky, however, had no fear. He had it all planned out. He was set on attaining his lifelong goal, which was to earn a living playing professional football while I would stay at home to have his babies. Because I'd grown up in a close-knit, two-professional parent family, where both a college *and* a graduate degree were *expected,* my plans were dramatically different. With hopes of gaining admittance to a top ten law school, I was set on a course to become a ferocious prosecutor. I dreamed of the day that my name would feature *Esq.* as its suffix. Of course I wanted the family, the picket fence and lots of children, and maybe even a dog, but that would come much later. That would come *after* I earned my J.D. But for now, I decided to let Ricky bathe in his fantasy of life as a professional athlete in the NFL.

We exited the freeway and Marie noticed what good time we'd made. "Do you realize that we made it home in an hour and forty minutes?"

I smiled, pleased with my driving prowess.

"Putting *my* life in danger 'cause you're desperate to get home to this man of yours," Marie half-joked.

"Yep. And it feels good." My grin was shameless. I was done. I was open and smack in the emotion that some believed made the world go round.

I opened the front door of the apartment and was slammed with the sounds of N.W.A.

"Dang, he's gonna get us all kicked out of here if he doesn't turn that shit down," Marie said as she chuckled and ran upstairs to her room. "See ya' in a few days!" she yelled from the top of the stairs before she let out a sarcastic laugh. Ricky and I rarely left our room to join them in the common living areas. Everything we did was done in our room. It was our own little cave.

I opened the door to our bedroom and heard the shower running. "Damn," I whispered at the mess. Clothes were strewn across the bed, the dresser and the vanity. Socks and shoes covered every inch of the gray shag carpet, forcing me to kick everything aside to make a path to the bathroom. Empty Popeye's Fried Chicken bags sat on the stereo, and a half full soda cup sat on the windowsill.

The door to the bathroom was halfway open. A cloud of steam seeped into the bedroom, causing a light fog to dampen the mirrored closets. Unsure of what was about to go down, my stomach grew queasy. He was in the shower and I knew this meant that he was going out. I sat on the edge of my bed and tried to calm the apprehensive feelings that crept inside of me.

I knew if I just barreled into the bathroom and demanded to know where he was going, the end result would be unpleasant. I pondered my feelings as I sat and waited. Where was this place that he called "out" anyway? Lately, it seemed that night after night Ricky would jump in the shower then pull on his jeans and Nikes, spray on some cologne and kiss me good-bye. And I would sit there and watch him leave like a lost puppy wondering how long he'd be gone.

"Well, where exactly are you going?" I would ask.

"Out," he would say. And then, with a swift kiss on my lips, and a reassuring smile that he'd be back soon, he'd be gone.

As I rehearsed the words to keep him from going anywhere, he appeared. "Hey," he said unable to hide the confused look on his face.

"Hi." I jumped up, my Adidas duffel bag dropping from my shoulder. My eager smile asked him to reach out and hug me. He didn't.

He frowned. "What are you doing back?" he asked, almost in an accusatory tone, trying to project his words over Ice Cube's blaring lyrics.

I turned the volume down. "I missed you so much I couldn't help but come home early and surprise you."

"Oh... but I have already made plans with Jason and Malik."

"I came home early to see you. Plans can be canceled, right?"

"I can't because Malik is already on his way to get me."

"Well call him and tell him you aren't going. See if you can catch him."

"I didn't know you were coming home tonight."

"I didn't either. But I'm here, so cancel. C'mon, call," I urged.

"How come you didn't come home tomorrow?" he whined.

"How come you're trying to stall me so Malik will leave before you call him?" I asked.

"Whatever, Stefanie." He turned his back.

I watched him search through the closet for something to wear. The fluffy white towel clung to the lower half of his 180-pound lean black body. Droplets of water trickled down the small of his muscular back. His skin was a shade lighter than bittersweet chocolate and as smooth as glass. He had deep brown eyes and full pretty lips. And even though, at that very moment, his disposition was heartless and uncaring, he looked good enough to eat.

Silence filled the room. I wondered who would speak next.

"Where's my Yankees cap?" he asked.

I looked around the room, saw it, but didn't say anything. "You really are going to leave, aren't you?"

His words were facetious. "Naw... I'm getting dressed just to stay home."

"I come all the way home from Palm Springs a night early to see you because I missed you and not only do I have to watch you get ready to go 'out' but I don't even get a hug or anything."

Silence.

Getting frustrated, he asked again, "Do you know where my hat is or don't you? C'mon, Stefanie, they are on their way. You and I go through this EVERY time and I'm never ready when they get here because of it. And then they talk all kind of mess about me and you being shacked up and you trying to control me and shit."

"Whomever *they* is—when *they* get here, *they* can take their sorry black asses back home or *they* can go on ahead without you." I shut my eyes and took a deep breath trying to inhale the air finding its way through the crack in the open window. I hoped it would cool my simmering blood.

I sat down on the corner of our queen size futon bed in disbelief. He was now fully dressed. Yankees cap and all. Every other second, he glanced my way, but never long enough to catch my eye. I got up and followed him into the bathroom. He ran the half-wet toothbrush across the front of his teeth and over his tongue quicker than the time it takes to blow out a candle. I watched him pull off his baseball cap, brush what little hair he had, squirt a hint of cologne across his chest then around to the top of his shoulder blades. I was able to predict each step. It had become such a routine. I knew his every move.

For some reason though, this time was different. This time at the very second that he put his baseball cap back on, a feeling of urgency swept through me; my time was running out. "I can't understand why everything seems like it is going so well with us one minute, then the next minute you want to go be with your friends. I came all the way home to see you and it just seems like you don't care." I sighed. "Come on, Rick, please don't go." He gently pushed me out of his way, passing through the doorway and into the bedroom to search for his keys.

My pleading tone quickly turned to anger. "I can't believe this. You are so rude. And besides, where is it that you are going anyway?"

"Out."

"And where is this place you call *out?* I mean really, Rick. You go there so often. Can I at least know *where* 'out' is? Is it a club called 'Out?'" I asked sarcastically. "Or is it some secret place that I can't know about? Or maybe it's another girl's house."

"Stefanie, grow up." He stared at me as if I was his five-year old little sister and grabbed the keys off the dresser.

"Grow up?" I nodded like one of those dashboard dolls with the bobble head. "You know what? I will do just that. As a matter of fact, I'll start tonight. When you come home I'll be so grown up that I will have your bags packed and on the street. Because a grown woman wouldn't take this. A grown woman wouldn't have your sorry ass. She'd have a real man. A man that would be happy to see her and spend time with her and take her out with him to these parties that you go to. A man that would respect her enough not to leave her at home, waiting for him every night."

Sighing deeply, he said, "Go find yourself one of those men then." He used his body to push me out of the way again. This time it wasn't so gently.

Using all of my anger as my strength, I pushed him back. He fell backwards but caught himself.

"Are you crazy?" The vein on the left side of his neck popped out.

"Actually, yes I AM crazy. *You* are making me crazy."

"Well sorry, I ain't tryin' to be with anyone crazy."

I can call myself crazy all day long, but there's something about when someone else calls me crazy that sends me to whole new level. A bolt of adrenaline surged through me. I balled up a fist and drew it back. My intention was to really show him crazy. But within seconds, I was falling backwards. I grabbed at my face over my right eye, desperate to make the sharp pain go away.

He'd hit me with an open hand.

"I can't believe you just hit me," I whispered, glaring at him from my good eye. The tiny stars blurring my vision prevented me from seeing the expression on his face.

In three seconds, like a snake, he slithered out of the bedroom. The front door slammed and echoed in the apartment. I lifted the window shade to cast my final glare. Malik waved from his Jetta, totally unaware of the horrible incident that had just taken place. Ricky lowered himself into the passenger side and shot a look my way that went right through me. I ripped the diamond engagement ring off of my finger and stomped into the bathroom. As I angrily flushed it down the toilet, watching it swirl away, I screamed a string of obscenities. I didn't care if Jana and Marie heard me. I didn't care if the neighbors thought I was crazy. I didn't care about a single thing.

Five minutes later, I cried myself to sleep.

The fluorescent glow of the clock radio peeked through the darkness. 4:45 am.

I patted the empty spot in our bed where Ricky should have been. My stomach turned inside out. I buried my face in my pillow trying to keep from crying, but as the first tear streamed down my face, a slight throb tightened the right side of my cheek. I touched it with my fingertip, winced and walked gingerly into the bathroom. I flicked on the light so I could see myself in the mirror. Purple and puffy, my right eye was swollen completely shut. *What had I got myself into? I never imagined Ricky turning into a violent person. What was I going to tell my friends? Did Marie hear the whole thing? Did my other roommate hear? Did he tell his friends? Behind the worried reflection in the mirror, there was one concern that only I could see.... Was he ever coming home?*

Ricky was under an enormous amount of pressure ever since his college football career was coming to a close. Only a few would be selected to go on to the next level and Ricky's chances were better than most of his fellow teammates, but not guaranteed. Although he had an outstanding senior season and remained at the top of the national ratings charts at the wide receiver position, according to the experts, he wasn't "big" enough to persuade the NFL scouts to take a chance. In the past, he seemed confident in his athletic ability; but lately, because his future was to be determined in the upcoming months, his confidence was lacking. He put on an Academy Award winning performance in front of his friends, acting as if he wasn't fazed by the uncertainty of his future. But in reality he was terrified of failing in the only career he'd chosen or prepared for.

Over the last academic quarter, he had lost what little interest he'd had in his studies. But as a college athlete on full scholarship, eligibility was always the top concern. Fortunately, we had enrolled in the same classes. I became his very own private, personal tutor. I helped him do all the research for his papers, helped him proof all his papers, and I even prepared extensive and detailed study sheets for him to use in the days leading up to his midterm and final exams. We'd beat the system by developing our own. Some days he would attend the first fifteen minutes of class, wait for someone from the athletic department to walk past the lecture hall to check the attendance of the athletes, and then he would leave. I stayed to take notes so that I was able to prepare him for the exams. Ricky never cared about the content of the material enough to digest it. He just wanted to pass the class. According to him, it wasn't necessary to flood his brain with course work that he would never need again. If it didn't benefit his future success on the playing field, it didn't matter. To him, football was his life. This desperate ambition allowed for him to disregard everything else. And lately, even me.

His intense focus on football even began to affect his sleeping pattern. He would lie in bed, eyes wide open, and try to calm his mind. He feared not getting an invitation to any of the post-season All-Star games. He knew that just one invitation would propel him into a higher round in the upcoming draft. He worried that none of the top agents would be interested in representing him. He wondered if he would be able to stand out at the post college combines and whether or not he would run an appropriate time in the 40-yard sprint. And most importantly, he worried whether his phone would even ring at all on the day of the draft.

Between his snores, he tossed and turned endlessly. I would lie on my back wide awake, fearing not that he'd fail, but that he'd never recover from the shame if he did. If it wasn't his tossing and turning that kept me up in the middle of the night, it was him gently nudging my arm, often wanting me to watch some old late-night television show with him.

"Baby, wake up... wake up... have you seen this movie?"

"No, I haven't seen that one," I would say half-asleep, not knowing and not caring whether I had or not.

"Well get up and watch it with me."

"Rickeeeee," I'd groan. "I have class in the morning."

"Please," he'd beg. "You don't have to go to class. I'm gonna take care of you. Remember?"

I would ignore him and try to fall back to sleep.

Then he would break out with something childish, irrational or desperate. "Damn, Stefanie, I can't sleep and you don't even care."

Although he was being nothing short of unfair, I reminded myself that he was going through a lot at the time and I would hang in there until we got past the draft. "Okay, let's talk. What's bothering you?"

He would never admit that he was scared. "Nothing. I just want you to watch this movie with me."

And with that, I would always sit straight up in bed, rub my eyes and give him my full attention. The faithful companion of the soon-to-be NFL wide receiver. I hoped, for his sake.

CHAPTER TWO

The sun began to rise and the first signs of daylight seeped through the windows of our bedroom. I quickly rose to my knees, grabbed the cord and yanked the blinds to shut out the morning rays. A sharp pain shot through the center of my head, reminding me that Ricky had almost knocked me out the night before. I wrapped myself in our comforter, sat cross-legged at the foot of the bed and peered between the thin slits in the shades. No sign of Ricky's return. Hopelessness set in and slowly I repositioned myself in a fetal position beneath the covers and fell back to sleep.

I looked at the clock when I heard a light tap at the bedroom door. The faint neon glow now displayed 11:45 am. I felt drugged.

"It's Marie," a voice whispered outside of my room.

"I'm asleep." I hoped she would not just charge into my room.

"Can I come in?"

"No."

"I know what happened, Stef, so just let me come in." She cracked the door and peeked through.

I rolled onto my other side and faced the wall. She tiptoed across the room and spread out across the foot of the bed. I shut my eyes and put my arm across my face so she wouldn't notice the black and blue bruise.

Marie said, "Ricky told me what happened."

I opened my eyes. "What? When did you talk to him?"

"He came home late last night and came right upstairs. He knocked at my door and asked if I would come out into the living room and talk to him. He told me about your fight and what he did to you." She rearranged her position into an upright, sitting one. Her pink curlers peeked from beneath a navy blue faded bandana. Adjusting the tie of her bathrobe, she wiggled her "Winnie the Pooh" slippers as her feet dangled, just barely reaching the floor.

With her one hundred and two pound frame and size zero clothes, Marie was the tiniest in my circle of friends. We called her "Chip" because she was both the same color and the same size as a Hershey's chocolate chip.

"Oh, so now he's just going to go and tell everybody."

"C'mon now... it's not like I'm *everybody*. He felt so horrible about it that he sat up and tried to explain himself to me over and over again. He told me that he doesn't know what came over him and that he just lost it."

"*Lost* it? Yeah—if he *lost* anything it's me."

"He said he couldn't ~~believe he did that. He claimed he never~~ hit anyone before. He thinks this whole football thing, with the draft and everything, is getting to him and making him crazy." Marie sighed, knowing that there wasn't any excuse that would have made it okay. "Stef, I know what he did was wrong but..."

"But nothing," I said trying to act like I wasn't hopeless and weak. "He should have never done that."

"I agree with you one hundred percent, but you know that he is under a lot of pressure right now. I know there is no excuse for what he did, that's not what I'm saying. It's just I know he loves you so much and I would hate to see you two break up over this."

"What do you mean, break up over *this*? *This* is serious!"

"I know it is and in no way am I saying that it should be taken lightly. All I am saying is we all know that Ricky is not a violent person. Come on now, he has never even raised his voice at you. He said you pushed his buttons."

"Yeah, I figured he would blame me."

"No, he takes all the blame. It's just that he said you swung first and that it was a natural reaction to slap you back."

"I did, but how the hell is one of my punches going to actually *hurt* him?"

"Look Stef, I know you are hurt right now, but please don't throw this all away until you talk to him. You know he loves you more than anything and the whole world knows how much you love him. You guys are a match made in Heaven. You exude this aura of love whenever you're together. You have this little love bubble following you guys," Marie chuckled. She was right. For some reason, everywhere we went we attracted the endearing smiles of passing strangers.

Our conversation was halted by Ricky's sudden appearance. Marie bounced off the bed and was gone.

Ricky stood in the doorframe. I looked away.

"Hey."

"Hi," I said without my lips moving.

"Can I come in?" he asked hesitantly.

"I guess," I said nonchalantly.

He sat down on the corner edge of the bed. "You know I'm sorry about what I did to you, Stef."

I forced myself not to look anywhere near him.

"I don't know what came over me. I love you so much, Stef, and I don't want what happened to be the cause of us breaking up. I can't even begin to tell you how bad I felt all night."

With that, I had to break my silence. "How bad *you* felt? Oh, please.

You can save all that. How do you think I felt? Sittin' here in the room all night not only in pain from a throbbing face but alone and wondering where you were."

"I was upstairs. I slept on the couch."

"And that is supposed to make me feel better?"

"Look, if you want me to move out, I will. But please believe that I will NEVER do it again. I have never hit anyone and I promise I will never hit you again. Ever. I promise. You are the reason for my happiness. If you left me, I'd go through the rest of my life trying to find somebody that makes me feel the way you do and I know I'd never find her. It's you that I'm supposed to be with. I promise I will never hurt you. I promise. You just have to give me another chance to show you."

Though I tried to be unmoved by his apology, it was a sales pitch that any girl in love couldn't deny.

"I have asked God to give me the strength to control my frustrations. I prayed all night. Can I lie next to you?"

I felt I should say no, but couldn't. Didn't want to say yes because that would've shown how weak I'd become for him. So I didn't say anything. He took that as a "yes" and cautiously slithered his smooth, ripped body into the bed, and put it right up alongside mine. His stare was contrite. "I swear I didn't mean for last night to happen."

Instead of responding, I stared back at him and watched him fall into a deep sleep. I snuggled up close to him and pulled the covers over us. Sharing the same pillow, I could feel his warm breath on my face. I admired his long eyelashes and his thick, soft lips. His complexion had turned silky from the long hours at training camp in the afternoon sun. I kept a few inches between us and admired his sculptured cheekbones. I often wondered whether he truly was as handsome as I thought or whether it was the love I felt for him that made him so beautiful to me.

CHAPTER THREE

A *short ways from UCLA, in Ladera Heights, Michelle DeVeaux's alarm* clock radio sounded at 6:00 am. She groaned, reached her hand out of the pale green fuzzy blanket to hit the snooze button and drifted back to sleep. Eight minutes later it went off again. This time before she hit the snooze button, the voice of KKBT radio's Steve Harvey wafted through the dimly lit bedroom. His sidekicks, the "Angels," chuckled lightly in support of Steve's sardonic humor. Michelle turned up the volume. Steve was busy mocking a caller who had just called in for the "Freestyle Friday" contest. She lay in bed and listened to two more callers. The next one sang an old Heatwave song and the last one tried to sing Brian McKnight's new hit. All three singers were faced with the whirling sound of a trap door and a subsequent dial tone. Michelle thought the people that called in to sing *a cappella* on the air were nothing short of idiots. She couldn't understand why anyone would ever embarrass themselves on the radio like that, all for a dumb prize. If she had it her way, she would pull the trap door on everyone. A commercial blared through the speakers, giving Michelle an excuse to slide her naked body from beneath the covers and head to the bathroom.

She tied her hair up and hid it beneath a purple shower cap before she jumped into the hot, misty stream. A fainting spell caused her to rock backwards. So she balanced herself by grabbing the handle on the glass shower door and stood as close to the forceful shower jet as possible. The warm spray of water hit her directly in the face as she attempted to wash away an ugly hangover.

She ignored the knock she heard through the noisy running water. It could only be her mother making sure she didn't oversleep. Ten minutes later, she heard her knocking again. "Jesus! Can't a girl take a decent shower around this place," she whispered as she turned off the faucet and snatched a fluffy pink towel from the nearby rack. Soaking wet, she hopped out of the shower, cringed from another sharp pain, and walked towards her bedroom door. "What, Adrienne?!" she yelled through the door.

"Nothing, honey. Just wanted to make sure you were up. And the door was locked so I couldn't peek in to see."

Michelle shrugged and marched to the full-length mirror near her vanity area. Droplets of water trickled down her slender cocoa bronzed body. She coated herself with lotion and kissed the mirror. "Damn girl, how on earth is it possible that you look so damn good *this* early in the morning?!" With heels, she stood over five feet nine inches tall and on a good day weighed 125 pounds. She touched her "c" cup size boobs and thanked the Lord above for their perk as she jiggled them lightly and strapped them into a lavender push up bra.

"See you later tonight!" her mother yelled through the house as she walked out the front door.

"Good-bye Adrienne," Michelle mumbled. She wondered where her mother was going so early in the morning. As long as Michelle could remember, Adrienne never had a job. They lived off the large sums of money Adrienne had won in lengthy, legal battles against her husbands, one through four.

The lack of respect Michelle had for her mother was derived from her poorly conceived attempts to find a man to "father" Michelle. Michelle's father left Adrienne the moment she became pregnant. Her mother's desperate effort to move them from their poverty-stricken neighborhood and into the prominent community of Ladera Heights was a long, tumultuous road. The beautiful, little angel that Michelle had been before she hardened into a selfish, loveless young adult had endured more pain and irreversible emotional damage from the countless men her mother had flaunted in front of her daughter. Night after night, as Michelle blossomed from a young, jump-roping, ponytail-wearing girl into a confused pre-adolescent, strange men would parade through their home as her mother would continuously disregard her daughter's desperate plea for attention.

Now, standing an inch away from the mirror, she studied a pimple that was just forming on her chin. She dabbed a speck of toothpaste on it, an old remedy her mother taught her, and sifted through the sixty-three pairs of shoes in her closet to find a pair to match her brown Bebe suit. She ran a handful of Sebastian Wet through her curls while she searched the house for the keys to her car. She glanced up at the message board and saw that her mother had scribbled a note, informing her that "Michael called."

Michelle rolled her eyes.

"Puff... where are my keys?" she asked her cat. "And what the hell does Michael want may I ask?" *Michael Sinclair,* she thought, *so fine, but so broke.*

Michelle had swung in and out of Michael's life for the past year waiting for him to surprise her with the news that one of the major record labels finally signed him to an artist deal. But the moment she found there was a possibility he may never "make it" as the singer he'd aspired to be, she fled. Nine of the record companies rejected Michael's demo and Michelle just didn't see it happening for him. She decided she would just pop back into his life when and if he ever did finally get signed. In the meantime, however, she decided there were many more opportunities that she needed to explore.

On her way to the office, she stopped at a red light, looked over and saw an older distinguished black man in a brand new white Mercedes sedan. His suit and tie were impeccable and his sunglasses were sleek. The sun glared off his shiny cufflinks as Michelle stared in his direction, waiting for him, willing him, to look her way. The half-second glance he gave her caused her to smile desperately. When the light turned green he sped off.

"Damn," she whispered.

CHAPTER FOUR

M ichelle glanced at the clock that sat over her head in the receptionist area. 4:45 pm. *Finally*, she thought to herself. It had been a long Friday. Previewing the night ahead and her plans to go out with her friend Kim, she was eager to get out the door. Fridays were designated nights for The Roxbury, the place to go if you wanted to see celebrities or those who were merely trying to become celebrities. Nouveau riche black men and women filled the tiny bar that hung off the edge of Sunset Boulevard in West Hollywood. Michelle knew that she had found the perfect spot the first time she'd spent an evening there. The men that crowded the dance floor and the bar areas, whether they were adorned in finely threaded European clothes or Nike sweatshirts with baseball caps turned to the back, all left the club in Mercedes, Range Rovers, BMWs, or Porsches. Diamond medallions swung from their necks and Rolex watches hugged their wrists. Any race, any age, any height or any weight. Whatever you wanted, you could find it at The Roxbury. Kim and Michelle renamed the bar "the Market."

Michelle had met Michael there the year before. She noticed him peering through the crowd at her from across the room. Within minutes of their introductory conversation, she found that he was searching for a record deal. Although his achievements in the industry were limited, he embroidered them, dropping names such as Boyz II Men, En Vogue and Bobby Brown during their light and casual repartee. Michelle built castles in the air and pictured herself walking down the red carpet at the Grammies with her new man. Poised, but oozing with duplicity, she slipped Michael her phone number and walked away. But less than a year later, she discovered that her superstar was still broke.

"Sunrise Cruises," she said picking up one of the blinking lines.

"Michelle?" a familiar voice asked.

"Michael," she replied, dryly.

"I can't believe I finally caught up with you."

She whispered a lie. "Michael, my boss is standing right here."

"Okay, call me later."

She hung up the phone and laughed. *Get a clue, dummy,* she thought. She laughed some more. Michelle never actually *liked* to be rude to Michael, or anyone for that matter. But she didn't understand why most men couldn't just get the message. Ever since Michelle had dumped him, Michael had been calling her morning, noon and night. Every time he called, she brushed him off with some excuse. And still, he kept calling.

She wasn't trying to grow with Michael or any other man. As she would often say to her friend Kim, "The time has come for me to be courted and supported." Because of her great beauty she felt that any man would consider her to be a prized possession and would be willing and ready to do so. Problem was, she couldn't find the right winner for such an extraordinary prize.

Hours later, she and Kim pulled into the parking lot of The Roxbury. Michelle looked over at Kim before she turned the engine off and sighed. Even though Kim had just stepped out of the salon with a fresh press n' curl and a new "bronzy brown" paint job on her finger and toenails, Michelle thought she was in desperate need of a full makeover. At that moment, however, she decided to bite her tongue. She knew if she mentioned that Kim's rust colored, African-esque outfit was absolutely horrific she might rustle Kim's feathers and ruin the evening. Instead, she redirected her thoughts to herself. "So Kim, guess what? I have decided to change my plan?"

"What plan?" Kim asked.

"My find-a-husband-plan."

"Oh yeah, that plan." Kim chuckled and rolled her eyes.

"Forget all that trying to find a *fine* man n' shit. I'm looking for a man who has something to show for himself," she explained.

"Something to show? What? Like a Mercedes?" Kim laughed.

"No," Michelle pouted, "Come on. I am serious. I want a man who has made something of himself. You know, usually I am trying to scope out the finest, richest brotha' in the place, but now...." Michelle explained.

"But now you've lowered your standards and you want just the richest. Forget how he looks, huh? Why don't you just look ahead and see what he drives up in."

"Shut up." She hit Kim on the shoulder. They both chuckled as they got in back of the long line that snaked around the corner of the club. "I just want to make sure I ain't trying to *grow* with another man. Forget that. I'm trying to find a man that doesn't need a teammate to win... just a woman to take care of, have his babies, and spend *his* cash. You know?"

"Michelle. You need help." Kim felt sorry for Michelle. She knew her friend was lost, searching for herself through someone else.

"The men here in L.A. are all dogs anyway, so it's time for us to join this doggy dog world of theirs and go for what we want."

"Suit yourself. But I think you should stop setting standards, making plans and scheming. Just relax. Have a good time and the right man will come around. Dang, Michelle, you act like your clock is ticking and your time is running out," Kim said. "Be alone and explore who you are for a change. You don't ALWAYS have to have a man in your life. Find yourself."

"Puhleeze. I do that every night!" Michelle exclaimed, laughing at her own joke. "I'm tired of buying batteries."

"And Michelle, quit thinking that ALL men are dogs." Kim eyed a brotha' standing about ten feet ahead of them in the line. "There you go. Check out eleven o'clock. Brown leather jacket," Kim discreetly whispered trying to talk without moving her lips.

"Not." Michelle twisted her expression. "He can't be an inch over five seven. And look at the man's shoes or look at his gear for that matter. He knows he ought to be 'shamed coming up in here dressed like that."

Kim looked down at the man's unkempt, grungy loafers. She tried to hold her laughter, also noticing his tired leather pants. "Umm excuse me... how are you gonna dog out the poor brotha' like that?"

"*Poor* being the indicative word there," Michelle said raising her eyebrows. "Girrrl, he didn't even have any socks on and he thinks he's getting in *here* tonight? Please. He's gonna have some cold ass feet sitting out here in line wondering why they won't let him in." Michelle pointed her eyes in the direction of a late model navy blue Porsche that pulled into the parking lot. "Now that's what I am talkin' about." Even though the windows were tinted, it was clear to them that the driver and the passenger were tall, black and according to the car they arrived in, rich.

"Remember the last guy you met who drove a Porsche?" Kim laughed. "What did he tell you he did for a living?"

"He said he was a *pharmaceutical salesmen*. Had me going too. Driving a Porsche and living at home with his mama selling drugs." They both laughed loudly, causing everyone in line to stare. Some of the girls standing close by began to whisper.

After waiting in line for more than twenty minutes, they finally flashed their IDs to the bouncer. Kim put hers back in her wallet, making her way inside, failing to notice Michelle had been stopped for questioning. "There is absolutely no way that you are 22," the bouncer suggested flirtatiously. Annoyed by his assumption that she would be the slightest bit interested, she didn't respond. Instead, she snatched her driver's license from his hand and marched through the door.

On the way to the bar, four different men smiled at Michelle. A few even reached out to graze the small of her bare back. She ignored them and concentrated on getting the bartender's attention. "What do you want?" she asked Kim.

"I'll take a Bone Crusher."

"Gimme the keys then, drunkard. You're not driving home."

Michelle hesitated, not knowing if she wanted to take it easy with a glass of champagne, or if she wanted to start with her usual Long Island Ice Tea.

"She'll have a glass of champagne," a voice from behind her spoke to the bartender.

She turned to stand face to face with a tall, brown-skinned, well-groomed man. Her eyes focused on his impeccably trimmed mustache, sitting atop the most kissable lips that she had ever been that close to.

"Thank you," she said. "How'd you know that I drink champagne?"

"You look like a champagne-type of girl," the stranger said shrugging his wide shoulders.

Captivated by his charm, she flashed him her please-don't-stop-talking-to-me-ask-me-my-phone-number smile.

"Just keep my tab open," her new friend informed the bartender. She watched him pull out his American Express Platinum card. That was all she needed to see. She wasn't going anywhere until she got some more information.

"Thank this gentleman for your drink, Kim."

Kim glanced at the man beside Michelle. She lifted herself up onto a barstool and grinned as though she smelled something brewing. "Oh, thank you very much. You didn't have to do that." And then Kim took the plunge for her friend and began introductions. "My name is Kim and this is my friend Michelle DeVeaux."

"Keith. Pleasure to meet you both," he said while looking directly into Michelle's eyes.

"Nice to meet you too," Michelle said.

"So, Keith have you been here long?" Kim started with question number one. If Michelle was interested in someone, Kim would dig for information. And vice-versa. They had their routine down. Usually by the tenth question, Michelle could determine whether or not she had a future with the proposed individual.

"No. Actually I walked in just after you did."

"I didn't expect it to be this crowded. There usually isn't a line outside," Kim said.

"Oh really? I don't know. This is my first time here so it's all new to me," he said looking again at Michelle.

Michelle jumped in, "You're not from Los Angeles?" She didn't remember seeing him in line in back of her and wondered how he got to the front of the line and into the bar so quickly.

"No, I live in Kansas City, actually."

"Oh well what are you doing out here then?" Kim asked.

"I'm out here on business," he answered.

Michelle couldn't help but notice the firm defining arm muscles underneath his loose fitting long sleeve white T-shirt that bore the Nike symbol across the chest. Using her X-ray vision to further determine what exactly was underneath his sweat suit, she could detect an enormous set of muscular thighs that made Michelle wonder what business man had time to keep his body looking so tight.

"Excuse me?" she said just then realizing that both he and Kim were talking to her.

"Helloooo? Earth to Michelle. Keith asked you where you are from," Kim widened her eyes at Michelle.

"Oh, sorry..." Michelle laughed. "I'm from here. I was born here. I'm a true native...straight outta South Central and into Ladera Heights."

Kim, realizing she better cut her sometimes dense and giddy friend off, quickly interrupted, "Do you come out here often?"

"Yes, at least two to three times a year," Keith answered.

Michelle gave Kim a go-on-ahead-ask-him-what-he-does-for-living glance. But Kim knew she'd have to approach that question strategically. She didn't want to offend him, nor did she want to make her friend's gold-digging efforts too obvious.

"So where's your friend?" Kim asked.

"There he is," Keith pointed and waved his arm to get his attention. Michelle saw the man nod his head at Keith through the crowd. She thought to herself, *Oh no, another fine ass brotha with a big out of shape fat guy friend. Too bad for Kim,* Michelle thought.

The big guy wound his way over. When Tank joined them, Keith made the introductions.

"Nice to meet you both," Tank said.

Kim asked, "So how do you all know each other?"

"Oh we used to work together," Tank answered. "What about you two?"

Michelle decided to reply with an answer just as vague.

"School."

"College?" Tank asked.

"No. High school."

"Oh, for real? Which high school?" Tank asked.

"Westchester."

"I went to Westchester!" Tank paused. "Probably about five years before ya'all though. Where'd you go to college?"

Kim replied, "I go to Cal State Northridge."

All eyes focused on Michelle. "Oh... naw I decided not to do the college thang." She took a sip of her champagne. "I don't think I would last a semester learning a bunch of garbage that I don't care about." She laughed. "Plus the dorm life thing is not for me either. The little two by four cells they make you live in. To me, you might as well enlist in the military or spend time in the big house." She paused. "And the dorm food? No thank you. And I'll be damned if I am gonna put on the, what do they call it? The Freshman Fifty. Forget that." She laughed some more.

"Keith, we should get going. You 'bout ready?" Tank asked. It became obvious that he was uninterested in the present conversation.

"Why so soon?" Michelle blurted out, cocking her head to one side and pouting her lips.

"We're headed to a party out in Calabasas," Keith explained.

"Yeah, we really need to get up out of here and hit the freeway. It's a long ways out," Tank said. Michelle hoped that Keith would pull out a business card. Maybe it would give her some indication of what he did for a living.

"Nice to meet you both," Keith said, instead of saying something to give Michelle any hope for future contact.

"Let us know if you come back into town," Kim hinted.

"Oh, I definitely will," he said staring at Michelle. "Would you leave me your number on my voice mail so that I can get in touch with you?" he asked her, taking the plunge.

"Sure." He took a pen out of his secretary-shaped alligator wallet and scribbled a number down on a cocktail napkin. Before she could even think of an unforgettable closing that would keep her on his mind, he was gone.

CHAPTER FIVE

The bruise around my eye had turned from a bright purple to a reddish-lavender. Although a week had passed, I still had to douse a bit of creamy foundation over it and mask my face with a pair of dark sunglasses to cover the obvious make-up job. But as Ricky and I walked down the Santa Monica boardwalk, just feeling the warmth of his arm around me allowed me to forget the pain he'd caused seven days before. The moisture of the fresh ocean air slowed our stride to a lazy one. It was one of those days when we had nowhere to go, nothing to do, only time to kill.

"Ricky, look, aaaw he only has one foot." I pointed at a handicapped pigeon. "He has to hop around. Aah, that's so sad."

"Let's take him to the vet and get him a fake leg. I'll pay for it," he said, laughing. We stopped for a moment and watched the pigeon stumble around in search of crumbs. "Seriously, though, I'm glad you wanted to come down to the beach with me 'cause we really need to talk."

"About?"

"I just want you to know again how much I love you and how sorry I am about everything. I'm so stressed about football you don't even know how messed up my life is going to be if I don't make it to the league."

I was glad to hear him express his fears. "Come on Ricky, you need to stop depending on football. You have to make a Plan B."

"Naw, I've got to git to the pros. Fuck a Plan B. I ain't tryin' to work in nobody's office wearing a stupid-ass suit and tie everyday for the rest of my life... talkin' that yes Massa shit."

"Oh come on, you're puttin' extras on it."

"Am I?" Ricky paused. "I don't think so. Slavery is still in full existence right here right now, this very day and age. And I really ain't the one to work for 'Whitey' for the rest of my life being hung up by a glass ceiling." Ricky, only since he'd taken a slew of African and African American history classes at UCLA, had become aggressively scornful of white men. He often cited facts about the Middle Passage and the slave trade in general, sprinkling his historical anecdotes with quotes from Malcolm X and Louis Farrakhan. Although I was glad he was learning something while he rushed his way through school, it was unfortunate that he had to fixate on the violence and negative side of it all.

"Oh and playing football is working for the black man?"

"Naw, but..."

"How many *black* owners are there?" I looked at him and waited for a response. "That's right. None. So who will you be working for? All those WHITE owners. And trust me, they don't give a DAMN about you. You will be their slave until your body gets old and rickety and then they'll waive your ass and get some new slave out on the field."

"I'm just saying... I have to play ball. Stef, you don't know how bad I want this shit."

"Yeah, that's good that you have a goal, but I'm telling you, you have got to prepare yourself, just in case. And even if you do make it, you gotta have a safety net in case things don't work out once you get there. That's why I think you should make sure you finish your degree."

"I will, during the off season," he affirmed.

"I think you should think about going to law school with me. If we do it together, it'll be easier for both of us." I wasn't sure he could cut it, but with me helping him it might be possible.

"A lawyer? Me? Naw. Law is boring."

"Ricky. Everything is boring to you except football. What about if you were a sports agent? Players need black attorneys to represent them as agents. Or you could even end up working for a pro team in the front office," I added. "With a law degree, you could even work your way up to an executive position negotiating player contracts for the team itself."

"Yeah, that would be cool, I guess, except I never really thought of me doing anything else besides playing ball."

"That is all I'm tryin' to get you to do. At least *think* of something. I'm not saying that you're *not* going to make it...it's just always good to have a backup plan. Or you could even teach or..."

"Yeah, right. And make $20,000 a year?"

I rolled my eyes. "Come on. You would make a lot more than that, especially if you taught and coached. And what do we need a lot of money for? Just as long as we have enough to be comfortable, I'll be happy. Look at how happy we are now and we don't even have an income. We are poor. Practically below poverty level. Starving students. Living off chips and beef jerky from our parents' Chevron gas cards!" I laughed at the ridiculousness of our situation. "I haven't been to get my hair done in two months. We never have food in the fridge. We can't even afford to pay our phone bill half of the time. And look, we are the happiest couple in the state of California."

He smiled. Staring at a bum nearby, he pulled out some change he had in his pocket and dropped it in the cup. The homeless man nodded his head, thanking Ricky. He put his arm around me again. "I know, but I want us to be secure when we have a family and we will be as soon as I sign my first contract. I got to get there 'cause to tell you the truth I don't think I could sit through three more years of school...especially *law* school! And you have to realize that my whole life, since I was nine years old, I have been gearing my future toward football, never thinking of anything else. Today is the first time I ever even pictured myself in a business suit. No one ever told me I could be something other than a football player. You are the first person who told me I could actually be something else."

"Well, I'm gonna keep telling you 'cause we are going to do good together. I love you so much and whatever you end up doing I want you to be happy," I said as I smiled at him.

"I love you too, and I can't wait to marry you," he said, while glancing down at my finger. "Where's your ring?"

"Flushed it."

"Down the toilet?"

"Yep," I said.

"You're crazy."

"Uh, *you* would be the crazy one, not me."

"It's not gonna happen again. I can promise you...check when we're thirty. Check when we're forty. Check when we're fifty. Mark my words. It'll NEVER happen again. If it does, you can walk. Without any argument. Okay?"

"Okay."

"But about the ring. Can we claim it on insurance or something?" he asked.

"What insurance?"

"Oh, well. The next one I buy you will be a lot bigger," he promised. "And I want to buy you a big-ass house filled with everything you need. Lots of rooms for all the kids..." He started dreaming again. He always talked about what we were *going* to have.

"Kids? And how many are you having?" I asked him teasingly. "'Cause I know I'm only having two, maybe three... no more," I said in a firm, but playful tone.

"*We* are going to have as many as we can. That is, if the man upstairs is willing, of course. You won't have to work, so you could just spend your time driving the kids to ballet, pee-wee football, and girl scouts. As a matter of fact, we need to get started on making one tonight," he said. "I'm gonna buy you a Mercedes station wagon with two custom car seats built in the back for the kids. You're gonna look all fine and shit with your hair slicked back. I can see it all now." He gazed out towards the ocean.

"Let's get some pizza." I changed the subject. It was fun to dream, but I feared the possibilities of him not making those millions he desperately wanted. The horror stories I heard of college athletes trying to make it to the professional leagues outnumbered the success stories. I had faith in his athletic ability, but sometimes you just never can tell.

"Stef, listen," he continued. "When I get you your Benz, the license plate is gonna say REDBONE."

"I don't think you'll ever see me in any car with that on my license plate. I don't like the term and I would never consider myself one, *whatever* it means."

"It means you got some Indian in you. That red blood in you is the reason for that red-tone in your light skin and that long straight hair of yours. REDBONE." The word rolled off his tongue. "You should be proud of your heritage and your beauty."

"I am, but not because of the Indian blood I have in me or because of the length of my hair. I'm proud because I'm real. Real on the *inside*. Real cause I know I love your crazy ass no matter if you end up being an underpaid teacher or the next NFL legend. And real on the outside...no make-up, no fake boobs, no plastic surgery or attitude, no bullshit! But as far as a Mercedes, big houses, and all that crap, let's just worry about all that when the time comes, okay?"

"Damn, Stef, dreaming and hoping gives me motivation." He spotted a vendor pushing a cart of toys. He ran over and grabbed a red pinwheel off the cart and slipped the man a five-dollar bill.

"Here." He put the pinwheel in my hand. "Every time you think our relationship is in trouble, just blow on this and make a wish for it all to get better."

"It's a pinwheel Ricky. It's not gonna make things better."

"Yes it is. Last time we played Cal, our team visited the children's ward at the Shriners Hospital up in the Bay Area. This little girl was holding one. She was so cute. She was bald and dying from Leukemia. I'll never forget her. She looked up at me and said that her mommy gave it to her and told her when she gets scared, to blow on it. She said it was making her get better."

"Aww, that's cute." I blew on the pinwheel and watched it whirl in the wind. His confidence warmed my heart, but still I feared the worst. "You're on the verge of being a professional athlete. Instant wealth and instant women." I handed the pinwheel to him. "Here you take it. You're gonna be the one who needs to make a wish every now and then."

I hated deflating his dreams, but I knew it was the hard truth.

CHAPTER SIX

As the force of the winds picked up, the rain hit the window, almost at a horizontal angle, waking me up from a deep sleep. I looked at Ricky next to me, sleeping peacefully, unaffected by the loud splatter of the rain. My body shivered from the cold, damp air in the room, and goose bumps rose on my bare arms. I snuggled closer to his warm, still body and listened to the gusty winds outside as they whipped around the apartment building making an eerie yet soothing noise. Rainy nights were rare in Los Angeles. And when we were blessed with one, I was always taken back to my childhood.

Growing up in the Bay Area, stormy winters were expected. Sometimes our lights would go out for days. The sounds of the creaking trees and rushing creek below the house scared me into my parents' cozy king size bed, where I'd ask my mom or dad to tell me a story to put me back to sleep. Usually it was always my dad who volunteered. Those were the days. The days that my father thought his little girl could do no wrong. Things, however, had changed.

When I called home to announce the news of our engagement, as expected my father interrogated me. His very first question concerned the life plan of my fiancé. In his eyes, no one was good enough for his only daughter unless they had an airtight career plan. At first I wasn't worried. I believed Ricky would be music to his ears, especially since he, at such a young age, was on the brink of attaining every one of his professional goals.

My reply to his inquisition was filled with conviction. "Yeah dad, he's got it all mapped out. He is going to play professional football after he's through with college. He plays for us right now. He's a wide receiver. And he's really good." Then I took the liberty to embellish my story, incorporating my addendum to his plan. "And then after he retires, he wants to go to law school and become a sports attorney."

"No, no, no, no." His voice was stern. Because we were talking on the phone, I wasn't able to see him, but still I could envision him abruptly shaking his head as he often did when I was a little girl. He raised his voice an octave with each word as he got closer to the end of the sentence. "You should not be getting wrapped up with any football players, Stefanie!"

"But Dad, he loves me and he comes from a nice family and he...." I pleaded.

He wasn't hearing anything I said. "Not my daughter. Athletes are trained to be athletes and that is it! What is he going to do if he doesn't go pro? Or if he gets cut during his first training camp?" he asked accusingly. "And what if he is one of the fortunate few and does actually enjoy a long, successful career in the league? Then exactly how is he going to treat you? Professional athletes have *lots* of women, not just one. Have you ever thought about all these things?"

"You are too intelligent, Dad, to *prejudge* people. And if that isn't a huge generalization, I don't know what is. You haven't even met him and already you are insinuating that I should walk away."

"I'm not insinuating. I'm demanding."

"What is any man that I meet in college going to do after college? Lots of regular students don't know exactly what they are going to choose as a career until much later in life. And as far as his loyalty toward me, don't worry, Ricky is in love with me. And every relationship will be tested regardless of what the circumstances are."

Through the awkward silence, I could almost hear my father's thoughts. Then he said, "He's a wide receiver you say?"

"Yes."

"Have you ever been sitting in the stadium watching one of his games and anticipated the quarterback's long pass to him? The whole stadium stands up and holds their breath? Long pass, probably fifty or sixty yards, and there's your boyfriend scrambling to find his place to catch the ball safely, right?"

"Yeah."

"Well, what are the possibilities?"

My father hadn't changed at all since I left home. He always had to cite a parallel or an analogy to get his point across. "I don't know. He catches it and runs it in for a touchdown or he's robbed."

"Right. An interception."

"So? I don't get it. What? I'm the ball? Or Ricky's the ball? What?"

"Imagine all the people in your world are the people in the stands. They are standing up watching you, excited for you, anticipating your future with your pro-athlete, soon-to-be millionaire boyfriend, right? In the end, there will be two possibilities. You will succeed or..."

"Or I will be robbed."

"Exactly. And the chances of the latter are far greater than if you were to just find a nice business student or law student. Listen to me, Stefanie. In life it's smart to avoid situations where there are no possible interceptions whatsoever. Do you get what I'm saying?"

"Okay dad. I'll make sure I always take the safe route instead of the risky route so that I never get what I truly want in life. That sounds like so much fun." My sarcasm pissed him off and he hung up without saying good-bye. I was left feeling frustrated and confused, as I always did when I went against my father's wishes. But I knew once he met Ricky, he'd change his mind.

Now, as I watched Ricky sleep, I thought about him being only eight classes away from completing his degree. I couldn't wait to prove my father wrong. He needed to learn that I'm not going to be his "little girl" forever, and there will come a time when I am able to make responsible decisions. The thought of what my father would do if he knew Ricky had hit me with his bare hand caused me to wonder if he was right.

The loud ring of the telephone broke the hum of the rain outside. I leaned over Ricky to grab the phone trying not to awaken him. "Hello?" I said softly.

"Ricky Powers please. Mr. Fessler calling." The voice was overbearing and unfriendly.

"Hold on, please," I said. I covered the mouthpiece of the phone and nudged Ricky. "Ricky, some Mr. Fessler is on the phone for you." He didn't move. "Ricky, telephone. Wake up." I positioned the telephone so the receiver would fit perfectly on his ear and his mouth without him having to hold it. "Say hello."

"Hello," he muttered, full of sleep. He paused. "Oh, hi. Fine. No, no not at all." Whoever it was, got him to wake up quicker than I ever could. He sat straight up in the bed. "Oh yeah. That'll be fine." Another pause. It must have been a call having to do with football because he spoke with respect and maturity as he always did to older white folks who had some part in determining his immediate success in football. "Sure, see you then, Mr. Fessler. Thanks." He handed me the phone and plopped his head back on his pillow.

"Mr. Who?"

"Mr. Fessler, an agent."

"An agent? Isn't that a good sign?"

"If you want a lousy agent I guess it is."

"Oh, now we're being picky?"

"Stef, he's lame. He doesn't have any good players." Ricky thought about what he was saying. "But no, I guess you're right. It is a good sign that at least someone is interested in representing me. He said he had been wanting to call during the season to schedule a meeting, but it would have been against NCAA rules."

"What rules?"

"The NCAA doesn't want agents sniffing around college campuses bribing athletes with cars and money to entice them to sign with them until they are finished slaving away for their prospective colleges." He looked at me through the slits in his eyes.

"Really? Cars and money?"

"Yeah, but you gotta be 'big time' for those type of agents to come around."

"Aaaah, baby. Aren't you 'big time'?" I teased.

"We don't really need all that stuff. We already have a car," he said blankly.

"Well, *you* have a car. We had to bury my Camry, remember?" I laughed.

"I mean the truth is that the only reason my name isn't known yet like some of the other high ranking wide receivers is because we had a shitty season."

I smiled and winked. "Okay baby. Whatever you need to tell yourself."

Later that day, I found myself thinking of the sweeping changes that were about to take place in our lives. Sitting in the chair at Hot Salon with my head tilted back into the wash bowl while Jimmy, my stylist, massaged my head, I realized that my deepest fears had become sewn into my every thought over the past weeks. I knew if Ricky did end up getting drafted, we would have to relocate instantly. We would be forced to assume an entirely new lifestyle. My friends and family probably would be farther away than they had ever been. I would have to become accustomed to a new neighborhood, cultivate new friendships and find a local law school.

"Jimmy?" I said, opening my eyes to look up at him. Jimmy was a handsome guy. He was short, only about 5 foot 7, but he had this baby smooth, bittersweet chocolate colored skin to die for.

"Yeah, baby?"

Jimmy was not only my hair stylist, but also one of my closest and dearest friends. He had been ironing the curl out of my hair since I first arrived at UCLA as a naïve, wide-eyed freshman. Over the years we had developed a bond, which I treasured more than the one I shared with most of my girlfriends. A majority of his clients felt the same way, which explained why he had become the most popular and busiest black stylist in all of West L.A.

"When do you get to take that sling off your arm?" I asked.

"Doctor says I should start treatment next month." He was suffering from muscle atrophy, and for the past year he had been losing a considerable amount of strength in his left arm. Although the doctors weren't able to make a diagnosis, they believed that he would regain his strength as soon as he started treatment. Even though Jimmy's health had been threatened, he remained jovial and vibrant, never letting anyone detect the fear he had regarding his mysterious illness. Jimmy continued, "As soon as I start those damn treatments, you can bet I'm gonna take me a vacation." He raised his voice so everyone could hear. "From all you crazy females. Havin' me up in here slavin' away knowin' damn well my arms ain't workin' right."

His laughter filled the salon. Jimmy's big smile, constant silly sarcasm and bad jokes made the sometimes three hour wait quite pleasurable.

"I'm gonna miss you if Ricky and I have to move after we graduate," I pouted.

"You ain't goin' nowhere." He was convinced that Ricky was going to be picked up by one of the local football teams. "And if by chance, circumstances prevail in which you do have to go 'cross country, shoot, ya'all be so rich, you could just take me with you. I could be your personal stylist and Ricky's personal barber."

"Really? You would want to come with us?"

"Yep. So when you get home tonight, tell Ricky that I'm coming."

Ricky had taken a liking to Jimmy also. Every time he came to the shop, the two of them would sit up and talk about football for hours while Ricky waited for me. "But I can't leave Felicia behind."

"Oh, yes you can." Even though Jimmy knew that I wasn't fond of his girlfriend, he didn't know the actual reasons why. It would have hurt his feelings to know that she had asked me to set her up with Ricky's older brother, a four-year veteran in the League.

He looked at me questioningly.

I decided I should change the subject quickly. "Jimmy, I need a trim."

"Naw baby. You need a *cut*. You hair is gettin' too long." Jimmy was forever trying to cut my hair into a style and get rid of my long-haired, Plain-Jane look.

"No such thing as 'too long'." I smiled up at him as he raised my head out of the bowl, wrapped my wet hair in a small white towel and led me to his chair. "Besides, Ricky would kill me and then he would come lookin' for you."

"This is *your* hair, baby. Not Ricky's! Don't start losing yourself now, Uncle Jimmy ain't gonna allow all that." He picked up the scissors and flashed them at me. "You know you gotta keep yourself together so you can fight off all those vultures that are gonna be hungry for your man as soon as he signs that million dollar contract."

I placed my hand on my stomach. "Damn Jimmy, that just made my stomach hurt."

"Don't worry Stef. Ricky ain't goin' out like that. He's one brotha that has his head screwed on right and tight enough not to let a good thing like you go. Plus aren't you planning the wedding?"

"No, we decided to wait until we knew more about where we were going to be living."

"Where's your ring?"

"I put it away for now," I lied. "There isn't any sense in wearing it if we aren't officially planning yet, right?"

Jimmy looked at me with one eyebrow raised. He didn't believe me.

"So tell me how I am gonna fight off these sharks?" I asked again.

"With your beauty and your love. The way you love that brotha' he'd be a fool to leave you behind." He looked at our reflections in the mirror, leaned down and lightly pinched my cheek. "Baby, you ain't got nothin' to worry about. Ricky ain't goin' nowhere." He paused. "But let's hope the two of you don't end up here in Los Angeles, the groupie capital." Looking around the shop he motioned for one of his clients to go sit at the wash bowl. "Tomiko, have a seat at my bowl."

After he played in my hair for a minute, he drenched it in a deep conditioner. "You are gonna have to sit under the dryer today so we can tame this wire."

"I hate the dryer...." I uttered as I followed him to the other side of the shop.

CHAPTER SEVEN

I had finished the History 140A final exam questions almost thirty minutes before Ricky and left the lecture hall to wait outside for him on the front steps. I couldn't imagine what was taking him so long, especially since I had quizzed him every second of the day it seemed—while we ate, while we were driving and one time while we were in the bathtub together. I even prepared a five-inch by seven-inch micro-scribed study sheet for him to carry around with him everywhere he went. By this time I'd do almost anything to help Ricky get his degree.

I sat in the chilly December air and repeatedly sighed long, heavy breaths. I needed to cleanse my mind and body of all the demands suffered with each final exam I'd just finished. I felt like a pressure cooker and someone needed to lift the top. But instead of a much-needed week of pampering, we were headed for northern California to visit my family. Ricky would finally meet my parents for the very first time. This, of course, was just another burst of anxiety that I didn't need now. I wished I could fast forward to New Year's. By then we'd be in Texas to bring in the New Year with Ricky's parents.

"Hey, girl!" a voice yelled from across the courtyard. I looked around and saw Tiffany walking towards me.

Tiffany Weber and I had known each other since freshman year. It was a friendship fated by our dormitory assignments. She landed on the fifth floor in 520, me in 522. On orientation evening, our common brown skin was reason enough to form an alliance that kept us sane in a dorm filled with sorority and fraternity pledging, ultra wealthy, BMW-driving white students. When we quickly discovered that most of our dorm mates were pledging white sororities and fraternities, Tiffany and I found quick comfort in venturing outside of the dorm environment to build our own social circle. By the middle of the academic year, we were inseparable. We traveled up and down the California coast to hang out at different black Greek college parties and once I flew home with her to meet her family in Maryland. Sophomore year we moved out of the dorms and found apartments only a block apart. Once I met Ricky and I introduced her to one of his friends, Malik Wallace, our carefree college days of being "single" were over. Our free time was transferred to our athlete boyfriends and our friendship was suddenly reduced to passing conversations on the campus yard and late night phone calls when one of us was angry with Malik or Ricky.

"Hey, Tiff," I said as she finally made her way over.

"Hey, girl. Where's Ricky?"

"Still in there." I pointed towards the lecture hall. Sharing a laugh, we exchanged a knowing glance. Tiffany's Malik was the star cornerback on the team and, by choice, not much of a "student" either. He had struggled four long years to get through his classes, not because he lacked intelligence, but simply because he, like Ricky, didn't give a damn. Tiffany let her twenty pound backpack fall from her arms to the concrete, sat down and got comfortable.

"I just took my chem final. Aced it!" She put her hand up and waited for me to "high five" her.

"If Ricky ever gets his butt out of there, we'll be done too. We are flying up to the Bay Area tonight."

"Ooooh! First time meeting the family." Tiffany laughed. "You mean to tell me that your dad is letting you bring your football playing boyfriend to his home?"

"Yep. This should be interesting, huh?"

"Yeah, especially once he sees that his *son-in-law* will be earning an income far greater than one he's ever earned. Right?"

"*If* Ricky makes a roster."

"He will." Tiffany stretched, shrugged and then bellowed, "But dang, I'll be glad when this stupid draft is behind us. Malik is so damn needy right now. I wish he would just relax. He knows I got my own thang that I'm trying to do. Preparation for the MCAT is no joke. I HAVE to do well otherwise I ain't gettin' into any med schools."

"Trust me, I know. That's why I decided to wait awhile before I take the LSAT. I can't have anything else on my mind when I decide to start studying for it. Besides, I want him to graduate before we leave California, and at the rate he is going," I glanced towards the lecture hall and arched an eyebrow, "He is gonna need my help."

"Stefanie, you really need to worry about yourself. What if ya'all break up?"

"Not a possibility. Not after all we've been through. No way."

"What happened to your ring then?" She caught me off guard.

Just then, Ricky appeared.

"Damn, baby, you the last one finished?" I asked.

An angry expression replaced his exhaustion as the sunlight forced him to squint. He quickly blocked the rays with his hand and peered down at us. "That test was no joke. How did you finish so fast?"

"I studied!"

"So did I," he said. He paused, looked at Tiffany and chuckled. "For about three minutes."

"For about three *seconds,*" Tiffany teased him.

"Ummm, the trick is to study all semester, Ricky," I mumbled.

Tiffany said to Ricky, "You nigros are some sorry excuses for students. You and Malik. With all the help you get from the athletic department and from us, you both should be getting straight A's."

Ricky wasn't trying to hear anything else about school. "So whatcha' all about to do?"

"I don't know. I'm kind of hungry," Tiffany offered.

"Yeah let's go get some food," I agreed.

"I'll go lift and then I'll meet you right afterwards," said Ricky. "Hey Tiff, is Malik in the weight room?"

"Yeah, if you hurry, you should be able to catch him."

"Meet us at the Coop after you're done." He kissed me lightly on the corner of my mouth, waved to Tiffany and walked in the opposite direction.

"Tell Malik to meet me up at the Coop too." Tiffany yelled to Ricky.

Tiffany took a bite of her pizza and before she finished chewing she said, "I found a phone number in Malik's jeans the other night." Her eyes caught mine and she waited for a response. I didn't have one. Tiffany paused to break the long strings of cheese that hung from her mouth and were attached to the remaining part of the pizza. "Yeah girl, this brotha' thinks I'm stupid. But you know I had to call the bitch and tell her that Malik has somebody already."

"No you didn't!"

"Yes I did. Some little sophomore tramp that lives in the dorms." She paused again. "Whatever. I'm so tired of these little tramps jockin' brothas even when they know they have somebody. They have no respect for themselves." Tiffany knew that her man was fine and she expected girls to be after him; but at the same time, when she discovered one of them was actually moving in for the kill, she was always ready to fight. Malik was a tall light-skinned brother with soft curly hair. He had a lean, muscular body with an ass so tight you could bounce a quarter off it. He was a fantasy come true for a sistah that liked that kind of look.

"College hussies are not the issue here, Tiff. It's the professional groupies that scare me. I have heard some wild things from Tanya and them." Tanya had graduated from UCLA and moved to Atlanta with her boyfriend when he got drafted to the league last April. "I don't talk to her that much anymore, but when she calls, she always has a crazy story to tell."

"Like what?" Tiffany was concerned.

"Oh no, it'll ruin your appetite." I shook my head and left it alone.

"Come on. Do tell."

"You know the term lay and wait?"

Tiff nodded anxiously.

"Okay well these women do just that. They plan their attack as delicately as a serial killer. They follow sports for the sole purpose of finding an athlete to marry or get pregnant by. They read the newspaper and try to forecast which guys will be relocating to their prospective city. Vultures. There are even girls who follow the players after the games to restaurants and night-clubs. Get seated at a table close by and there you go! Battin' those fake eyelashes and flaunting those silicone tits from the next booth over. Don't even care if a player is with his wife or family. Just scandalous! And the scary thing about it is most of the time these women are top tier. Body, beauty, all that."

"Yeah, but no brains I'm sure." Tiffany thought a little more about what I'd just said. "I'll knock a bitch out if she tries to follow my man anywhere!

Those little light-skinned high yella tramps... ooooooh, they git on my nerves." Tiffany punched her fist in an upward motion. "No offense, Stef." Tiffany added because of my own light skinned complexion. She punched the air again. "And then I'd knock Malik's butt out." It was always comical to hear Tiffany talk about "kickin' somebody's ass." With her petite frame and bony limbs, she was sure to get beaten by any opponent.

"What do you think Malik would do if you hit him? You think he'd try to hit you back?"

"Heck no. Malik would NEVER hit me. Why you ask that?"

"Naw, I was just curious that's all."

"So what else did Tanya say?"

"She said they just hang out after the games and wait for the players to come out to their cars. Sometimes, the bold ones, they will go right up to the guys and ask for an autograph, flash a little skin, and slip their numbers in their duffel bags. Actually, one of the guys on the team met his girl like this."

"No way!"

"Yep, Tanya says she sits next to her at the games. Scandalous tramp. This full-fledged bimbo is sittin' up in the stands talkin' 'bout 'Go Team!'" I put my arms in the air as if I was a cheerleader.

With an incredulous nod, Tiffany laughed. "Sharks. Circling. Waiting for *our* men?" Tiffany got up to throw her empty plate away. She yelled behind her. "That's why I'm going to make sure I'm doin' my *own* thing." When she came back to the table she said, "I ain't the one to let this superficial football world gobble *me* up. And you aren't either, girl. We have to do our own thing for real."

"I know." I looked at my watch and realized Ricky and Malik should be meeting us at any minute. I went to the pay phone to check our messages. There were five messages. Two were from sports agents.

Ricky and Malik appeared. Malik greeted Tiffany with a kiss. From Ricky I got two envelopes.

"What is this?" I asked.

Ricky was clearly excited. "Read them."

Tiffany looked at her watch and her eyes widened. "Oh damn. I gotta go. I have a final in the morning. History of women during the labor movement. Like I really care about some damn labor movement."

"I'll help you," Malik teased.

"Yeah, help me fail," Tiffany exclaimed.

Tiffany grabbed him and pulled him off in the direction of the library.

"Have a good Holiday."

"You guys too."

"So read," Ricky urged.

I took each letter out of the already opened envelopes, unfolded them and scanned them as quickly as I could. He had been invited to play in two college post-season All Star games.

As I read, he said, "The Hula and the Shrine Bowls are the best ones to play in."

"What do you mean the best?"

"They're the most respected. The stands will be loaded with scouts."

"Yeay!" I jumped on his back and made him carry me piggyback down the stairs toward the parking garage. "But guess what else?" I whispered in his ear. "I checked the messages and two more agents called."

"For real? Was one of the names somebody Schwartz?" he asked anxiously.

"Actually yeah, it was. How'd you know?"

"I *didn't*, it's just I was hoping that he'd call. He is one of the top sports attorneys in the country. He has most of the big time players."

"So what possibly could he want with *you?*" I wrapped my arms around his neck tighter and hugged him while still riding piggy-back.

"Hopefully he is interested in representing me," Ricky said modestly. "Then I don't have to go with Fessler."

He carried me to a patch of grass area in front of the main library and playfully threw me down off his back. After he'd tackled and tickled me until I begged for mercy, I couldn't help but surrender to his contagious bright smile. I caught my breath while surveying the European architecture of the four buildings that surrounded us and surveyed UCLA's warm collegiate atmosphere. Our college memories were quickly falling behind us.

"Are you gonna miss it here?" I asked.

"Nope. Can't wait to get out of here actually."

"Aren't you gonna miss the lifestyle? Going to class, going to practice and chillin' without any responsibilities hanging over our heads. No working for a living, trying to make sure you are doing a good job. Trying to weasel a raise and a promotion. Trying to kiss your boss's ass."

"The only ass I'm kissin' is my next coach."

"Excuse me?" I raised my eyebrows and pointed to my left butt cheek turning from a sitting position and aiming it at him. "You better kiss this one, too."

Ricky leaned down as if he were actually going to kiss it, but then quickly dragged me over his knee. "You mean I better *spank* it." He lifted his large hand threatening to swat me until I again, through my laughter, begged for another round of mercy.

CHAPTER EIGHT

"*United Airlines Flight 2019 to Kansas City is now boarding. This is the final boarding call for Flight 2019 to Kansas City. All passengers should be on board at this time.*"

"Shit!" Michelle yelled as she heard the announcement blaring from the airport-wide PA system. She picked up her pace and dashed through the airport. In three-inch knee high boots and two larger-than-necessary Louis Vuitton carry-ons that belonged to her mother, she realized getting from gate 39 to gate 72 was not going to be a quick or easy feat. If she missed the flight, she wouldn't be able to go until the next morning, making her weekend in Kansas City far too short. She passed gate 62 and then gate 63, looking ahead as the ramp agents were closing the doors. "Wait a minute, please!" she yelled, her voice echoing throughout the waiting area. "Please wait one more second!" She begged her way through and trotted down the ramp hearing the door slam behind her.

During the third week of lengthy phone conversations, Michelle was surprised to find a plane ticket to Kansas City, Missouri in her mailbox. Without hesitation, she accepted the invitation and packed her things for the following weekend. Keith had shared enough of his personal life with Michelle that she felt comfortable enough flying out to spend the weekend with him. He had introduced her to his dogs one night when he let them bark through the phone. He even used three-way calling to phone his mother and introduce Michelle over the phone. With each conversation, Michelle was more fanatical at the possibility of Keith having a bank account large enough to support the two of them. Although he skirted around what he actually did for a living, she was determined to find out everything she needed to know the moment she arrived.

"Good evening, may I see your boarding pass?" the flight attendant asked as Michelle stepped onto the plane. "Oh, you are seated this way." She followed the flight attendant into the First Class cabin. "Can I get you a drink?"

"Sure," Michelle replied. She was surprised to be offered a drink so soon. "Chardonnay is fine." One of the male flight attendants whisked her baggage out of her hands and into the overhead as Michelle scooted past an older white man to get to her window seat. *Hmmmm, First Class,* she thought. "Now this is what I am talking about," she said under her breath as the flight attendant approached her with her drink.

"Excuse me, did you say something?" the older white man asked respectfully peeking from behind his Wall Street Journal.

"Oh no... just talking to myself."

The flight attendant unfolded Michelle's arm table and set the drink in front of her. "Oh, here ya' go." Michelle handed the woman a five-dollar bill.

"Drinks are free in First Class, sweetie," the woman with glaring red lipstick whispered.

The man beside her lowered his newspaper and smirked as Michelle turned a light shade of pink.

Keith was waiting patiently at the baggage claim with the rest of the flight 2019's eager loved ones. He greeted Michelle with a warm, bear-like hug.

It was as if the two had been long distance lovers for years. Natural, and so familiar. Michelle gave him a cheerful once over. His gear, his body and his beautiful full lips reminded her exactly of why she was so anxious to fly half way across the country to see him. He wore a black velour Phat Farm sweat suit with a pair of fresh Timberlands to match. Michelle noticed he was impeccably groomed and couldn't help but wonder if he made a special trip to the barber just for her. Both his clean fade and thin goat-tee were trimmed to perfection and gave him the clean but rugged look she liked.

"How'd the flight go?"

"Oh, it was great." She decided to be cool and not to give any extra thanks for the First Class ticket, wanting him to believe it was expected. "Thank you so much for sending for me. You have to show me EVERY-THING, especially since I've never been out here before." As a matter of fact, Michelle hadn't been anywhere outside of Los Angeles. The farthest she'd even traveled was to San Diego.

"Well, there really isn't much to see. And if we miss anything this time, you can always catch it on the next trip."

When they finally made it to the parking lot, Keith led the way to a black Chevy Dually truck. He opened the door for Michelle, took her bags and put them in the back seat of the extended cab. She was disappointed he didn't have a car that held more prominence, something with just a bit more class.

"What in the world do you do with all this truck?" she asked, raising her voice over the loud engine.

"Oh," he laughed. "This is really for when I take the dogs out. Which lately is every day. I just dumped them at home before I came to get you."

Thirty minutes later, when they pulled up to his house, Michelle couldn't believe what filled her entire line of sight. Staring back at her was a gorgeous Beverly-Hills style, newly constructed mini-mansion. She knew something must be wrong. There was no way that a twenty-six year old man would have the wherewithal to purchase such an expensive house. But she knew she had to keep her enthusiasm to herself while she continued to gauge how wealthy he truly was.

The home sat on endless acres of rolling green land. The surrounding houses were scattered throughout the picturesque countryside giving each neighbor what seemed like miles of space between them. Two stories and equipped with white clapboards and beveled glass windows that reflected shades of red, orange, purple and yellow in the evening sunlight, it was nothing short of exquisite. Two columns flanked a set of solid oak floor-to-ceiling doors that led into an enormous foyer. Sturdy Italian furniture filled the spacious floor plan, and Salvador Dalís and Van Goghs dotted the walls.

"Nice house," she said beneath a quiet smile. Adrienne taught Michelle it was always important to conceal any excitement that may occur when discovering the wealth of a potential husband.

Keith disappeared up the wide staircase with her bags.

Michelle moseyed into the elaborate kitchen for a glimpse of the backyard. A sparkling swimming pool with a diving board sat in front of a separate guesthouse. It too had the same beveled glass windows.

She found her way through the splendor, almost tiptoeing. It was as if everything were spanking new. Past the dining room and two steps down was a wide-open family room that sported a movie-screen-size television framed by a wide array of electronic equipment. Above the granite fireplace she noticed four painted footballs in glass cases. As she got closer, she noticed Keith's name professionally sketched across each one. The names of two professional football teams were painted below his name and the scores of each game. "Game Ball" was written across two of them. In the still, quiet room, she heard her own gasp.

"A professional football player," she whispered. "I'll be damned. How does a girl like me get so lucky?" Stunned by the revelation, she dropped down on the forest-green leather couch and absorbed her winnings. She pretended there was a casino slot machine in front of her and pulled the handle while she chuckled devilishly. *"Cha-ching!"*

Michelle stood on the curb at LAX underneath the United Airlines sign patiently waiting for her mother. She checked the diamond-studded Cartier watch she had borrowed from Adrienne's jewelry box and realized she'd been waiting for thirty-five minutes. Although she wasn't surprised, she planned to have a little talk with Adrienne and find out why her own mother could never be on time.

Her mind drifted back to the days she had been stuck outside her elementary school waiting for hours. Always the last one to be picked up. She could never figure out why her mommy couldn't be waiting by the curb when she walked out of the classroom like the other mommies. And why was it that her mother's boyfriend-of the-month had to pick her up more often than not. Little Michelle would hesitantly get in the car only to wonder why her mother couldn't make it. "Your mother had an appointment," they'd always say. But as Michelle grew into an adult, she finally realized the only appointments her mother ever had were for her hair, nails or for a body wax.

"You better tell that boyfriend of yours he's fired. Having a pretty lady like you wait in the cold all this time," the taxi coordinator yelled. "You should take a taxi. You know, I don't live too far from here. You could hide out at my place for a few days, make him real mad."

Michelle shot the hound half of a smile and turned away. Just then, she heard Adrienne honking obnoxiously as she whipped up to the curb in her fifteen-year-old white convertible Mercedes Benz.

"Hi, honey," she squealed. Michelle flashed a fake smile as she opened up the trunk and deposited her luggage. "Hugs!" Adrienne said, reaching for her daughter as she got inside the car. "Now, I hope you behaved yourself out there. You know, Michelle, after you left, I realized I shouldn't have let you go out there to spend the weekend with a total stranger." She pulled away from the curb and headed up Sepulveda north.

"*Let?*"

"Yes, *let*. Michelle, you are still my daughter no matter how grown you think you may be. And I have had to make many more decisions in life than you have so I suggest you learn from me."

Michelle stared at her mother. "Sorry Adrienne, but it's a little late to try to be a role model." She cut her eyes at her mother. "Besides, I'm old enough to make my own decisions. And you can bet the decisions I make for myself will carry me much farther than you think you've come."

"I don't know where you picked up this attitude, young lady, but..."

"You don't know where I picked it up? Probably from watching how you have behaved." Michelle never fully admitted it, but the wiser she had become from her own experience, the more clearly she was able to draw conclusions about Adrienne's poor attempts at earning the title of mother. "And going to Kansas City to see Keith was in fact good judgment on my behalf." Her wide grin seemed to make her mother forget how rude her daughter had just been and made her want to hear more. Michelle added, "Just let me say that Keith is rolling in the dough."

"Oh is he?" Adrienne arched an eyebrow. "And how much cash is he rolling in?"

"He plays ball."

"Basketball?"

"Football."

Adrienne's eyes danced with delight. "Oh yeah, honey, you definitely caught a good one." Suddenly, frowning, she added, "But you need to be a little cautious of those athletes. They think they are God's gift. I dated a couple of them in my day and they were somethin' else."

"Adrienne? Who *haven't* you dated in your day?"

Adrienne rolled her eyes and sped off when the light turned green.

CHAPTER NINE

"Ten. Nine. Eight. Seven. Six. Five. Four. Three. Two. One. HAPPY NEW YEAR!" Corks flew from five different champagne bottles and ricocheted off the ceiling of the large double suite at the Sunset Boulevard Belage hotel. Ricky and I ducked when one flew in our direction. Tiffany had extended a last minute invitation to us to join one of her sorority sister's New Year's Eve soirées.

"Our second New Years together," I whispered in Ricky's ear. "And I can't believe I still love you." Ricky laughed. "You should go call your parents and wish them a Happy New Year." We'd canceled our trip to visit his family in Texas so Ricky could prepare physically and mentally for post-season play. The two upcoming All-Star games were critical in the determination of his future success and there was no time for Ricky to fly to Texas and eat fried turkey and sit on his butt. My parents were also forced to understand the importance of the next few months when we cut our weeklong Christmas visit short. And though the trip was shortened to three days, I was glad Ricky finally met my family. My father covered his premature judgments of Ricky with a cordial attitude and phony smile, which thankfully allowed Ricky to feel comfortable enough to admit to a good time.

"Hey girl! Happy New Year!" Tiffany yelled from across the room with a drunken smile plastered across her face. "Come here." We met half way and hugged while Tiffany spilled her champagne all over both of us and then onto the floor. "Where's your drink?"

"I'm driving. I need to chill."

"Oh." She looked at me as if I just told her that a relative of mine had died. "Well go get some sparkling apple cider or some soda or something 'cause I am about to make a toast."

As I waited for the bartender to fill up a champagne glass with ginger ale, I watched Tiffany float in butterfly fashion about the room. Eventually I spotted her gliding her way to the corner where Ricky and Malik were perched.

Making my way toward them, I said, "Okay Tiff, make your toast."

Tiffany raised her glass. "To friendship and not just any friendship, but *long*-term friendship. They say that the best friends you'll ever make are the ones you make in college so let's make that statement a truth. No matter how far we all end up away from each other, let's always remain as close as we are today." She glanced back and forth between the three of us. "Okay?"

Our blank stares melted into smiles as we held up our glasses.

"Wait a sec, I'm not done. I have to make a toast to all of our futures. May you, Stef, make it through law school so you can represent them when they are poor and unemployed and when they need to sue the team for cutting them." Tiffany let out a drunken laugh. "'Cause you all know what the N.F.L. stands for?" She swigged half of the champagne in her glass. "It stands for *Not For Long!*" She laughed at her joke and rambled on, "And may *I* make it through medical school so that I can fix all ya'allz broken limbs when ya'all get hurt on the field." She began to slur. "And to ya'all..." she fixed her eyes on Ricky and Malik, "...may you both get that damn phone call on draft day so all this stress can go away... and so we can ALL

FINALLY BREATHE AGAIN... that's it."

Our glasses clanged and then we sipped. Tiffany gulped.

If getting drunk was a race, Tiffany never failed in beating us to the finish line.

"I guess I should stop drinking so I make sure we all get home," Malik offered. He looked at each of us questioningly.

"Naw, Malik, I'm cool," I said. "Go on ahead. Plus Ricky isn't drinking too much either," I said. "We'll get you home."

"Yeah, I gotta get up and lift in the morning. And so do you," Ricky said to Malik.

Tiffany's eyes widened. "New Year's Day? Damn. Ya'all can't take ONE day off?" She hesitated and looked at Malik. "Wait a minute. Aren't you all supposed to be playing in somebody's bowl game? You always play somewhere on New Years Day, dontcha'?"

"Not this year. USC ruined our chances when they beat us in our last game," Ricky answered. "It's these All-Star games we have to start worrying about."

"Oh yeah. Hula Bowl and the Shriners Game. Stef, you going to Hawaii?"

"Yep. You?"

Malik answered before Tiffany had a chance. "Yep. You know me and my girl are gonna be chillin' on the beach...at night...doin' the adult thang... n' thangs."

"You know I'm goin'." She started doing her own rendition of the hula as she swayed across the floor away from us. She stopped in front of another group of her friends and continued her hula. Malik grinned at his alcoholically extroverted girlfriend and finally went to scoop her up. "Baby, I need to take your drunk butt home. Ya'all ready?"

"Yeah, let's get out of here," Ricky answered.

"Wait a minute!" Tiffany protested. Then in a haughty stage voice, said, "The pahtee has just begun. It's not even half past midnight yet! Where ya'all goin'?" She tried desperately but failed to see straight. Ignoring her plea to stay, Malik picked Tiffany up, threw her over his shoulder and followed us to the door.

"I hate these damn talk shows," Jana said to me as she glanced up from her textbook and stared at the television set. "Look at these ignorant people. Makes me 'shamed to live in this country. That's why I'm moving to Paris after I finish my M.B.A." Jana laughed and gathered up her study materials. "I'm going to the library to get some real studying done. Wanna come?" Jana noticed my eyes were glued to my laptop. "Stef, you writing a paper for yourself, or for Ricky?"

"Ha ha. Very funny. For me. Two more classes and I'm done."

"What about Ricky?" Jana asked.

"He has two more quarters left. You know how athletes do it. Go play in the pros for a few years and then come back and finish." Jana quickly re-focused her attention on the transvestite about to confess his love for his sister. "Jana, how and why do you all watch this stuff?" I asked, finally glancing up at the television. "That's poison to your intelligent mind. Turn the channel."

She hit the power button and the TV went off. "You should apply to 'SC's law program," Jana suggested. Marie and Jana finished undergrad a year before I did and were in graduate school at USC earning their M.B.A.s.

I decided not to respond. She already knew I'd decided to put my law school plans on hold. She also knew I was waiting to see where Ricky would be drafted. And she knew that I was madly in love. Jana had never been, at least not in the way I was. She didn't have time for love. She was on a straight and narrow path to land a C.E.O. position at a major corporation.

Such fierce, nothing-can-stop-me, career ambitions did not live within me. I had big plans, but because I'd met the man of my dreams earlier then I thought I would, my plans could be put on hold. There was no reason I couldn't have love and family along with a career as a lawyer. But to Jana, it was one or the other. So trying to make her understand was impossible.

Jana continued to push. "But think about it. We could keep this apartment. We could all commute together. Even though we wouldn't all be in the same program, we would still be together on the same campus."

"Sounds great! Yeah, let's do it!" My facetiousness pissed her off. And so did the fact that I said it without lifting my eyes from my book. I continued to read about the WW II and Nazi Germany so I could finish my paper on Erwin Rommel, *The Desert Fox.* I felt the need to repeat my plan despite her complaints. "Yes, I do plan to eventually go to law school, but I just have to wait and find out what city we end up in."

"What's wrong with going to 'SC and flying to see him, wherever he is, on the weekends?"

Marie came up the stairs and joined us in the living room. She overheard Jana and decided to enter the conversation right away. "Come on Jana, you and I both know Stefanie is going wherever Ricky goes. No need to try to persuade her to do anything different."

I said, "You guys come on. Can you imagine me letting my husband go 'cross country without me and give him all that time and temptation to mess up."

"Husband?" Jana said with mock surprise.

I thought about retreating to my cave where I could get some real studying done. "Whatever. Neither of you understand what it's like to love someone the way I love Ricky. I guess I got it bad."

"First of all..." Marie started.

Oh great, here we go, I thought.

She continued, "We do understand. We live with you and him. We see the two of you locked up downstairs in your little dungeon. You are like two little lovebirds fluttering in and out of this apartment. We see how much you love each other. Shooot, we *feel* how much you love each other. Jana's just worried that you are putting all your eggs in one basket." Jana nodded her head in agreement with Marie. "Me, I support whatever you wanna do 'cause that's just me. You're a grown woman and we, as your friends, have to trust your decision to be with Ricky. It's just that sometimes...well, you never know."

Jana added. "I support you too Stef. I just want to make sure you don't give your life to him without realizing that you are your own person. It happens a lot. And you are just a little too wrapped up in his life already. The money and stuff will only make everything more complicated. Money changes people."

I shut my book. They had my full attention. "There's a part of me that doesn't even want Ricky to make it to the pros at all. I just feel like the more money he makes or the more famous he gets, the less chance that we'll end up together. I know we could be a lot happier if he just got a normal job so we could live a normal life."

"And that is why we are saying you should make sure you have your independence...just in case he falls to the wolves."

"As long as we don't end up somewhere like here where the wolves come in packs," I laughed nervously. "Or even if he goes fourth round or lower."

"What do you mean?"

"Tiffany was telling me the higher round you are picked, the bigger the contract, the more famous you get, the bigger your head gets and so on and so on. So, I figure if he just goes in a low round, he'll keep his head on straight because he will be forced to maintain a certain level of humility. You know, worrying about just making the team will be all that is on his mind.

He won't be worrying about how he is gonna spend his money or who he is gonna spend it on." They listened carefully, sensing my honesty and real fears. "So come on, you guys, hope with me that he goes fourth round or lower," I said, hearing someone creep up the staircase at the same time.

It was Ricky.

Jana and Marie immediately flicked their eyes to the television as if we weren't talking about my perceived dilemma. Funny thing was, there was nothing on because the TV was still off. But still, they stared at it, determined not to look Ricky's way.

"Why you hope that?" Ricky asked. His expression was bemused, yet slightly offended. I could tell he hoped that he'd heard me wrong.

"I was just… just jokin' around," I stumbled over my words. "Why would I ever hope for anything but your success?"

Marie finally turned the TV back on. I sat on the floor pokerfaced, and felt as if I had the wind knocked out of me. Ricky stood five feet above me, but it felt like fifteen. When I looked up at him, the blood rushed to my face and suddenly I felt very warm. He walked into the kitchen, yanked a jar of Tang out of the cupboard, made himself a glass and walked past us without saying another word. He galloped down the stairs leaving an eerie stillness behind him.

"Ooops," Jana whispered.

"Damn! I didn't even hear him come in," I whispered back.

"Girrrrl, you better raise up and go down there and fix that shit," Marie said, leaning over to push me toward the stairs.

A quick rehearsal of what I would say played in my mind as I stepped carefully down the stairs. I didn't want him to know I was coming.

"Ricky?" I tentatively poked my head in the door of the bedroom.

Sprawled out on the bed, he flipped through a pre-draft football magazine.

"Hi," was all I could offer.

"So all this time I've been praying, practically *begging* for a spot in the N.F.L, you are right beside me canceling out my wishes with your own prayers that I don't even get a phone call on draft day."

"That's not what I was saying Ricky. I'm just scared you're gonna get all 'big time' and leave me in the dust. I know it happens to a lot of women and I don't want to lose you. I was telling Jana and Marie that I hope you and I don't end up like all those other typical athlete-girlfriend relationships. You have to understand what this is like for me," I explained, hoping he'd see the worry in my eyes.

"And *how* exactly is it for you?" He continued to give his attention to the magazine.

"Whatever." I sighed. "You aren't gonna understand. Probably just like I can't fully internalize your feelings about what's going on in your life. But Ricky, it's just hard to watch you go out night after night with your friends wondering what you are doing and who you are doing it with. Wondering why you never take me with you. And I just feel like once you get a little bit of cash, it'll get worse."

"No, it'll get better." His disposition changed as he patted the empty space on the bed next to him. I accepted his invitation, but straddled his lap instead. "I'm just trying to get in as much time with Malik, Jason and them because in a minute we are gonna be spread 'cross country. Then it'll be just you and me. I promise. I know everything is crazy right now, but it'll calm down soon. I'm sorry if you are feeling scared. I thought Hawaii did us some good. I guess I was wrong."

Actually, he was right. Our Hawaii trip was a welcome dose of what we needed. Tiffany and I had kicked it by the pool while the guys spent their days at the University of Hawaii's stadium, practicing for the big game. We had stayed at the Sheraton Moana Surfrider, a hotel we could never have afforded on our own. Sports agents, scouts and marketing executives swarmed the hotel like discouraged car salesmen trying to make their quotas. A few even tried to make casual conversation with Tiffany and me while we baked our brown skin in the hot Hawaiian sun. We, of course, drove them away with politeness. Each night when Ricky and Malik returned, agents jumped on Malik as he walked through the hotel's lobby, hoping to say the one thing the predicted early first rounder wanted to hear. But Malik shooed them away like flies on the beach while Ricky shuffled behind secretly wishing for the same attention.

Ricky's performance at the Hula Bowl ended up convincing some of those very agents that they should track him down once we returned to Los Angeles. Even a few local journalists called. But still the level of stress and anticipation rose to almost an unbearable degree. And even though Ricky tried his best to maintain a level head and a calm manner, I still feared that a physical confrontation would occur again. I couldn't wait for April to come and go. The sooner, the better!

"Oh, I forgot to tell you. Mr. Schwartz called again and asked if you needed anything. I told him you were fine, but that you would call when you did. Are you going to sign with him?"

"What do you think I should do?"

"I think you should. I like him a lot. He seems like he will get you the best deal." Mr. Schwartz was my favorite agent. All the others, with their annoying persistence and numerous requests to grant Ricky favors, were just as bad as the swarming women vying for his attention over the past few months. They were relentless, hoping to find someone like Ricky, a quiet star promising a steady long-term allowance that may equal the quick money of a first rounder that only plays for a few years and then fizzles out. Mr. Schwartz, however, wasn't desperate or conniving. He was just plain honest. He offered his unscathed reputation to capture clients, not cheap favors like most agents. With a client list including a handful of the leagues starting quarterbacks, he knew how to get any player what he was worth.

"Okay, I'm going to set up a time to meet with him. Actually, can you call? Set the appointment for a time when you can go too." Ricky nodded, trying to convince himself into signing with Mr. Schwartz. "Yeah, it seems like he would hook me up with a nice contract." I could tell Ricky was disappointed that the attorney Malik had signed with, the supposed "Top Agent" in the country, never called.

"Schwartz is going to be good. I know it. You know what he told me?"

Ricky came out of his reverie. "Huh?"

"When he took us out to dinner last week, when you went to the restroom, he told me that out of all his clients, you and I were the only couple he would want to be stranded with on a desert island."

"What is that supposed to mean?"

"That he likes us. That everyone else he deals with is loony, selfish, unreal."

"Stef, come on, don't be so easy. He probably tells that to all his clients. He just wanted to get on your good side."

"I don't think so. He seems pretty genuine. And I think I'm a pretty good judge of character, even after a short first impression. I mean I chose you, didn't I?"

"No, *I* chose *you*. Where's my wallet? His phone number is in there."

I grabbed it out of his jacket and handed it to him. He took out Mr. Schwartz's business card, studied it for a second, then dialed the number and handed the phone to me.

CHAPTER TEN

Michelle and Adrienne found the seats corresponding with the numbers on their tickets. As soon as they got comfortable, they enjoyed the football spirit rocking San Diego's Jack Murphy Stadium and quickly directed their attention to the activity on the field. Michelle looked for Keith and found him in a bright red jersey plastered with the number 83. But only minutes into the first quarter, she was bored with the players and their seemingly predictable maneuvers. She couldn't understand why the quarterback kept handing the ball to number 28 just so he could run straight into the cluster of linemen. She knew nothing of the rules of the game and became much more amused with the clan of women she sat amongst. Girlfriends and wives of the players, decked in Prada, Donna Karan and Gucci sat close by. They were much more into checking each other out, unless of course one happened to spy her man achieve something down on the field to earn her applause.

"I think we're underdressed," Adrienne whispered to Michelle.

Michelle checked herself out. "No way, Ma, even though I've got jeans on, if you add what I paid for for my hat, Gucci, these sunglasses, Prada and my shoes, Jimmy Choo, I'm comin' out on top."

Michelle read Adrienne's mind and answered the question about where the hell her daughter got the money to buy such fine things.

"Keith took me shopping last time I was in KC. He bought me this Gucci hat. Cute, isn't it? And I spent my whole paycheck and a little bit of my last paycheck to buy these shoes."

"And the Prada sunglasses?"

Michelle whispered. "They're fake. But they *look* like Prada, don't they?"

"Uh, no they don't. But sweetie, I think *she's* got us all beat." Adrienne and Michelle salivated as they gawked at the woman beside them. A colossal diamond suspended by four prongs and sitting atop a platinum band blinked back at them.

Michelle hastily tried to mask her envy with a whisper. "Ma, this is my life." She glanced at the ring again. "And *that* is what I have to look forward to!"

Three hours and some minutes later, Michelle and Adrienne loitered amongst the crowd outside the locker room. Finally, Keith appeared in a midnight-blue three-piece suit, smelling of cologne and Lever 2000 soap. "I'm sorry you guys lost," Michelle said. She expected him to be a bit more disappointed.

"Oh yeah, whatever, no big deal. I hurt my wrist though. When I caught that one ball in the end zone, two linebackers smashed my hand between their helmets." Michelle looked at his bandaged hand, but quickly switched her attention to her mother.

"Keith, this is my mother, Adrienne. Adrienne, this is Keith." Her eyes never left Keith. "Isn't he absolutely adorable, Adrienne?"

"Hello, Keith. It's a pleasure to meet you." The two exchanged a warm handshake and carried on with small talk while Michelle's eyes wandered to some of the other players greeting their wives and families. Her furtive glances captured more images of the lifestyle she knew would soon be hers.

Handsome, fit men greeting their decorated wives, making their way toward a private parking lot filled with shiny, brand new Ferraris, Mercedes, and Range Rovers. Keith tried to draw her into the conversation, but Michelle was too wrapped up in the exhilaration of finally finding a crowd that was not *chasing* a dream, but instead a crowd that had already *arrived*.

During the following months, the two of them became inseparable. Michelle flew to Kansas City every other weekend where they did nothing but discover new things about each other. They rented movies, ordered take-out Indian food, basked in the sun near the pool and even worked out together. The countryside and clean air was enough to make Michelle look forward to their morning three-mile run, not to mention the view that remained directly in front of her. She couldn't quite keep up with Keith's pace, but she had been working out long enough at least to follow close behind. Sometimes after their run, they worked out in his private gym near the guesthouse. But most of the time, she would skip the weights and shower while he lifted.

One morning, while in the shower, she pondered her place in Keith's life. She wondered whose place she'd taken and why someone hadn't already dragged him to the altar. There were no signs of crazy ex-girlfriends and no indication that he had even been casually dating. "Whose place did I take?" she asked that night when they were in bed together.

"Whose *place* did you take?" Keith repeated her question.

"Yeah, I know there's some broken-hearted girl somewhere out there wishing she was right here with you right now."

"Trust me, the last girl I was serious with is not thinking about me."

"You broke her heart that bad?"

"She broke mine. So that has made me very picky and if I don't find out within the first couple of weeks that the person I'm interested in is a loyal, trustworthy type of person, then I'm out."

"So did I pass the test?"

"The jury is still out." Keith smiled at her. "But so far you fit the mold. I mean most of the girls I meet have nothing going on, can't wait to just get in the mix, go to the games, meet the other players wives, talk shit and gossip, ya' know? Most of them have shitty jobs, and no interest in bettering themselves on their own. Just looking for a man to do it for them."

Michelle stared ahead at the television. Dave Letterman interviewed Halle Berry as they showed a clip of her latest movie.

Keith continued, "You didn't know I even played football for the first month we got to know each other. You were just trying to get to know me for me."

"Shhh, I wanna see this movie," Michelle insisted, motioning to the TV screen. She needed to steal his attention from the subject of the current conversation.

"You have dreams, I mean, even though you didn't go to college, you have dreams, don't you?"

"Okay, now *that* is gonna be a good movie. Can we see it this weekend?" She tried to ignore his question, continuing to stare at the television.

Keith pressed the power button on the remote. The television went black. "Michelle."

"Yes."

"We've never even talked about your dreams. Do you even have a dream?"

"Of course." She quickly searched for an answer to a question that no one had ever asked. "I'm going to be a real estate agent."

"Really? See, that is something I never knew about you. Do you have your license?"

"Not yet."

"So this is your lifelong dream?" Keith asked.

"Well I used to want to be a veterinarian, but there was too much schooling involved."

"Oh really. How much?"

"I don't know, but I just knew there was too much for me to try to hang with it so I changed my dream."

"To something that didn't require any schooling, you lazy lima bean," he said making his tone teasing, but still trying, she suspected, to get to the root of her lack of desire to further her education.

"Whatever, Keith. Why are we talking about this?"

"Because it's important." He reached under the covers, pulled her closer to him and grabbed her butt. "And because I'm looking for a wife, a wife who has some ambition. So I need to know these things. I need to know everything about you." He playfully swatted her butt with his strong hand. She laughed uncontrollably as he reached further under the covers and grabbed her feet. He tickled her until she begged him to stop. "Dang, Michelle," he said softly exploring her butt cheeks. "You got a tight little booty." His thoughts quickly shifted from Michelle's real estate agent dreams to her hard, beautiful body.

"Yep... I played tight end in high school. Flag football," she said proudly.

"Puhleeze, you don't know a thing about football."

"Okay. Ask me something."

"Okay, what position am I?" Michelle knew, but the more she thought about it, she decided it would be cute *not* to know. She didn't want him to know that she did her research.

"You are a... linebacker?"

"Nope, guess again."

"A lineman."

"Do I look like a lineman?"

Michelle shrugged her shoulders.

"I'm a tight end." Keith sighed, as he laughed. "You really don't know shit about football, do you? How can you sit up there watching me and not know what's going on?"

"I just watch and I know that if you get in near that pole at the end and you catch the ball, you get your team seven points. That's about all I know, though." She really hadn't known much about the sport itself, but she was determined to learn as much as she could, especially if the game of football was going to get her paid. "Come on Keeeeeeth," she whined. "Let's do it." Michelle slid her body across his and positioned herself on top of him.

Weeks before, Keith had told Michelle he didn't want to make love until "the time was right." According to Keith, there were two kinds of women, real women and real gold diggers. And he didn't want to risk getting blinded by the sex before he found out which category Michelle fell under. She had expected them to get to know each other for a month or so before they took it to the next level, but Keith threw her for a loop when he continued to tell her he wanted to wait a little longer. He still wasn't sure. After a few warnings from the fearful and suspicious voices in his head that she may be after his money, Keith kept her on hold.

But whatever it took, Michelle was far from giving up. No way. Not yet. She did have goals, just ones that she couldn't tell Keith about. To her it was all a game and her goal was to win. Win big. Win her own game ball.

CHAPTER ELEVEN

Through the blaring beats of En Vogue's song "Hold on," Michelle heard her phone ring. Without bothering to turn her stereo down, she answered it. "Hello?"

"Whatchu' wearin'?"

"Dang, Kim, you're not dressed yet? You're supposed to be here by now."

"Well if you just tell me what you are wearing, then I could figure out what the hell I am gonna put on and then I could be on my way."

"Just come over and wear something of mine," Michelle said. She knew that's what Kim wanted to hear.

"Okay, I'll be there in a minute." Kim hung up and in less than fifteen minutes she was ringing Michelle's doorbell.

Michelle opened the front door to find Kim in her pajamas and a bathrobe, holding a pair of heels. She slid past Michelle and made a bee-line for her closet. "Turn that up. This is my jam."

"I know huh. En Vogue are some bad ass bitches, huh?" Michelle finished strapping her shoe on and looked at herself in the mirror. "But this bitch right here is even badder."

Kim stared at Michelle while she gushed at herself in the mirror.

Michelle was wearing a black dress so tight you would've been able to see the line of her underwear... *if* she was wearing any. "You sure you didn't paint that thing on?"

Michelle turned a 360 and chuckled.

Adrienne yelled from the living room. "And where do you think you young ladies are going tonight?"

"To a party!" Michelle yelled back.

Adrienne appeared and posted herself against the doorframe. "Whose?"

"It's pre-draft party at some hotel in Beverly Hills. Keith flew out this morning for it. His little brother is up for the draft this year. Our goal for the night is to find Kim a man."

Kim, busy fishing through Michelle's closet, poked her head out when she heard her name. "That would be nice, but I know none of these dresses are gonna look as good on me as they do on you." She slipped a purple Bisou Bisou dress over her head and groaned as she tried to get it past her stomach. She took a deep breath, sucked in the fat and groaned a second time.

"Just hurry up and put the damn thing on," Michelle said as she fumbled with the zipper. "We gotta meet Keith in 45 minutes." She stepped back and gave Kim a once over. "Yeah that's it. That one right there. You walk in to the party tonight with that dress on and you'll be able to get that man with ALL FIVE B's."

"And *what* may I ask are the 'Five B's?'" Adrienne crossed her arms and waited for an explanation.

"Please, Adrienne, you know you know what they are," Michelle scolded. "But of course I will be glad to refresh your mind. The Five B's are...number one... 'B' for "Booty". A man has got to have a sufficient amount of ass."

Adrienne rolled her eyes and laughed. Nothing her daughter said surprised her any more.

Michelle continued. "No pancake booties ova here!" She picked up the beat coming from her stereo and started dancing around the room. She stood in front of the mirror, shook her butt and stared at herself in the reflection.

"Now girls, I want the both of you to behave yourselves this eve..." Adrienne tried to cut her daughter's silly explanation short.

Michelle, holding up her finger, interrupted, "'B' number two... Body. Not only does he have to have a nice butt, but he also has to have a good body. Number three would be 'B' for Benz. If he is rollin' in a Benzo, you know he's got it goin' on. And to have a Benz, one must have *Bank*, which brings us to our fourth 'B'. 'B' for Bank. Oh yeah, mother, that is the only one you taught me about. It's these other ones that I'm just now learning about." Michelle laughed, realizing how ridiculous she sounded. She didn't care though. She continued, "And the final and most important "B" stands for Black. The brotherrrrr must have a bit of colorrrrrrr."

Kim ignored Michelle's stage performance and slipped into dress number three, which wasn't as tight on her as the others. In this one, at least she was able to breathe. She studied herself in the mirror awaiting Michelle's opinion.

"That's cute. Wear that one," Michelle approved.

"Yeah, I like that one too," Adrienne added. "And good luck on finding a man with all those superficial characteristics. What happened to the good qualities—honesty and respect?"

"I don't know ma, what happened?" Michelle turned to Adrienne and raised her eyebrows. "You never thought they were important, so why should I?" She searched the room for her driver's license. "Anybody seen my ID?" Adrienne took a deep breath, shook her head and left the room.

Kim pulled her broken-down green Nissan Altima into the valet area at the Beverly Hills Hilton. They were twenty-five minutes late when they spotted Keith and Tank at the front door, waving to catch their attention. As Michelle stepped from the car and walked toward Keith, she dreaded the long line that was wrapped around the hotel's perimeter. Keith greeted her with a hug and said, "Don't worry. I got this." After a short, secret exchange with the bouncer, Keith slipped him a crisp hundred dollar bill. Within seconds, Michelle and the others were escorted through the red ropes.

"I'll just be a minute," Kim whispered to Michelle and walked toward the ladies room.

"Oh yeah, me too." Michelle followed close behind.

"Just meet us at the bar!" Keith's words carried over the loud beat of the music.

Michelle couldn't believe her eyes. Men galore. "Damn Kim, these brothas are suited AND booted!" And to her surprise, as she glanced through the crowd, it seemed that most of them had come alone or without dates. They went into the bathroom and parked themselves in front of the mirror. "All these men up in here, we should have come alone," Michelle added. She adjusted one of the bobby pins that was holding her hair up and re-applied her Mac lip gloss. Kim stood next to her waiting for her to finish.

A tall light-skinned brotha' loitered outside the door. "Excuse me?" he said. Michelle and Kim tried to ignore him at first, but they turned around when he tapped them on their shoulders. "Excuse me?" he said again.

Kim just smiled politely at the man knowing that his interest was in Michelle. It always was.

Michelle raised her eyebrows and looked up at him. *God, he was tall,* she thought.

"Hi, I just wanted to introduce myself. I saw you walk into the ladies room and had to stop and wait for you to come out. You are straight *fine!*"

Thank you," she said nonchalantly as Kim tugged her along to the main room.

"Wait! Excuse me! Can I holla' at chu' fo a minute?" His words became anxious, almost strident as he chased Michelle through the crowd. His long legs made it easy to keep up. "My name is Spider. Spider Daniels."

Michelle stopped and gave him another once over. *What can I say to get this ugly ass giant away from me,* she thought. She threw him an apologetic expression. "Sorry, I'm married," she lied.

"That's okay. So am I."

Kim couldn't hold her tongue. "Excuse me?" Kim hissed.

Spider responded, "I said, so am I."

Kim put her arm in front of Michelle the same way a mother would protect their child from an approaching stranger. "Well then, I think you need to stop chasing down my friend and take your sorry ass home to your wife. And when you get there, she oughta hang you by your balls."

Even though Spider was speaking directly to Kim, he stared at Michelle, and licked his chops. "Actually I was thinking of bringing your friend home with me so my wife could watch her *lick* my balls."

Michelle let out a loud burst of laughter. She couldn't believe her ears. Kim, on the other hand, didn't think any of it was funny. Michelle, still laughing, spotted Keith. "Come on. There's Keith." Before Kim had a chance to shake off the moment that made her want to leave, Keith asked the two of them what they wanted to drink.

"I'll have a Cosmo," Kim managed to say, still feeling out of breath. "Thanks."

"Champagne is fine," Michelle said.

"Okay, don't move." He and Tank found their way to a less crowded side of the bar.

"Did you check out that brotha' in the chocolate brown suit over there?" Michelle asked. Kim shook her head, looking over the herd of men. "Girl, over there." Michelle steered Kim's gaze with a nod toward a group of men nearby.

"Next to the guy in the pimp hat?" Kim laughed.

"Yeah."

Kim looked at her with an I-can't-believe-you-don't-know-who-that-is look. "Girrrl, that is Dante Williams."

"Who is Dante Williams?"

"He is the starting running back for..." Kim paused, "some team, girl, you know I don't know nuthin' about no football. All I know is he has about two different commercials running right now. Look at him closer, you'll recognize him."

"Whoever the hell he is, he is foiinne!"

Kim frowned. "Michelle. Focus. You need to keep your eye over there." Kim glanced at Keith. "*He* is a nice guy. All these other guys in here, as we just witnessed first hand, are like five levels lower than scandalous. Keep your eye on the prize."

"Blah, blah, blah. Keith may be the prize, but shit, he's a boring prize. He's too nice. There's no challenge. Plus, he's probably gay because for your information, he still hasn't tried to have sex with me. What the hell is that about?" Michelle noticed Dante checking her out now. She smiled and spoke to Kim as she stared back at him. "If *that* brotha' has commercials, then *that* is the type of brotha' I need to be talking to."

Kim noticed Keith trying to get their attention from across the bar. She guided Michelle towards him and Keith smiled as they noticed he was waiting to introduce someone to them. He pointed to a small crowd of people who were congregating in back of them. The lingering friends waited patiently for Keith to introduce them. "Michelle," Keith said turning around to bring the strangers in closer. "I want you to meet my little brother."

Michelle put her hand out to shake the handsome man's hand. "Ricky, this is Michelle. Michelle, Ricky." They shook hands. "Ricky, this is Michelle's friend Kim."

"Nice to meet you," Kim said.

Ricky turned to bring a few more people into the circle. "This is my girlfriend Stefanie and this is my boy Malik and his girl, Tiffany." Everyone exchanged "nice-to-meet-you's." Michelle smiled and acted as if she were pleased to meet Keith's little brother and his friends. Her attention, however, remained elsewhere, as she furtively glanced across the room at her newfound desire—Dante Williams.

Two mornings later, when Michelle woke up next to Dante, she smiled. She glanced around the hotel room and noticed the sheer luxury that surrounded her. She watched him snore lightly as she got up and tip toed to the bathroom and shut the door so she could make a phone call on her cell phone. She thanked the stars above that Keith didn't answer his phone. She whispered, "Hi Keith. Just seeing if you made it back to KC safely. Just woke up. Getting in the shower. Call me." She grabbed the fuzzy bathrobe and turned on the bath. As she watched the water fill the tub, she laughed at herself. She couldn't believe that she slept with a man she'd met only two nights before. But she didn't care. The past twenty-four hours she spent with Dante were far more exciting than any of the weekends she'd spent with Keith or any other man for that matter.

First they had dinner at Geoffrey's, a secluded house turned restaurant off the Pacific Coast Highway in Malibu. For dessert, he took her to his home in Brentwood. Although she tried to hide her astonishment, Dante easily tracked it. Michelle simply couldn't help herself. She had never laid eyes on an estate like Dante's, except on the featured cover homes in the Sunday

L.A. Times Real Estate section. She'd never been in a Ferrari, either.

Michelle compared Keith's house to Dante's mansion as he gave her a private tour. She swallowed her laughter. *This shit makes Keith's house look like a tract home,* she thought, as she noted the intricate beauty of the architecture and the richness of his Egyptian-style furniture. She used her wildest imagination to redecorate as she ambled through the hallways knowing just how she would add her very own touches if given the chance. In the west wing, they rounded the corner to a closed double door. Dante didn't hesitate. He walked right by. Michelle's confident smile faltered, as she wondered why he didn't include the master bedroom in the tour. Saved by the ring of his cell phone, he excused himself and disappeared down the hall. Michelle retreated down the stairs and to the kitchen.

Only seconds later, Dante walked up from behind her. "Actually we should get out of here and go somewhere that has some real dessert. What do you think?"

"What do you mean?"

"All I have here is some old chocolate chip ice cream. Tiramisu and coffee Haagen Dazs rolled in by a room service attendant sounds better to me." He hurriedly led her from the kitchen into the six-car garage and opened the passenger door to his silver Range Rover.

Michelle glanced ahead fearfully as the truck bolted down and out of the cascading stone driveway.

The Malibu Inn, a luxurious, intimate hotel that sat on the sands of Malibu's beach was their next stop. Instead of declining the invitation to spend the night with a man whom she barely knew, she enjoyed the feeling of royalty he instilled when she was in his presence. Just on their short jaunt from the valet and through the hotel's quaint lobby, three strangers approached him for a quick autograph. Dante's celebrity gave Michelle a sense of importance that she'd never felt on her own.

Now, as she slipped into the bathtub and drowned herself in the lavender smelling bubbles, she decided that even though hanging out with Dante in public might jeopardize her relationship with Keith the risk was well worth it. Her choices in life were improving by the minute. A nice, under-the-radar athlete who makes millions and lives a quiet life in Kansas City *or* a celebrity athlete who lives in a 12,000 square foot mansion who has commercials. She looked in the mirror at the foot of the tub and pictured herself on the set of *The Price Is Right*. She smiled into the mirror as if she was smiling into the camera. "I'll take the one with commercials, Bob."

CHAPTER TWELVE

"Baby?"

"Huh?" Ricky answered.

"You nervous?"

"About what?" he asked.

"About the fact that if your mama's phone doesn't ring tomorrow, you are going to have to go to law school with me."

He was confident. "Trust me, the phone will ring." He patted me on my knee and continued to read the April edition of *Sports Illustrated*. I knew he was scared, but by then I was used to his inability to express such fear.

The landing gears beneath us shifted and the wheels extended from their hidden position. We descended from thirty-five thousand feet and made our final approach to Texas' Hobby International airport where we'd be met by Ricky's parents. My mind jumped ahead in anticipation of the plane ride back to California. I knew that if we weren't celebrating the confirmation of his football career and planning the necessary steps to move all of our belongings to the city of his new employer, we would be calling the university to find out when the next LSAT exam was offered. I figured it would be the former of the two, considering the myriad pre-draft reports that had been published in the past couple months. Ricky was projected to go in the third or fourth round, but his agent Mr. Schwartz warned Ricky with "I've never sat through draft day without being stunned. I've seen good. I've seen bad. I've seen the unimaginable."

The round in which he was picked was important to Ricky. The city we would relocate to was important to me. I was just ready to get on the road and start my new life with my soon-to-be husband. I was ready to go for my law degree and ready to build the picket fence. I knew if I worked at it, I could have both despite what some of my independent, ambitious friends believed. Los Angeles, however, was not a place for a young couple that aspired to raise a family. I believed Los Angeles was more of a city for those who enjoyed the fast life and for those who didn't mind a place where the emphasis was on material wealth. My dad often deemed it as "a concrete jungle infested with plastic people." And with its smog-filled air, twelve-lane congested highways, around-the-clock traffic, graffiti-filled walls, car-jackings, gangs and bubbling racial tension left over from the Rodney King riots the year before, I was ready to leave. I envisioned Ricky and me living somewhere with clean, fresh air to breathe; a place where real people lived; people who valued life as something other than a material existence.

"Where do you hope we end up moving?" I asked.

"Anywhere. You know I'm not picky." Ricky turned his head to look at me and out of the plane window at the same time. "I'll just be happy to be selected." I sensed desperation between each word he spoke. "Mr. Schwartz seems to think Green Bay is interested. Chicago also."

"Great. It snows in *both* those places."

"He also said Minnesota." Our laughter was drowned out by the engine of the jolting plane as the tires screeched on the ground.

"I'm fine with anywhere but L.A."

"You know Keith will be there. He flew in from Kansas City last night."

"Yeah. You told me."

"Apparently he's bringing Michelle, that new girl he's been seeing." He raised his eyebrows slightly.

"The one who was scoping out every brotha' at the draft party. Like she was a kid in a candy store."

"Yep, looking for the suckers. You think Keith would've learned after Samantha burned his ass." Samantha Banks was Keith's college sweetheart. Two months after he got drafted and two weeks after Keith proposed to her, he opened a stack of fan mail and found an anonymous type written letter that said Samantha was sleeping with Major Leaguer, Chris Slotter.

"It's crazy 'cause Keith is such a smart guy. You would think he could see right through those type of girls."

"Yeah, but just because you're smart doesn't mean you have common sense," Ricky laughed. "I swear, once a fine ass woman enters the room, nothing else matters to Keith. She could be carrying a shovel that has gold dripping from the last guy she got over on and still he wouldn't get it. He told me he thinks he can trust Michelle because she didn't find out about his million dollar bank account until *after* her first visit to Kansas City."

"Hmpf. We'll see how this one pans out."

"But get this. Then he tells me that the night after the draft party she didn't show up to drive him to the airport. She called the next morning and said her mother had food poisoning and they were in the hospital all night."

"Okay maybe Keith's not so smart after all."

"Dinner will be ready in an hour," Ricky's mother's voice carried from the kitchen of their 1970s suburban country-style home.

"Good," Keith said rubbing his belly. "I'm hungry. Michelle, you hungry?"

"I will be in an hour." She smiled at Keith.

"I'm not," Ricky frowned.

Keith laughed. "Rick, the phone will ring. I promise you. Everything is gonna be fine."

"It better. 'Cause if it doesn't… oh I don't even know what I'd do." Ricky held a black ballpoint pen between his fingers, flipping back and forth and twirling it through his knuckles. It was a nervous habit he said he had started in high school during the college recruiting period.

Keith shot him a dose of reality. "You'll just be travelin' north to find a spot in the Canadian leagues."

"It'll ring," Michelle offered.

Keith nodded his head up and down quickly. "But who it'll be on the other end is gonna be the big surprise. Or will it ring on day one of the draft or day two?"

"There are two days we have to wait?" Michelle asked.

"Yep. And the difference is day one you get a fat ass million dollar paycheck or day two you basically get the slave wage," Keith explained. "I remember when I had to wait for that same phone to ring four years ago." Keith looked up at the mustard yellow rotary phone attached to the wall. "Remember Ricky? I was goin' crazy. And remember Aunty Carol and Uncle Otis kept calling to see if any teams had called yet?"

"Yeah, by the way, did Ma tell everyone not to ring that phone tomorrow for any reason?"

"Yep, she did," Keith replied. "I know you all are probably wondering why we still have that ancient-ass phone tacked to the wall old-school style." Keith looked at me and then at Michelle. "It's for my superstitious brother. It's there, he thinks, for good luck. Ricky wouldn't let my mom and dad take it down." Keith pulled Michelle, who was sitting on the other end of the brown plaid cushy couch, closer to him.

"Are you even gonna be able to sleep tonight?" Michelle asked looking at Ricky.

"Are you kidding?" I cut in to reply. "We haven't been sleeping for months".

Keith added, "All we gotta do is pour some Hennessy or something down his throat and then he won't have a problem falling asleep."

Ricky shook his head. "Naw, I'm cool."

Keith tried to comfort his little brother's nerves. "We already know that you'll get a call so quit trippin'."

"But what we don't know is which city," I added. "That's what I'm worried about. Anywhere but L.A."

"Why not L.A.?" Michelle asked.

"I'm ready to get out of there. It's infested with plastic, phony people. The divorce rate is approaching 70%. The crime rate is ridiculous. The air is gonna kill us. My roommate has had her car stolen twice. It's just all wrong there. Don't you like how quiet and clean Kansas City is?"

"Yeah, it's nice, but actually I'm from L.A... not Kansas City," Michelle answered.

"Oh, oops. Well, no offense," I said. "I had thought you were from Kansas City."

Michelle shook her head.

"But Michelle isn't a typical 'L.A'. person," Keith interjected. "She likes the quiet life."

"Yeah, I actually love K.C. so far or at least what I know of it," Michelle said, lying through her smiling teeth.

The phone rang. Ricky jumped.

The tantalizing aroma of a Powers home-cooked meal captured my senses and drew me into the kitchen. Ricky's mom and pops scurried about, she measuring a cup and a half of milk, he opening a box of cornmeal. I stood for a moment and watched them in action. Then I said, "Please, put me to work." I wanted to get my mind to another place, somewhere other than whether or not the damn phone would ring the next day.

"Come with me honey," Mr. Powers nodded. "I'll put you to work." He grabbed four oven mitts and led me through the sliding door and onto the covered patio. We stood over a large vat of oil and stared down at a sizzling brown whole turkey.

"I should've guessed." Each time Ricky and I traveled home to spend time with his parents, his father had to prepare Ricky's favorite, a fried turkey.

"We wanted to make a special feast for all you kids, especially since ya'all weren't able to come out for New Year's." His country twang coated his words.

"Honey, did you know we are out of eggs?" Ricky's mother asked Mr. Powers as she poked her head outside.

"No, I didn't. What do you need eggs for?"

"The cornbread that you left in here is half done." She grinned. "Stefanie, dear, you wanna ride to the market with me?"

"Okay, let me go tell Ricky and I'll grab Michelle, too."

The three of us cruised through the streets of downtown Galveston in the Powers' 1983 Cadillac Seville.

Michelle suggested, "Mrs. Powers, we got to persuade Keith to buy you and Mr. Powers a new car."

"No sweetie, I told my boys that we didn't want anything until they were both finished with their careers. There are no guarantees in the world of professional football and we don't want them to spend a penny on us until they are set for their very own future."

"Yep," I agreed. "'Cause what you'll soon realize is that the Powers are simple, happy folks who don't need much other than their barbeque, their fried turkey vat and a house full of people to cook for."

"Keith is always trying to send money, buy me clothes, jewelry and things, but I tell him all that's not needed. Their father and I already have everything we want," she explained. "This right here I couldn't turn down, though." Mrs. Powers held up a tear-shaped three-carat diamond pendant. "It was much too beautiful."

We hopped in and out of a few local markets and then found our way to the video store. We picked up six videos, two classics and four new releases.

"At the rate Ricky is going, he'll sit up and watch all six of those straight through the night," I said.

"Why? Hasn't my poor baby been sleeping well?"

"Not at all," I answered.

"Bless his heart. I'll be glad when this is all over for you two. If I get to have it my way, you will end up here in Texas so we could come to all the games."

Michelle tried to make herself part of the conversation. "Yeah, and then Keith could get traded down here so we could all eventually be in the same town."

"Now wouldn't that be a mother's dream?" Mrs. Powers smiled at Michelle through the rear-view mirror. Something told me, however, that her smile wasn't as genuine as the ones that she and I exchanged.

"I wouldn't mind Texas," I admitted. "You'd get tired of Ricky and me, though. Always comin' over tryin' to eat some of that home cookin' that we've missed so much since we've been in college."

"No, we'd never get sick of cookin' for ya' all. Michelle, you didn't eat well when you were in college either, did you? I can tell by that little tiny waistline you've been able to maintain." She eyed Michelle through the rearview mirror again.

"Oh no, I always eat well... sometimes too well," she answered and patted her flat tummy. She decided not to mention that she didn't go to college. It wasn't necessary for anyone to know that she thought it was a waste of time.

Although I had been asleep for hours, Ricky never surrendered to his weary, burning eyes.

"Stef, wake up," he said, nudging me.

I lifted my eyelids halfway but couldn't focus.

"Wake uuuppp," he urged again.

Half asleep, I told myself this would be the last time that I would have to get up in the middle of the night because of *his* winless bout with insomnia. *The last night, c'mon Stef,* I told myself, *open your eyes. The last night.* I opened my eyes, focused my vision on the digital clock. 2:52 am.

"Watch this with me. Have you seen this?" I glanced at the television. He was watching *New Jack City.*

"Yeah Ricky. I saw it with you. In the theatre."

Ricky stared ahead as if he had never seen the movie. "It's good though Stef. Come on. This fool is about to get popped."

By the time I opened my eyes, Chris Rock had finally surrendered to his drug addition and was in a crack haze, shaking and sweaty, white lips and all. "Nino Brown dies at the end. Okay? End of story." I plopped back down on my pillow.

"There you go ruining the movie."

"Ricky," I laughed. "You've seen it already."

He decided not to reply. I was awake now and that was all he wanted.

It's the last night for this, I told myself again. Struggling to sit up in the sofa bed, my back was stiff. I was supposed to be sleeping on it alone with Ricky on the floor, but he ended up climbing aboard anyway. "Wait a minute. Get on the floor before your parents come in here."

"They're not coming in here. Besides, Michelle and Keith are in the living room sleeping in that sofa bed together. My folks should be worried about them, not us. We're engaged."

"We are?"

"Yes, Stefanie. We are."

"It's a matter of respect though. If I were Michelle, I would make sure that Keith didn't come anywhere near me in the middle of the night. Especially since this is the first time she's been out here to meet your parents."

"So. The first time you came out here with me we stayed in the bed together. Remember?"

"But I had met your mom and pops a million times already."

"Yeah, I know. I'm just messing with you," he answered. Then he stared back at the television trying to hear what Nino Brown just said. I shut my eyes hoping that he'd stay engrossed. "Stef, don't go back to sleep."

I propped myself up against the Powers' old-school corduroy arm pillow and watched. I also turned on the lamp on the night table beside the bed to keep me awake. It worked.

The phone rang.

The whites of Ricky's eyes widened and shone through the dimly lit room.

"No way. It's too early," I said.

"Grab it," Ricky said.

I reached for the phone. "Hello?"

"Stefanie," a familiar voice whispered. "It's Malik. Is Ricky there?"

"Hi, Malik," I whispered back. "He's right here. Wide awake. Hold on."

"Thanks."

I handed Ricky the phone and could hear Malik giving him a pep talk. Minutes later, after they reminded each other not to call their houses at all until they were both "gone," they wished each other luck one more time before they hung up.

"Stef, come on and kneel on the floor with me so we can say our prayers. See you were already asleep and didn't even say your prayers. You ain't right. I'ma tell," he teased. We both slid off the bed and knelt on the floor beside each other.

My prayer was silent, short and sweet. I said to God: *I could ask for special things like a good spot in the draft for Ricky. For a great city like Seattle or San Francisco. I could even ask for you to make it possible for Ricky and Malik to get picked by the same team. But I won't. I won't because I know you have it all planned out. So I'll just say this...Please God continue to take me and my family, Ricky and his family down the righteous path you've already carved out for us.* Out loud I said, "Amen" and got back up in the bed.

Ricky remained on the floor praying, begging and trying to convince the Lord above of his athletic and spiritual worth.

CHAPTER THIRTEEN

By two o'clock the next afternoon the mustard-colored rotary phone hadn't rung one time. We did, however, watch Malik's name blink across the moving ticker at the bottom of the television screen. He was selected as the sixth spot in the first round. When ESPN announced the news, live from New York, we cheered and applauded as if he could hear us. He and Tiffany would be moving to Chicago.

Half an hour after Malik was chosen, Ricky had left the living room. He watched the second half of the first round in his parent's room while we stuffed ourselves with hors d'oeuvres and left over turkey. Through the cracked door, I heard him on the phone with Malik making congratulatory remarks.

It took over five hours to get through the first round. When the second round's draft choices began we stared blankly at the television screen wishing, hoping and praying for the phone to ring. Every time the commissioner walked toward the podium to announce another selection, I cringed. Conversation was sparse. No one could seem to think of much to say. Ricky remained sprawled out across his parent's bed with the T.V. on mute flipping a sharpened pencil. I was anxious, yet dazed. Ready for it all to happen so we could breathe again.

Hours later, with three picks in the second round still left, my mind began to wander. I couldn't understand why the National Football League made the players suffer through such agony. I thought of the other college football players that were yet to be selected as they sat in their living rooms waiting anxiously by the phone, waiting for that call. Waiting for the contract. Waiting for that pedestal to be placed in front of them. Waiting to take that giant step up to fame and fortune. Waiting to be worshipped by the entire country.

As I pondered the value and respect society had for American athletes and how it was comparable to astronauts and doctors, occupations that I saw more fit for such high regard, I saw Keith's eyes widen. A sharp, quick silence snuffed out everyone's chattering as he pointed at the television screen. We listened carefully to hear something, anything, but we forgot that we had muted the television volume. Mrs. Powers sprung up off the couch and yelled toward her bedroom, "Can you see? Ricky? Can you see?"

The phone rang.

Everything around me stopped. I tried to speak, but couldn't. Ricky's name appeared on the blinking ticker that slid across the screen. His name was followed by a city. A city all too familiar to me. A city where I didn't want to be, but now, once again, would call home. A city called Los Angeles.

Ricky was on the phone less than five minutes before I heard him place it back on the receiver. He emerged from the bedroom, hands in the pockets of his jeans, his grin humble and wide. We jumped off the couch. Mrs. Powers got to him first and the rest of us waited in a semi-circle to congratulate him. I hung in back, patient, so I could get the very last and longest hug. "Congratulations," I quietly whispered, my lips touching his ear softly. His smile beamed with finality and success. Mine, with relief. It was clear to all of us that this was Ricky's proudest moment. All the distressing and worrisome thoughts were now gone. Ricky was a new person, with a new life that had begun just seconds before.

His father spoke first. "Second round! That's higher than you expected."

Ricky gulped. "Yep, way higher. I can't believe this. Really, I can't." Disbelief collided with reality as the words tumbled out of his mouth.

"I'm so proud of you!" his mother squealed.

Mr. Powers nodded, with one of those uncontrollable expressions that a father often has when he sees his son earn a taste of success. I couldn't help staring as he stood beside Ricky. The resemblance was arresting. Never in my life had I exchanged such cheerful and personal emotions with a group of people, my family or my friends. It was as if a force of positive energy, fueled by such a sudden emotional thrill, created a permanent bond between us that no one would ever be able to break.

"Okay, so you know this places me in a very precarious situation," Mr. Powers announced. "Which team am I going to support now?" His booming laughter filled the room.

"Naw, Pops, you're goin' for Kansas City," Keith replied. "When I retire, *then* you can go for Ricky's weak team."

Michelle appeared from the kitchen with two chilled bottles of champagne, one in each hand.

"This calls for a little golden bubbly, wouldn't ya' say?!" she announced. Keith hurried into the kitchen to grab the champagne glasses. Michelle set the champagne on the coffee table and followed Keith back into the kitchen.

"Looks like they are staying on the West Coast with moi," Michelle bragged to Keith, her nose in the air.

"No, 'cause *you* are going to be in Kansas City with me," he whispered through a sneaky grin. He hugged her and smothered her with a million tiny kisses. Michelle's stomach filled with anticipation. She smiled, grabbed a glass and headed back to the living room. Keith followed closely behind staring at her thin, sexy body. He knew he was getting close to giving in. He had to have her soon.

"LOS ANGELES!" Keith yelled loudly throughout the house as he walked back into the living room. "I can't believe ya' all don't have to endure the most painful part of pro sports. RELOCATING! Cause I'll tell you—it's a BITCH!"

Mrs. Powers cut her eyes at her son implying that she didn't approve of his profanity as conversation about Los Angeles filled the room.

My mind drifted in and out of the cheerful banter to what lay ahead. Although I was happy for Ricky, a touch of fear surfaced beneath the joy. Jimmy's voice was talking to me loud and clear—*just hope ya'all don't end up in Los Angeles. The sharks are circling. Waiting to attack. L.A. is the groupie capital of the country. Ricky is gonna have to have a little piece on the side. Ha. Ha. Ha.*

"Champagne? Stef?" Michelle asked me not realizing that she was interrupting a chain of horrific thoughts. She shoved a filled glass into my hand.

"Thanks," I said. Just as I thought of Tiffany, the phone rang loudly through the house. "I'll grab that." I ran to the kitchen and picked up. "Hello?"

"Stefanie!"

"Tiffany, damn! Can you believe this?!"

"Girl, you are SO lucky! We gotta go out and live in the snow, ice, wind, and blizzards." Tiffany yelled through the phone. Although she was already bitching, she sounded as if she was on Cloud Nine. After all, Malik was the 6th selection overall, why shouldn't she be? Rain, sleet or snow, Tiffany and Malik were going to be filthy rich. "What in the world am I gonna do in a place that has a wind chill factor? It's cold as hell in Chicago!"

"Hell isn't cold, fool!" I said, laughing at her sheer elation.

"But look at your situation, it's all sunshine and beaches for you!"

"Yeah, Ricky is definitely relieved. He didn't sleep a wink last night. I'm waiting for him to fall over like a timbering tree. So did you see that Chicago took that wide receiver from Michigan? I was hoping they took Ricky. Man, that'd been the best thing ever if we *all* got to move to Chicago. Dang."

"Yeah, can you imagine how perfect that would've been? But I'd have never seen you though…'cause Northwestern Medical School, here I come."

"I thought you were gonna go wherever you got in and not worry about being in the same city," I said teasingly. "See, you know you want to be with your man."

"No, the thing is…" Tiffany tried to explain.

I cut her off, "The thing is that you want to be with him and there is nothing wrong with that."

"Shut up and listen!" Tiffany laughed. "I was going to apply to Northwestern anyway. Along with UCLA, NYU and Yale and maybe 'SC. But the thing is, Northwestern has a really good program. Hard to get into, but I'm gonna write a bomb-ass essay and maybe Malik's agent will have some pull. He went through their law program and now is one of their top donors. Ha! Now come git with that!"

"So there you go. You are officially starting the perfect little life you've always wanted."

"Yours is perfect, too."

I don't know why I didn't feel the same exhilaration. I don't know why I wasn't feeling as confident and hopeful. Or why I was feeling more fearful than ever at that moment… but I was.

The phone clicked.

"Tiff, another call is coming in. Call you right back." I answered the other line. "Hello?"

"Ricky Powers, please. Jay O'Brien from the Los Angeles Times calling."

"Ricky," I yelled through the house. "Phone's for you. It's the L.A. Times."

CHAPTER FOURTEEN

Michelle caught the last flight back to California that same evening so that she could make it to work Tuesday morning. As her plane descended into Los Angeles, she thought about her weekend with Keith and was comforted by his willingness to bring her home to meet his warm, friendly family, especially during such a momentous weekend. She decided to give Keith one much needed point for that. Keith had the family she wanted to join. Dante, however, had the celebrity status she wanted to join. *Hmmm*, she thought, *what's a girl to do.*

She picked up the air phone attached to the seat in front of her, swiped her credit card and dialed the number. His answering machine picked up. *"Hello, you've reached Dante Williams and I'm unable to take your call at this time. Please leave a message or call me back at a later date."*

"Hi Dante, it's me, Michelle. I am landing in twenty-five minutes so I just wanted to make sure you were on your way. See ya' in a minute." She placed the receiver back in its slot and took out her make-up bag.

She walked down the long tunnel-like ramp into the airport and spotted Dante the moment she entered the terminal. He sat in the distance in an empty boarding area killing time on his cellular phone. As Michelle approached him, her smile widened with each step.

His smile though was more of a smirk. "How's Keith?"

Michelle looked around, panicked. She whispered, "Don't say his name. It makes me feel weird."

Dante's laugh was confident. Then he suggested, "Can you take a couple of days off work?"

"Why?" Michelle asked.

"Can you or can't you?"

"Probably not," Michelle answered. "Why?"

"I want to take you to Maui."

"Maui?" *Maui and Dante Williams. A couple of days of nothing but sunshine, drinks and good romantic sex on the beach at night. Palm trees and pineapples. Pina Coladas. Dante Williams.* She focused on his face. *Was he serious?*

"I was just sitting here waiting for you to come in and I heard a change of gate call for Flight 3200 to Maui over the loudspeaker. And they are moving the boarding gate to right here!"

"I have to work."

"Forget work. They can replace you for the week."

"I have no bathing suit. No nothing."

"I'll buy you whatever you need. We'll go shopping as soon as we get there. What's the big deal? Come on, let's go. We have exactly forty three minutes to go get tickets and get back up here," he said.

Michelle and Dante sped along a two-lane highway staring out of the window at the geometrical rows of Maui's Del Monte pineapple harvests. Michelle cuddled herself next to Dante, still in disbelief about her whereabouts and Dante's ability to persuade her to get on the plane six hours before. The blue passenger van finally slowed and crept up a winding brick driveway lined with anthurium, orchids and birds of paradise. In front of them was the Grand Wailea resort. Dawn had just broken and the early morning sunshine revealed the reigning splendor of the hotel. Dante's sleepy smile warmed her, but only for a few seconds. The fact that she had to be at work in an hour and still hadn't made the phone call to let her boss know she wouldn't be in all week diminished the paradise in front of her.

"Does your cell have any battery left?"

"No."

"Mine either. As soon as we get to the room, I gotta call Kim. Maybe she'll call my boss for me. Or maybe I'll call. I don't know. What should I say?"

"I'll call. I'll tell them you quit."

"And they'll tell you that I'm fired."

"And then I'll take care of you."

"Yeah, right," Michelle replied. *You may be joking now, but watch—I'll figure out a way to MAKE you take care of me,* she thought. "Quit talkin' out the side of that fat neck of yours." She pinched his muscular neck and then kissed him lightly on the lips.

As Dante stood at the reception counter, Michelle sat on a large, cushy couch in the lobby, using her tongue to play with the tiny paper umbrella that sat in the pink passion fruit juice they offered her upon their arrival. She sniffed the purple and white lei they had draped around her neck and looked at Dante across an open lobby that hosted ivory life-size statues and gigantic Hawaiian flower beds. She took a deep breath inhaling the ocean breeze as it swept from the shore and through the open atrium.

Finally when they got to their room, Dante pulled a wad of cash from his pocket to tip the bellboy and Michelle rushed past them making a b-line for the phone. She dialed Sunrise Cruises and the extension to her boss's voice mail. "Hi Kathryn, it's me, Michelle. I'm really sorry that this is such late notice, but I won't be coming in for the next couple of days. I hope you will be able to get a temp. I'm not feeling well. When I got back from Texas last night I felt like I was coming down with something really awful." Her explanation was far too long and Dante couldn't wait. He planted a row of wet, tongue kisses teasingly down her neck. She pushed him away with a that's-not-funny-look. "Hopefully I will feel better tomorrow. I'll call you though. Sorry again. Bye." Finally, she hung up the phone.

Dante tackled her and then pinned her down. He watched her struggle through loud bursts of laughter to free herself. Fully surrendering to his comforting strength, she relaxed her body and waited for him to lean down to kiss her. Dante's soft lips sparked a warm feeling throughout Michelle's body. A pleasurable ache flickered between her legs.

Without a word, Dante lifted himself off of her, opened his wallet and took a condom out and then carried her into the bathroom. Between the spray of the double shower heads, they washed each other's back. "Do you like what you see?" she asked him teasingly. He responded by cupping both her breasts from behind. Michelle groaned as he played with her nipples, teasing them with his fingertips. Michelle turned to Dante and pushed him into a sitting position. He carefully unrolled the condom for a snug fit. Michelle rubbed her inner thighs over his penis and then sat on it. Dante admired her beauty as she closed her eyes and gently rode him. Up and down. The water ravaged them and Dante's moans grew loud enough for her to know he was about to come. In one fluid motion, Michelle dismounted Keith, pulled off the condom and leaned over, her mouth to his penis, to finish him off. Shocked and awed, his moans were sluggish but sharp and half way through his orgasm, before he became flaccid, she re-straddled him and pulled his face into her full wet breasts, hugging him tightly as his body jerked with pleasure. "Damn baby," he said, "I don't know what it is about you. But the shit feels like magic."

"Ta da!" Michelle giggled.

Dante regained consciousness and moved his attention from Michelle's magic tricks to his now shrunken, totally exposed penis. His expression turned from a look of being ultimately satisfied to one of sheer fright. "Oh SHIT. You *are* on the pill, aren't you?"

"Of course," she lied through her pearly-white seductive smile.

Later that morning, after they had napped, Dante left the room in search of a newspaper and another box of condoms. While he was away, Michelle grabbed her cell phone off the charger and quickly dialed the Powers household in Galveston.

"Stefanie?" Michelle asked.

"Yes?"

"It's Michelle. Is Keith around?"

"Hold on."

"Hello?" Keith said.

"Hi Keith. It's me."

"Hi baby. You made it home safely?"

"Well, kind of. I made it home and this morning I went into work and then my boss asked me to work in our Southbay office. So I'm here for the rest of the week."

"Oh, well I called you late last night and you didn't answer."

Michelle thought quickly. "Oh, my cordless phone lost its juice because I left it off the charger over the weekend, and my cell was dead when I got off the plane. It's charged now... sorry. I was going to call you out there, but I didn't want to wake everybody up."

"Well give me the number at that office. I'll call you when I get to Kansas City tomorrow."

"That's the problem. I can't get phone calls here, so I'll have to call you. Or you can just call me at night. But tonight and tomorrow night I have to watch my auntie May's kids. She went out of town so I gotta pick them up at day care and go straight to their place. I have to spend the night over there." Her lies were getting more complicated now, but she was desperate.

"Well, just call me here when you get to your aunt's place."

She started to whisper. "I have to get going before they get mad that I'm sitting here just talking and not working."

"All right baby. I miss you."

"Me too." Michelle hung up the phone.

Dante swung the door open, "You too, what?"

"Me too, I hope I feel better. That was my boss."

He tossed a small paper bag on the bedside table and a box of Trojan Magnums fell half way out of the bag. She flashed Dante an inviting smile.

"Oh, but damn," he said. He grabbed his forehead. "I left the newspaper on the counter."

"Forget the newspaper."

"Naw, I found an L.A. Times. My agent called and left a voice mail message. Told me I made the front page of the sports section."

"Why?"

"Who knows? I'll be right back."

Michelle grabbed her purse off the table by the window. She glanced at the shimmering blue endless ocean. She would enjoy the view later, she decided. She took her purse back to the bed, sat down and searched through it until she found a safety pin.

"Yes!" she said out loud, holding the pin as if it were the answer to all her problems. She pulled the packets of condoms from the box and laid them out on the bed. As she poked a tiny hole through the center of each one she wondered if child support was taxable income.

CHAPTER FIFTEEN

Within three months after the draft, Ricky had moved us out of our apartment, replaced his Chevy Camaro with a brand new Range Rover, and after spending a few full shopping days at South Coast Plaza and The Beverly Center Mall, completely replenished our wardrobes. We moved into a luxurious three-bedroom apartment in the Marina, a place where most of the younger guys on his team lived. Ricky's agent wanted him to acquire some type of real estate so he could receive the tax benefits, but Ricky was hesitant about buying a home just yet. He wanted to get through his rookie season before he decided how much house he could afford and which area he wanted to live in.

"What are you wearing?" I asked as I stood inside the large walk-in closet sifting through my new clothes.

"I'm just gonna wear jeans," Ricky answered. "Wear that red strapless dress that I like." We were invited to a going-away party for Malik in Laguna Niguel at the home he bought for his mother.

"I don't like that dress. I wanna wear jeans."

"Uh-uh, wear the dress."

I rummaged through the closet while Ricky disappeared in the bathroom to turn on the shower. On my way to finding a pair of shoes, a stack of porno tapes fell on my head. "Damn!" I exclaimed. "Ricky, I thought you were gonna throw these damn pornos away!" I yelled.

No response.

I found the dress and met him in the bathroom that was three times the size of our old one. The apartment was brand new, very bright and spacious. The first piece of furniture we bought was a California king-size bed. Since Ricky wasn't much into spending his time in furniture stores, Tiffany and I took a week to shop around for the basics. Ricky wasn't worried about how much I spent. He had been floating on a cloud of dollar signs since the day he signed. His team offered him what I thought was an exorbitant amount of money, especially when compared to what most entry-level positions in the corporate America paid. And although it didn't quite compare to Malik's eight-figure deal, he was totally content.

"Stef, can you git me a new bar of soap?" he yelled from the shower. "And hurry up, we gotta go."

I grabbed a bar of soap, threw my robe off and jumped in the shower with him. I was relieved to finally be going "out" with him. Besides the draft party, and a couple campus fraternity parties, it would be only the second time we'd been to a party together.

"Who's all gonna be there do you think?" I asked, lathering up the fresh bar of soap between my hands and covering his back with bubbles.

"Don't really know, probably a bunch of UCLA people and some of Malik's people from the 'hood. And Tiffany's too. Probably people like Dante Williams will be there."

"So, when you get 'big-time' like Dante, are you gonna leave me for some younger, prettier groupie?" I asked, letting Ricky shampoo my hair for me.

"First of all, a pretty groupie is a contradiction in terms and second of all…"

"Owwwww," I whined. "You got shampoo in my eyes."

Ricky ignored me. "You can't be pretty *and* shallow. Beauty comes from within. And why would I wanna start over with someone after spending all these years with you." He paused and looked at me. Then, he continued. "Plus, knowing how much you love me, Stef, is so special. A girl that I know will be loyal, faithful and here for me until the end is a hard thing to find. So don't you go and get all insecure on me now, okay?"

Too late. My insecurities were endless. "Well, why do you watch all those nasty porno movies then?"

"'Cause, like you always say, you can't keep up with me."

"Throw 'em away. They're not good for you." I laughed. "It's dirty."

"My prude little princess."

"It's not that I'm prude, it's just that…damn… porn girls have perfect bodies. Perfect boobs and round butts." I hated my butt. Although I was glad to be tall and proportioned, I hated the fact I wasn't dealt even one "ass card". Ricky always told me that he loved my body, my boobs, my legs, and even my feet. Truth was, however, I knew I wasn't perfect and I thought maybe it was time to start working a little harder on both my inside and my out.

Ricky turned off the shower. He grabbed a towel and wound it up. He snapped it at my naked butt. I jumped out of the shower, grabbed a towel and ran into the bedroom, soaking wet.

He spoke up so I could hear him from the bathroom. "Your body is fine. It's fine and it's mine. Look at my gap. Look at the fact that I'm losing my hair. People have imperfections. But we learn to look past 'em."

"Okay, Gappy, whatever you say," I whispered to myself.

We didn't return from Malik's party that night until after 3:00 a.m. "Ricky, can you undress me and put me to bed?" I groaned. "I don't feel good."

"Should have left that champagne alone."

I winked at him and realized I could see better if I kept my right eye closed.

He unzipped my dress and pulled it over my head. "Did you have fun?"

"Mmm-hmm. Had a good time." Now, both my eyes were half shut. I was glad Ricky hadn't left me at home for this one. Tiffany and I probably had more fun than any of the other guests simply because we used the evening as a time to celebrate the fact that finally we could let off some of the built-up steam that we'd harbored over the past year. We locked ourselves in the pool house with a couple bottles of champagne making one toast after another until Ricky and Malik came to interrupt our private party.

"Yeah, so did I."

"I didn't know that Malik knew so many people."

"He knows some of the older guys, the veterans, through his agent. Like Dante, Kenny and Jaylin. They all have fat-ass contracts, play in the Pro-Bowl every year and they all are..."

I interrupted, "Scandalous and sneaky."

"Why do you think that?"

"Did you see the way they were acting? I can just tell. And did you see that one guy, Chris, the guy Tiffany pointed out who got MVP in the Super bowl last year? He had his wife on one side and his girlfriend on the other? I couldn't figure what he had goin' on."

"Well apparently it wasn't for you or any of us to figure out."

"Had a harem right up in front for all to see." I laid back and looked at the ceiling. "They probably all went home together."

"So, what's wrong with that?"

"*What's wrong with that?* Well, the fact that he is married to start off with. And the fact that," I paused, "I don't know, the threesome thing is just gross anyway."

"What's gross about it?"

"Whatever, Ricky."

Ricky leaned down and started removing my panties with his teeth.

His head lifted. "No really, Stef, what's wrong with a threesome?"

"Everything is wrong with a threesome." I pushed his head away from my thighs. "I'll be damned if I'm gonna have another girl in our bedroom with us. I ain't tryin' to share you with anyone. Are you crazy?" I couldn't believe I was even engaging in such conversation.

"You wouldn't even do it for me, baby?"

"What's in it for you? Isn't one kitty cat enough? Greedy ass! No! It's never gonna happen, so get it out of your mind." He pulled the rest of my clothes off, yanked his off and met me beneath the sheets.

"But..."

I interrupted him. "But nothing. Shut up and kiss me before I fall asleep on your sick and twisted ass."

Before the darkness lifted, I woke up to Ricky's voice. I opened up my eyes and noticed he was talking in his sleep. I listened to him trying to make out what he was saying. His words were jumbled and unclear.

"Hey, wake up." I shook him softly.

"Huh?"

"Wake up for a sec."

"What? What is it?" his voice groggy and confused.

"You're sleep talking."

He tried to smile and asked with his eyes still closed. *"Sleep talking? That's funny. I've never heard that before."* He opened his eyes and looked at me. "You want me to put you back to sleep?"

"No, Ricky. I want to talk."

"About what?" he said softly still full of sleep.

"I don't know. I guess all this football stuff is really on my mind. Tonight, at Malik's party, I was just trippin' off everyone. The whole scene seems like it's kind of a foreshadow of what our life is about to be. And it's really not a crowd I want to become a part of. Those people just seem too 'caught up'. Ya' know?"

He snuggled up against me and kissed my shoulder. "Don't worry. It's just you and me. You and me against the world."

"Promise?"

"I promise."

"Promise me you'll never get wrapped up in all that superficial and shallow side of the life of an athlete. And promise me you'll never leave me for someone prettier."

"Well you first promise me you won't leave me for someone who *isn't* going bald."

"Okay, if you promise me that you won't leave me for anyone that will do the threesome thing with you."

"Oh, well I don't know if I can promise you that," he laughed.

"That's not funny," I commanded.

"Stefanie, relax. You should be excited for what's ahead. You are thinking about a bunch of stuff that is never gonna happen. Ain't nobody leavin' nobody. I'm here to be your husband, to take care of you and to father your children." He paused. "Matta' fact, let's get started on it right now." Lazily, he scooted on top of me.

"No," I whispered. "We have to wait until we are married. And I'm on the pill anyway."

"Well, stop taking it then Stef. I want a baby. Come on."

"Not 'til we are married. I told you. So quit asking."

With that, I pushed him off me, rolled over and shut my eyes. Ricky cuddled up against me from behind and we both fell back to sleep.

CHAPTER SIXTEEN

The loud shrill of the telephone interrupted my peaceful sleep. Frustrated and angry at whoever it was, I grabbed the receiver off the nightstand. I didn't even say "hello." I just listened.

"Girl, WAKE your tired ass UP!"

"Damn, Tiffany, shhhhhhh." I put my index finger over my mouth as if she could see me.

"Guess what?"

"What time is it?"

"I don't know what time it is out there, but I do know that out here it's nine-fifteen." She paused. "I was just looking at Malik's schedule and his team plays Ricky's team this season. Twice. Once here and once there."

"Tiffany?"

"What?"

"You woke me up to tell me some unimportant shit like that?"

"Yep!" she ignored my frustration. "So, you gonna come out when Ricky plays out here?"

"I don't even know when his first game is. He's still up at training camp. He won't be back for two more weeks. I miss him," I groaned, stretching my tired body.

"Stop missin' that fool. You need to be using this time to prep yourself for the LSAT." Tiffany waited for a response that I didn't give her. "You ain't even thinking about that are you?"

"Of course I am. But I missed the deadline to put in applications for this year so now I have to wait for next fall. And that isn't for a year and three months."

"Well good you have more time to prepare. I'm telling you, LSAT, MCAT, all those tests ain't no joke."

I tried to brush her off. "Yeah, yeah."

"Yeah, yeah nothin'. I'm taking the MCAT next month and getting my apps in this January. Girl please, nothin' is guaranteed with these fools," Tiffany said. "How many more times am I gonna have to tell you?"

"Actually, none. Starting today," I spoke with heavy sarcasm, "you don't have to tell me ever again. Okay, mother?"

"All right, missy," Tiffany warned. "So whatcha' been doin? I mean besides missin' Ricky?" Before I got a chance to answer, she continued, "I've been shoppin' like a mad woman. Malik and I filled the entire house with new furniture already. Some of the stuff hasn't arrived yet. It's coming little by little. And he bought me a whole new winter wardrobe. Oooh, they got some fat gear out here."

"For real? Yeah girl, just been hanging out. I've been up to the training camp a couple times to see Ricky during his dinner breaks and other than that, still getting this apartment in order. I'm going up there tonight to have dinner with him. I'm gonna surprise him."

"Naw, I ain't been up to the training camp yet. I've been taking advantage of having Malik absent for the past four weeks. I met some new friends at the hospital where I am volunteering and they have been taking me out and showing me around."

I decided to change the subject and share something that had been on my mind more and more with each passing day. "Tiff? Has Malik ever mentioned that he wanted to have a threesome with you?"

"No, why?"

"The night of Malik's party, Ricky hinted around about it. He didn't push it, but I just wanted to know if Malik ever tried anything crazy like that with you."

"Uh-uh, but Malik has never hit me, either."

I froze and tried to figure out who had the big mouth. "Who told you?"

"Malik."

"Damn." My sigh was heavy and I immediately tried to defend myself. "It wasn't like it seemed. Actually I tried to hit him first."

"Stef...."

I interrupted her before she could start lecturing me. "Really, Tiffany. It wasn't that big of a deal."

"Well, apparently it was because Ricky went to counseling for it. DON'T TELL HIM I TOLD YOU. YOU BETTER NOT!" she demanded.

"He did?"

"Yep. Malik said that Ricky was all messed up behind it. He didn't know where it came from and eventually the school psychologist guessed it was some uncontrollable impulse from the pressure he was under."

"Hold on. My other line is ringing." I pushed the flash button. "Hello?"

"Stefanie?"

"Yeah?"

"It's Michelle."

Michelle? At first I wondered who Michelle was, but then I realized it must've been Keith's new girlfriend. "Oh yeah, Michelle. How ya' doin'?"

"Good. What's been up?"

"Not much, just getting settled in our new place and missin' Ricky in the process. He's been away at training camp."

"Yea. Up in Fresno, huh?"

"Yep. And call me crazy, but I find myself behind the wheel as often as I get the chance, driving up there to see him." I wondered how Michelle knew it was in Fresno, but quickly decided that Keith had probably mentioned it to her in passing.

"I'm calling to see if you wanted to meet up and have dinner or something since Ricky's away."

"Sure." I figured I could just surprise Ricky tomorrow night instead.

"Tonight? You aren't doin' anything tonight? Going up to see him or anything like that?"

"No, tonight's fine. We can go to dinner."

"Actually, oops, you know what? I just realized, tonight is not good after all." Michelle fidgeted over her words. "Anytime later this week is actually gonna be better for me. I'll just give you a call towards the end of the week."

"Okay, that's fine."

After we said our good-byes and hung up the phone, I thought about how strange the phone call was.

Michelle paged Dante and waited for him to call back as she sat at her desk and stared into the psychedelic screensaver on her computer. *What luck for Dante and Ricky to end up on the same team,* she thought. She realized she was playing with fire, but she knew if she were careful, she wouldn't get caught.

Bored, Michelle thought about the bleak possibility of advancement at Sunrise Cruises and decided to grab an L.A. Times from the lunchroom to check out the employment section. She wondered if anyone at the company had ever worked their way up the corporate ladder from a receptionist position to one of the executive positions. Then she realized she'd have to spend time in school, getting a formal education. She knew even if she did have the chance to go to college, she didn't possess the courage. The courage one needed to compete against a student body was something Michelle never felt burning within her. No one ever told her that she was intelligent. She was "beautiful," "pretty," and "gorgeous," but never "smart."

Michelle remembered a night when she was seventeen years old. She overheard Adrienne on the phone with her biological father. Michelle had only seen him twice in her life, but as she approached her high school graduation, she'd secretly hoped that he would make a surprise appearance. Even though she barely squeaked by, she wanted to make her father proud. But when she heard her mother pleading with him to show, she knew her prayers would go unanswered.

"This may be the last time she actually achieves something we can be proud of," Adrienne said. She spoke loud and clear into the speaker phone as she washed the dishes.

"No college plans?" Mr. DeVeaux asked.

"Come on Ray, you know Michelle isn't the sharpest tool in the box. That child couldn't get admitted into a city college if she tried."

"Well that is too bad," he replied. "Looks like she is just going to be a clone of her shiftless mother."

Michelle listened through the cracked door, expecting her mother to defend herself and perhaps say something in Michelle's defense as well. But she didn't. Instead she attacked the man who, so many years before, left them without word or warning. "You haven't changed a bit, have you? Is it that impotence problem that is still making you so angry?"

Michelle didn't feel like hearing another back and forth between her mother and "the coward" and walked away. Adrienne's inability to defend her only daughter and to preserve her own integrity were enough to make Michelle sick to her stomach. She knew from that moment on, she would never be on her side again. She also knew that, in the end, she would have the bigger house, the more expensive car and the bigger bank account. And she couldn't wait for her mother to ask her for a loan. She would never help her out nor would she ever claim Ray DeVeaux as her father. As a matter of fact, she couldn't wait to replace his name with the name of a real man.

Three lights on her 24-line PMX switchboard lit up and interrupted her painful thoughts. "Sunrise Cruises?" she said, answering one line and placing it on hold to answer the other two. After she transferred the calls to their appropriate departments, she channeled her thoughts somewhere a little less depressing. She thought back to the time when she and Keith finally consummated their relationship the night before he had to leave for training camp. She laughed, thinking of how he almost ruined the entire lovemaking session by checking every other minute to make sure the condom didn't break or fall off.

The red lights started blinking again. "Sunset Cruises?" Four more calls came through as she forwarded those on as well.

The fifth call was Kim. "What up?"

"Nuthin'," Michelle responded placing her voice right away.

"It's Friday, girrrl. We gonna hit the Market?"

"I'm going up to see Dante," Michelle said, sounding apologetic.

"No, you are not!"

"Yes, I am too." Michelle responded matching Kim's tone.

"As your dearest friend, I guess it's my duty to tell you that you are stupid with a capital 'S'. Didn't you tell me that Keith's little brother and Dante were now on the same team? And didn't you tell me that you and his little brother's girlfriend were friends now?"

"Yeah, Ricky and Stefanie. Uh-huh. But correction, I wouldn't consider Stefanie a friend. She's a bit too, you know, out-of-style and just boring, ya' know? Boring personality, dry sense of humor, can't dress for nothing. Put it this way, Stefanie is the type of girl who would take Target or Old Navy over Gucci. And besides, she and Ricky won't last. She's so homey, I give them less than a year."

"What if Keith's little brother sees you? Or even better, what if Stefanie goes up there and visits him?" Kim asked.

"I just called Stefanie to make sure she wasn't going up there, so all I have to do is make sure I don't run into Ricky. And Dante said he'd meet me at a restaurant anyway. So it's not like I have to actually go into the dorms. Hold on." Michelle picked up the other blinking line and then came back to Kim. "Okay I'm back."

"I dunno about this, Michelle. Why can't you just be happy with Keith? He's so sweet. He's such a good guy. How many guys do you know that won't sleep with a girl until they really and truly get to know her?"

"Yeah, whatever. He's full of shit. What he's worried about is me getting pregnant before we get married. Look…the bottom line is that if Keith decides to one day walk out, like my father did, no notice, no caring, no money, no nothing, then I'll have a backup-man plan."

"But why another athlete?"

"Because athletes have body *and* money. Doctors and lawyers have money, but don't let 'em take their clothes off. Uh-uh, honey, their bodies… most of 'em are out of shape or skinny or nerdy. And then you have the gym rats that have spent all their time in the gym and none at the library. Yeah, they may have body, but at the same time they're dumb as a doorknob and don't have a penny or a pot to piss in."

"Why are you so damn crass?" Kim asked.

"I'm not crass. I just like to keep it real. I say what most are afraid to say. Athletes, they have it all. They have the slammin' bodies. They got the cash. And they have enough intelligence to have a decent conversation. Call me what you want Kim, but this time I'm out for mine. I'm tired of givin' it up and gettin' nothing in return. Good stuff costs money and ain't nobody told me that my stuff ain't good. So there you have it."

"Don't let Keith *and* Dante walk out on you. No other football players will take you seriously. You know that, right?"

Michelle didn't hesitate. "There's always the NBA. And don't forget about the Major Leagues. I could learn to speak Spanish and get me one of those fine ass pitchers from the Dominican Republic." Her laugh was evil.

"Wow," was all that Kim could say.

"Kim, I hate to be so bold, but during my life enough people have convinced me of my above average looks, right? And isn't it a known fact that fine women attract men with money?"

"I can't answer such an idiotic question."

"You think I'm crazy, don't you?"

"No, but if you want me to be honest, I think that really deep down inside you feel ugly and insecure because of how your father treated you. You keep saying how FINE you are, but you don't really think that. Really, you hate yourself. And to make yourself feel better, you go after these get-rich-quick, overnight millionaire athletes so you can get back at your parents to show them that despite what they think about you, you can be successful. You are tired of them calling you stupid, dumb and a waste. I know, Michelle. I've known you for your whole little life. And I've always held my tongue until now. Girl, you've got serious issues and they are gonna come back and bite you in the ass if you don't watch it."

"Hold on." Michelle switched over to another blinking line. "Sunrise Cruises?"

Kim waited a minute and a half before she realized that Michelle wasn't coming back.

Michelle pulled into the 7-11 parking lot at exactly 8:02pm. She noticed Dante's silver Range Rover hiding inside a secluded corner. She crept up beside him and noticed his seat was fully reclined. He was fast asleep. She rolled her window down, turned off her engine and watched him for a moment before she spoke. "Bed check!" she yelled through his open window. Startled, Dante opened his eyes.

Slightly panicked, he asked, "How long have you been sitting there?" What time is it?"

"Time for you to explain this." Michelle threw the current month's issue of "Black Life Magazine" through his window. It hit him in the head. "I read an article in there today as I was leaving work about how *Dante Williams* and his *wife* Maxine live in Brentwood with their two dogs, Dolce and Gabbana. You are such a liar. You told me that you've been separated for over a year."

"Don't believe everything you read."

"Dante, whatever. You're lucky I'm not in love with you cause I'd…"

"Michelle, I brought you to my house. How could I be married if I brought you to my house and made love to you in my bed?"

"I wouldn't put it past your indecent ass." Michelle laughed to make her accusation less potent. And then, because she didn't believe one word he ever said, she had to get one last jab in. "And for your information it wasn't love that you made to me."

"Maxine moved out over a year ago. End of conversation. Now are you getting in or not?"

Michelle got out of her car and jumped in his truck. She sat in the seat with her back up against the dashboard. The better she could look him in the eyes while he drove, the more she could read each little lie. She picked up the magazine and turned to Dante's article. "His wife Maxine likes to garden and buy baby clothes. What kind of woman buys baby clothes before she is even pregnant?" she asked.

"She was buying baby clothes since before we got married. She just wanted a baby that bad, I don't know, it was just her thing." Dante turned up the music. He was done with that part of the conversation. But Michelle figured whether he was lying or not, she would continue to use him for anything she could get. Him *and* Keith.

Five minutes later they pulled into the parking lot of the college dorms that housed the team. Dante circled the lot twice looking for a spot.

"Ooooooh, look, Michelle, it's your girl." Michelle's eyes followed Dante's directly to Stefanie. She was getting into Ricky's car two spaces over from them.

"Oh my God," Michelle said quietly. "Do you think she saw me?"

"You still worried about Keith? Michelle come on. Keith is *not* thinking about you. Trust me on that one."

"You *wish* he wasn't thinking about me. Trust *me* on that one."

"Feisty, fine ass." Dante laughed. "Okay, well it doesn't look like she is going anywhere. Look." Dante stared at Stefanie sitting in the car.

"What is she doing?"

"Probably waiting for Ricky."

"She said she wasn't coming up here. I called her today to make sure."

"She lied." He raised his eyebrows and looked at Michelle. They both laughed. "Stay right here." Dante got out of the truck and walked over to Stefanie. Michelle watched him speak to her through the open car window. Then, he turned around and walked back to the truck and got in. Michelle ducked as he opened the door.

"Would you relax?" he said laughing. "Okay, so yeah, she is waiting for him."

"Well, I ain't gittin' out until she is out of sight."

"Then you ain't gittin' out."

"Why?"

"'Cause Ricky won't be coming anytime soon." He pressed his lips together and then let out a heavy sigh. "Ricky had *alternative* plans. He told me at practice today."

Michelle sighed. "Let's get out of here." Dante started up his truck and pulled out of the parking lot.

Ricky sat in the beige metal folding chair and slammed down a domino so hard the flimsy card table almost caved. "Blam, nigga what?" he yelled. "See Gina, I *always* get these fools." He smiled at Gina who shifted her hundred-and-ten pound body to his other leg and pulled her black spandex dress down a couple inches to stop it from riding up any further. She undid her long ponytail and let her shiny, black hair flow. Gina was a Filipino and Japanese mix. She had a deep tan and fine features.

Ricky met Gina at a red light just weeks before. She was on her way to the team's cheerleading tryouts when she saw him sitting high above her in his truck. All it took was an innocent smile and a wink for Ricky to roll down his window and ask her to pull over. Gina smelled money and Ricky smelled an easy target. One night later in a hotel room, after he told Stefanie he was going "out", Gina had given him what he'd wanted. Ricky was right on schedule. One day before he was to report to Fresno, he had officially found his training camp ass.

Ricky continued to loud-talk his opponents. "Ya'all can't get me. When are you gonna learn? We've been at camp how long? And not once have any of you sorry mutha fuckas got up in mine."

"Nigga shut up, damn! Sorry ass hasn't even made the team yet and you steady talking all this shit!" Big Henry said as he swished the dominos off the table and rose up out of his chair almost knocking Gina aside with his three hundred pound body. "Don't forget the donuts in the morning, rookie BITCH!"

Riotous laughter filled the room.

Ricky smiled victoriously. He asked, "Where's D-Manny at?"

"Out to eat with that broad he had up in here last night."

"Good. Keep him out of the room until bed check." He scooped up Gina, walked out of the sliding glass door and headed across the quad to his dorm. On the way to the room, a quick thought of Stefanie rushed underneath his consciousness trying to pry the lithesome cheerleader from his grip. But one look at her half-exposed silicone mounds, and her perfectly round ass shooed all thoughts of Stefanie aside. The few times he chose to lay down with Gina caused a string of guilty thoughts, but using the justification that he wasn't married allowed him to feel okay with his cheating ways.

The activity in the dark parking lot lessened as I watched the clock move to ten o'clock. I called Ricky's cell phone one more time, but continued to get his voicemail. I dialed my old apartment hoping to reach Marie or Jana.

"Hello?" Marie answered.

"Hey. It's Stef."

"What up?"

"Hey, will you call me back and see if my phone is working? I think I have bad reception and no calls are coming through."

"Why? Where are you?"

"Girl, just call me back. Five-five-five-four-zero-five-eight. Bye."

The phone rang immediately. I pushed send. "Yeah."

"It's me," Marie said. "What are you doing?"

"Waiting for Ricky to call me back. I'm up at his training camp and I knocked on his door and called him and he hasn't called me back," I explained.

"What time were you supposed to meet him?"

"He didn't know I was coming. I was gonna surprise him."

"Didn't you learn from the last time you surprised him?"

I got back to Marina Del Rey shortly after midnight. Stripped off my clothes and left a trail from the front door to the bed and lowered myself beneath the sheets. I just lay there in a daze, frustrated because of my unsuccessful surprise visit. Didn't even turn the lights on or check the messages. The neon glow of the clock radio lit up the room with its bright numbers. 1:00am. I picked up the phone and instead of dialing his cell phone, I called directly to his room. Finally, someone picked up, "Hello?"

"Ricky?" My voice was anxious.

"No. Hold on." I had awakened his roommate, but didn't care. At least Ricky was there finally.

After his roommate covered the mouthpiece of the phone, I heard rumbling and whispering. Then, I heard Ricky walk out of the room and shut the door behind him. "Hello?"

"Ricky, where have you been?"

"What do you mean?"

"I came up there. You weren't there. I left a message on your cell and you didn't call back. I waited for over an hour."

"You came up *here?*"

"Yep." I sat up in the bed and stared at the darkness.

"I was in Patrick's room. We were slappin' bones. You should have asked someone to find me."

"I did. I saw Dante. He didn't know where you were. I paged you on your two-way three times."

"My cell was back in my room."

"Whatever." My face got warm. I felt like he was lying. But why start a fight now? What would it resolve? And what if he was telling the truth?

He's not, Stefanie. He's not telling the truth. Can't you see that? He is telling a lie. And what if he is telling the truth? You know how he gets when you accuse him of something. You know he's gonna end up hanging up on you if you start. Just shut up, hang up the phone and go to sleep.

Nuh-uh Stefanie, tell him how you really feel. You're trippin' letting him get away with anything he wants. His pager was NOT back in his bedroom. That is the oldest lie in the book. The only thing that is back in his bedroom is a groupie chick that is probably still there at this very moment. C'mon, you are sharper than that! Don't let yourself be disrespected. "What is the point of having a cell if you are gonna leave it in your room?" I asked, raising my voice.

He raised his. "What is the *point* of coming up here without telling me first?"

I hung up.

He didn't call back.

See? You should have listened to me. I told you to hang up without mouthing off and you could have avoided this whole thing.

NO. You should be proud you stuck up for yourself. Yeah, what you need to do is develop some strength and stop allowing him bring out your weakness! Stand up for yourself and don't listen to that devil.

Okay, fine. Be a bitch and nag, nag, nag. See where that gets you.

No. Not a bitch. Just a good woman looking out for yourself.

Nag.

"Everybody just shut up!" I yelled into the quiet, still room. I covered my ears trying to make the voices go away.

CHAPTER SEVENTEEN

"*I'll take the original,*" I said. "*And a Diet Coke.*"

"Me too, but make mine really hot," Michelle told the waitress. "And I'll have a Diet Coke with lime. A water also please."

I stared at Michelle while she spoke to the waitress and wondered why she was dressed as if we were at some posh Beverly Hills restaurant. We were at Killer Shrimp, a small seaside shrimp shack. Were three-inch heels really necessary? I couldn't figure out whether to feel underdressed because of my Nikes and jeans or to just chalk it up as a difference in style between the two of us.

"All of our shrimp comes hot. There's no medium, mild or hot," the waitress said, her voice tight. "Anything else?"

We both shook our heads and the waitress left.

"Yeah, whatever, we'll see what their version of hot is," Michelle said.

"Trust me, it's *hot*. But it's good."

"My mom is in from New Orleans. Anytime she cooks, *that's* hot... which I guess ain't often."

"Oh, I didn't know you were from New Orleans."

"No, I'm not. Just Adrienne, my mom. She followed her first husband out here. They didn't even last a year. My mom had me with her third husband. She's been married four times. Spent her life chasing paper. It's really a shame."

"Chasing paper?" I asked.

"Yeah, chasing men with money. My mother has never worked a day in her life. She has been living off alimony and the skimpy child support my dad gives her. Been in and out of court suing her ex-husbands for all she can get."

While Michelle talked, I noticed every man in the place, black, white, Latino and Asian had been sneaking glances at our table ever since we'd walked in. I knew that she had to be used to the attention although she didn't seem to notice or care about any of them.

"So, what's up with you and Ricky?" she asked. She slid some ice from her glass into her mouth and chewed on it.

"Same 'ol. They have their first game this weekend."

"I know. Keith is flying me out to watch his opening game on Saturday. I'm leaving tomorrow."

"I'll be going alone or I'll try to drag one of my old roommates with me. None of my friends are really into football though. Well, except for Tiffany. Remember you met her at that party?"

Michelle nodded, seeming indifferent to Tiffany.

"Yeah, her man also got drafted this year. They had to move to Chicago. And then my other college friends, their men either didn't make the draft or are still playing at UCLA." I turned around and grabbed my jacket off the back of my chair. "It's cold out here, we should have sat inside."

"Hey, I have an idea. I'll go with you to Ricky's games when I don't fly out to Kansas City." Michelle smiled as if it was the best thing she'd ever thought of. She sipped her water and made a face. "I need some Pelligrino."

"Yeah, anytime, let me know. But won't you be bored not knowing anyone on the team? I can't watch a football game unless I know someone on the team."

"Well, I know Ricky, don't I?"

"Yeah, I guess you do. Well, like I said... anytime. Just let me know. When are you leaving for Kansas City?"

"Tomorrow after work."

"Where do you work? I know you told me, but I'm sorry, I forgot."

"Sunrise Cruises."

"I can't wait to get my career going. I'm kind of getting over this staying at home cooking for Ricky every night not having my own life crap."

"But Ricky's perfectly capable of taking care of you. Why work?"

"Yeah, but I wouldn't be satisfied with my life just being a housewife."

"I'm sure you could get used to it. That is what every woman wants, whether they want to admit it or not. So just get him to marry you, have a few kids and then you don't have to worry 'bout anything."

"Okay Michelle, *now* who is the paper chaser?" I asked, not caring if I offended her.

"No, it's not even like that. I mean, when I was talking about my mom, what I meant was that she tries to act like she really loves these men that she marries. And that isn't right. If you are going for the money, then just admit it. Wear the shit on your sleeve. Don't wear a mask."

Michelle was out of her mind. I was glad Tiffany wasn't at the table with us.

"I could never live with myself. Too many lies and schemes. I never understood women that can just lie to themselves, their men, their families. And those are the ones we gotta watch out for, cause they'll turkey baste your man right out from under you," I said.

Michelle looked at me inquisitively.

I laughed. "Yep. There are girls who are so damn desperate to get pregnant by a paid brotha' that they'll try to use a turkey baster."

131

"What do you mean? How?""

"It happened to one of Tiffany's boyfriend's friends. This guy in the NBA. Yep. He has big dollars and this girl he met during All-Star weekend tried to tag his ass."

Michelle swallowed, put her fork down and stopped eating.

I continued. "Check it out, okay this is what happened. After they finished gettin' busy, he got up to go wash up in the bathroom. But he had left the condom on the side of the bed. Do you know she pulled a turkey baster out of her purse and started sucking his semen out of the condom so she could re-insert it all up inside her."

"Nuh-uh, I still think you are lyin'. Can sperm even stay alive after it comes out like that?"

Then I realized I shouldn't be passing along groupie secrets to a groupie. I thought I better change the subject before she used my stories to trap Keith. I shrugged my shoulders and stuffed my mouth with a piece of bread. I noticed her eyes watering and I knew that the food was getting to her. "Hot, isn't it?"

"Damn. You weren't kiddin'," Michelle said as she quickly gulped her water until her glass was empty. We both sat there for a moment trying to digest both the spicy food and the entertaining conversation.

"So Keith tells me that you and Ricky are engaged or were engaged or will be engaged. He didn't really know. Said he couldn't keep track of you two."

"Yeah, we *were* engaged, but we had a fight and I flushed the ring down the toilet."

"How big was the diamond?"

"Half carat."

Michelle shook her head. "Oh no, you *should* have flushed that little pebble down the sewer. Honey, trust me you'll be gittin' much more than that next time 'round."

"Personally, I don't care how big a diamond he buys me, I just want to get married!"

"Well, I'm tryin' to get no less than three carats," said Michelle. "Four carats if I'm lucky."

"I guess for you, that's fine. Me, I'm the jeans and t-shirt kind of girl. A four carat diamond would look stupid on me."

"You're very wrong. A big diamond looks stupid on nobody." She shook her head. "All the wives out in K.C. have big ones. No one sports that half-carat stuff. Honey, these men have money and trust me they know who our best friends are." Michelle nodded, wiggling her fingers. "They know."

It was at that moment that the thoughts whirling around inside my head surprised me. As Michelle talked, I started to feel like a big 'ol diamond on my finger might not be such a bad thing. Never before did I think about the carat size of a diamond. But for the first time in my life, I wondered if maybe I did have one that people would see how much Ricky truly did love me. But then my conscience scolded me and snapped me back from that lost and insecure place I'd been finding myself in lately. *Stefanie! Wake up! What is wrong with you? You are a small town girl who was raised with a sense of self and security! You are an independent soul and a smart woman. The size of a carat does not determine a man's love for you! You're losing yourself. You better watch out.*

I took a swig of my Diet Coke and got up to go to the restroom. I needed a break from Michelle and from the fake and phony energy that she brought to dinner.

Michelle excused herself from the row of loud gossiping women. Their shrieking laughs and constant giggling conflicted with the intermittent waves of nausea she had begun feeling earlier that morning. As she stood up, she felt dizzy and light-headed. It was half-time anyway so she didn't feel as if she'd miss much of the gossip. She followed the crowd up the endless, concrete stairs desperately trying to get to the restroom.

The line spilled out of the ladies bathroom and into the concrete hallway of the stadium. Michelle impatiently waited for ninety seconds and then walked to the front of the line. "I'm sorry, but do you mind if I go in front of you? I'm going to lose my lunch all over the place if I don't get in there." She grimaced, patting her stomach.

Within seconds, she was bent over the stinky toilet giving up the nachos that she'd eaten an hour before. A victorious smile escaped her as she sat on the cold, concrete of the restroom stall and tried to let more nausea pass. Michelle knew that she was one of two things: violently sick with the stomach flu or pregnant. She said a quick prayer that it was the latter.

"Hey girl," someone yelled from the long line of waiting fans.

Michelle stood up, washed her hands at the sink and looked for a face to match the voice. It was Cindy, one of the rookie's girlfriends.

"Wait for me, okay?" Cindy yelled.

"All right, I'll be outside." Michelle stepped outside to wait for Cindy.

Michelle put two fresh sticks of spearmint gum in her mouth and leaned against the wall, waiting for Cindy. Busy calculating how many days it had been since she slept with Dante, she didn't even notice the heads she was turning. One gentleman, walking with his wife, whipped his head around so fast to check out Michelle in her painted-on sky blue dress and matching heels that he ran into another man who was carrying a tray of concession items. Beer, popcorn and attitude sprayed everywhere. Michelle glanced over at the commotion completely unaware that she had created the mess in the first place.

Cindy bounced out of the ladies room. "C'mon, we're late, the second half already started." Cindy grabbed Michelle by the arm and pulled her along. Michelle knew that Cindy wasn't concerned about the actual game itself, but instead she wanted to hear the gossip that spilled out of the mouths of the wives and girlfriends that circulated throughout their seating section. Gossip about so and so's man and who caught their man with so and so's girl and which girl got shorted on the size of her engagement ring, or which girl scored with a five carat ring and which girl got pregnant by who and why she was *really* with him when he looked like that and which girl's kids were bad and which girl's outfit was the most obnoxious and which girl's skirt was the shortest and why the hell she was wearing that to a football game and which man's girl was doin' another player on the team and which girl's man was about to leave her and whose husband was about to be axed from the team and which girl's man had herpes. When the word "herpes" surfaced in their constant chatter, that's when Michelle had to duck out of the conversation. She told the girls once, "If Keith ever brought home herpes or any STD for that matter, I'd cut his dick off. And then I'd shoot him."

Lots of gossip went on during game time in section 114, rows 11-21. But Michelle's favorite topic of conversation was when they tried to figure out which player had more than one of his women up in the stands. One time Rachel, one of the player's wives, pointed out that James Black, the starting running back, had two of his women seated eleven seats from each other. At first, the two girls were totally clueless. Each time James gained a few yards, they'd both clap cheerfully. But by the second quarter both girls became suspicious. When James ran for 80 yards and scored a touchdown, each girl jumped out of her seat cheering and the suspicious eye quickly became the evil eye. At the end of the game, everyone involved waited to see who the victor was. Only one of them would win and it was always decided at the locker room waiting area. One girl got to wait for

James and drive home with him. The other had to drive home alone.

Michelle looked to see who was in James' seats that day. She noticed that all of his seats were empty, and wondered if he'd finally been caught.

Halfway into the third quarter, Patrick recovered a fumble. Michelle noticed that Cindy wasn't cheering. "Girl, you better cheer loud enough for Pat to hear you down there."

"I'm mad at Pat."

"Why? What'd he do?"

"Yesterday I found out that he has had this secret voice mail number hooked on to his two-way pager."

"What did you do?" Michelle asked.

"I drove down to their practice facility and waited until he got out and told him to cut *it* off or I was cutting *him* off. Nigros always trying to have side dishes. I swear men ain't shit."

Rachel turned around from the row in front of Michelle and Cindy. She said, "You know Maria caught Bobby tryin' to have two phone lines in the house."

"What do you mean two phone lines?" asked Michelle.

"Okay so you know her and Bobby don't live together," Rachel explained, but lowered her voice peeking up at Maria sitting three rows up. "But she is always spending the nights over there so Bobby had two phone jacks right next to each other. One for his women and one for Maria and his family. So when Maria was around he'd plug in his regular line. When she wasn't around he'd plug in his hot line."

"How did she even know?" Cindy asked.

"She was looking for her earring one morning after he'd left for practice and she noticed a contraption coming out of the phone outlet that allowed two phone lines. So she plugged the other line in and waited. Girl, do you know that phone started ringing off the hook?"

"She answered it?" Michelle asked anxiously.

"Uh-uh. No," Rachel shook her head. "She waited until later that night when they were both at his house and she secretly plugged the other phone line in when he wasn't looking. Hot line started ringing and he answered it thinking it was the other line. Maria saw him glance behind the nightstand to see which phone was plugged in to which jack. When he hung up the phone he was in such shock he just flubbed up his excuses and got..."

"Busted!" Michelle laughed. She wanted to say, "Ladies, get with it here. Those are the oldest tricks in the book." She wanted to tell them that she has even used the two-line phone trick herself. But she didn't. She knew she couldn't trust Cindy or any of the girls in her section with her secrets.

Cindy asked, "Maria left him right?"

Rachel whispered, "No, she's right up there, a few rows behind you."

Michelle searched the crowd above them. "Dang, she is even cheering for his sorry ass. Look at her."

"Look Michelle, Keith is trying to get your attention."

Michelle waved toward the field and smiled down at him.

"That's so cute. Patrick never waves to me," Cindy frowned. "I wonder if he even knows where I am sitting. He probably doesn't," she continued to talk to herself. "I mean since this all basically new to both of us... you know the NFL and all...but I like it though. I could keep this up for the rest of my life. Just chillin' and not working. Just spending time with Pat, coming to the games on the weekends."

"Well enjoy it now," Brittany, a girl sitting in front of us who had overheard Cindy talking said. "Because you never know when your man is gonna get his walking papers. N.F.L. in case you didn't know stands for, Not-for-Long."

Cindy said, "Or you know my stepmother's daughter, she has been going to these damn games for 13 years straight."

"With the same guy?" Michelle asked.

"Yes, with the same guy, you slut." Cindy laughed. "Well I guess you could call her my stepsister, but I don't really refer to her as that 'cause we are only bound together by an 'I do' that'll probably turn into an 'I don't' sooner than later."

Rachel decided to add to the story, "I'd be lovin' life too if my man made the money that he makes."

"Who is he?" Michelle asked trying to get herself involved in the conversation without really caring.

"Dante Williams," Cindy and Rachel both said in unison.

Michelle whipped her head around and looked at Rachel. "Wait a minute. I heard Dante and his wife split."

Rachel laughed. "Maybe for a night so he could tramp around with one of his many girlfriends. Girl please, Dante Williams is a known philanderer."

Cindy shook her head. "Yep and Maxine stays with him no matter what. You should hear the stories she has told me. It'll make your stomach hurt."

Rachel added, "There are rumors that he has a wife, Maxine plus three girlfriends that he takes care of. They all live in different cities. And they all have kids by him. All of 'em except Maxine."

Brittany couldn't help it. She turned around to the row in back of her to add her two cents. "Oh hell no. That fool got way too much mileage on his dick. That shit is probably about to fall off. Nasty ass mutha fucka." A few spectators sitting close by were trying to enjoy the game but interrupted by the foul language. They glanced at Brittany, hoping she'd shut up.

Michelle shook her head and looked for Keith on the field. She watched him catch a pass and run a few yards. She clapped and smiled. Cindy high-fived her when the announcer alerted the fans, "First down!"

Cindy nudged Michelle. "Aren't you glad you have a good man, girl?

Gosh, some of these men, I swear. Just raggedy ass nigros."

At that moment, Michelle made a promise to herself to leave Dante alone and focus solely on Keith.

CHAPTER EIGHTEEN

*I*t *was still dark outside. Ricky's hand softly grabbed my bare shoulder.* His touch was rough, almost like sandpaper. He tugged at me, but I didn't budge. I didn't say a word. Didn't even open my eyes. I knew what was next. I knew he was on the other side of the bed wide awake. I knew he wanted to talk. And I knew what it was about.

"Stef?" he whispered. "You awake?"

"Kind of. Not really. Yeah I guess," I mumbled quietly.

"Can I tell you something?"

"Ummm hummmm."

"I love you."

So far I was right. Next he was going to apologize for anything he's ever done to hurt me and then he was going to tell me that he's worried about getting cut from the team.

"Me too."

"But that's not what I wanted to tell you. I mean it is, but…well…" he paused, "…that night I hit you in the face, remember?"

"Yeah, how could I forget?" Sluggishly, I turned my body over and faced him, still keeping my eyes shut.

"Well I went to talk with someone about that. And I know you never knew, but I want to tell you what the man said." Because his words were honest and his tone wakeful, I knew he'd been up for hours. "He said that I wasn't a violent person and that I didn't have natural tendencies to do that kind of thing, but that the pressure of what I was going through sparked it."

I lay there and listened to him reiterate everything that the shrink said.

He continued, "He said that if I ever go through another traumatic time, that I should really work on trying to control my pent-up frustrations and worries. He said the best way to avoid it happening again is to talk the shit out with someone close to me."

"I agree. And I think that someone should be me."

"Well, I'm going through another traumatic time."

"This is all because your coach isn't giving you any time on the field, isn't it?"

Even though it was almost pitch black in the room, I could see Ricky nod.

I lay the palm of my hand gently on his face. "You are not going through anything that anyone else in life doesn't go through. Everyone has to go through obstacles and challenges before they reach their goals."

"But this is different. What if I get cut?"

"You won't. You just have to rise to the challenge. It's not that easy for anyone, Ricky. People in the work force, people in professional sports, students, even mothers and housewives. Think about the struggles that medical students go through for all those years before they actually get that MD tagged on to the end of their names. Think about the nine months that a woman has to go through worrying about labor and delivery, worrying about if her baby will be healthy. What about the guys who were drafted in the last round? Think about how hard they have to work to even make it week to week in training camp. We *all* worry about tomorrow. It's natural."

"I know, but Stef, I want this so bad. I've been thinking about this time my whole life."

"And you know what I've been thinking?"

"What?"

"When the hell you're gonna get up and brush your teeth," I laughed, hoping to lighten the mood. "Talk about dragon breath, you could light our sheets on fire right about now."

Ricky inched away from me and laughed. "Shut up, it's not funny. None of this shit is funny right now."

"Okay look, you've already made it to the league, that's your goal. Now you just have to establish yourself. You don't have much else to worry about if you ask me."

"No, *you* don't have nothin' to worry about. You are set. You got cool parents. You got me. You're straight."

"You know what my biggest worry in life is?"

"What?"

"You."

"Well don't worry. I'm not goin' anywhere. I promise."

"What if you break the promise?"

"You can write a book about me and tell everyone I broke my promise."

"You're not interesting enough for a whole book." I laughed. "So what else did this head doctor say?"

"Nothing."

"Nothing at all?" I asked.

"Nope."

When the phone rang, I glanced over his shoulder at the clock again. 4:25 am.

"Who in the world would that be?" I asked. I leaned across him to pick it up. It was Keith wanting to talk to Ricky.

"Yeah, he's right here."

"Hello," Ricky said. He paused and listened through the receiver. I could slightly hear Keith's voice, but couldn't quite make out what he was saying. "Uh-huh. Yeah man, I know what you mean." He listened some more. "Yeah, I feel you." He nodded his head again. "Yeah, but you got to do the best thing for you, man, not her. Uh-huh," he said. "Well, are you sure it was an accident?" He pressed the receiver tighter against his ear. "Yeah, man, I know. You're right about that. All right then. Well, just remember whatever decision you make, I'm here for ya'," he said, speaking quietly into the phone, his tone filled with sorrow and regret. "All right. Later." He hung up the phone.

"What happened?"

"Damn, Michelle is pregnant."

"Shouldn't we be happy?"

"Well, Keith is happy, but he wanted to be married first. You know Keith is a by-the-book type of guy. The last thing he wants is Michelle's belly to poke out through her wedding gown. He's pissed because Michelle said she was on the pill and they had been using condoms and he can't understand how she got pregnant."

"Oh damn." My mind raced back to a few conversations Michelle and I had about women tagging men with turkey basters and securing their futures by having kids with millionaire athletes.

"They're going to elope."

"When?" I asked.

"Next week. They are just gonna fly down to Miami with Patrick and Cindy, do it and fly back. Gonna do it on Tuesday. He wanted us to come, but knew it would be too much to get down there and back for Wednesday's practice." Tuesday was the league-wide day off. It was the only day of the week that the players got to sleep in. Ricky shifted the conversation to us. "That's two birth control methods more than we are using and we still are coming up dry. What's up with that?" He laughed and rolled towards me and rested the front of his body up against the side of mine. "Why can't we get pregnant too?"

"No way," I said, shaking my head back and forth. "I'm like Keith. I want to do it the right way. The way my parents did. The way your parents did. The way it should be done."

"Come on let's make one right now. Feel him. He is even getting hard." He rubbed himself up against my thigh.

"Let's have a double wedding with Michelle and Keith."

He frowned. "Stef, I'm really just not ready yet. I love you and I don't want you to think that just because we aren't married that I don't. I just want to be one hundred percent ready and I wanna mean it when I say "I do.""

I rolled over and turned my back. I had nothing more to say.

Off-season. A six-month vacation. No alarm clocks, no weekend games. I couldn't wait to have Ricky all to myself. I was glad that his rookie football season was finally over.

The "high" lasted exactly four days. We lounged in bed all day. Rented movies. Watched every NBA game that we could find. Read the paper. Had sex. We even ate in bed. The only time we got out of bed was to shower and run to Blockbuster to grab some more movies. I had Ricky all to myself. Little did I know that he was just waiting for Malik and his other cronies to return to Los Angeles so they could resume their buck wild adventures on their nights "out." Except now, going "out" was different. They were no longer young, broke college students. Now, not only did they have all of the latest Enyce, Roc-a-wear and Phat Farm gear, a wad full of hundreds in their pockets, brand new Porsches, Benzs and BMWs, but now they had names for themselves. They were professional athletes.

With the new silver Porsche Ricky had purchased, Malik's midnight blue convertible Mercedes Benz, and Jaylin's black 700 series BMW, they were a trio that turned the heads of hungry women. Each night they'd caravan to the clubs, separately. I asked Ricky why they couldn't all go in one car. His reason was that if someone felt like leaving the club sooner than the others they were free to leave. I laughed in his face when he threw that excuse my way. It was plain and simple: their cars were their bait, bait to reel in the sharks they encountered at the nightclubs. "Face the facts, Ricky," I told him. "Those cars are like candy is to little kids." I prayed at night that he would grow up and get over this post-adolescent stage.

Of the first twenty-seven nights of the off-season, Ricky and his friends had gone "out" on nineteen of them. But of course, there were perks for Tiffany and me. Some weekends Ricky and Malik dropped their platinum American Express cards in our hands. It was almost as if they were paying us to get out of their hair. We would drive to Palm Springs and run up their credit cards as if we were getting back at them in some way. A suite at the Four Seasons, cocktails by the pool and a day-long shopping spree at the outlets suited us just fine at first. But after a few weekends in the 106 degree heat, I realized that no friend, no American Express card, no suite at a five star hotel could compare with a lazy weekend at home with Ricky doing absolutely nothing.

Deeper into the off-season, Tiffany's days were spent at the UCLA and 'SC Med libraries and her nights were spent at home, sprawled out on her floor surrounded by anatomy and physiology books. I often called her when Ricky went out hoping she'd want to have dinner or catch a movie, but her time in the library became more important. Jana and Marie were in the same boat. Working diligently on their M.B.A.s, they too were buried in books.

Now, staring through the darkness at the ceiling, suffering from the same insomnia that Ricky had had for so many years, I wondered if Tiffany was still awake. I fumbled around the sheets for my cell phone and dialed her number.

"Hey, Tiff."

"Hey now."

"Whatcha' doin'?"

"Just shuttin' these books."

"Damn, it's two o'clock in the morning. You haven't even officially started med school yet and you are already pullin' all-nighters?"

"I gotz to git prepared, do you know they only admitted four blacks into this freshman class?"

"FOUR? Damn. Do they have a high attrition rate?"

"Well, if they do, you know they are expecting me to make it higher. The other three of *us* are Ivy League undergrads, so you see I'm already the underachiever of the underachievers."

"I'm surprised you even got in."

"Me too. But I think it was Malik's agent who sealed the deal. He made a few calls a few weeks before I got my acceptance letter. He donated a shit load of money to the program some years back."

"Back-door influence at its finest."

"Yeah, that and the fact that your girl here has a lot of other stuff to offer. You know, like my top 90 percentile MCAT scores." She paused. "Oh, and don't forget I ran track, and volunteered at County hospital since I started at 'SC. They like that kind of stuff."

"You don't have to sell me. I know you got it goin' on."

"*And* because I am worldly, a humanitarian, I speak almost fluent Spanish, and I have the finest man on the planet," Tiffany boasted.

"Second finest," I said. We both laughed. "Speaking of, is Malik home yet?"

"Yeah, he just got in. He's in the kitchen making his greedy ass some food."

"See, Ricky's not even home yet."

"You need to stop worrying about that fool Stef and git your own stuff to think about."

"What? Somethin' on the side?"

"Uh-uh, somethin' like a life. You haven't even thought once about law school or nuthin, huh?"

"Yes, actually I have."

"Well, you better think some more about it 'cause... okay let's talk hypothetically. What if they were out tonight meeting the women of their dreams and we were assed out by next month? Then what?"

"Then I'll have to kill somebody."

"Men like strong, independent women, Stefanie. Women that have their own things going for them always win. Trust me. I'm telling you. Ricky could be out there just getting' buck wild right now and you're just sitting at home waiting for doomsday. Let me tell you what's going on out there in Chicago. Maybe this will set you straight. My friend Jodi told me that a bunch of the guys on the team out there bought an old house, fixed it up real nice and use it strictly as a place to satisfy their extra-curricular urges."

"No way."

"Yes way. Jodi said she found out about it and she followed her man there one night. Bold-ass Jodi got out of her car and started peepin' in windows. Yep. She said there was all kind of activity goin' on up in there. Women all over the place. Bimbos. She knocked on the front door, snagged her man and made him come home." Tiffany cleared her throat. Then she started to whisper. I assumed Malik was near. "So you see you gotta be careful and get your own stuff together. Secure your future girl, cause you never know."

"I hear Ricky's Porsche pulling past the security guard. Let me go." I lied to Tiffany because it was too late at night to be getting lectured.

I watched the digital click slowly tick towards morning hours. The room turned from pitch black to fading gray as the sun slowly began to rise. I thought about Ricky and whether or not I should just leave him. I wondered if his team had a house like the one Tiffany was talking about. *Maybe I could just pack my stuff and be out of his way before he got home. But where would I go? I guess I could go stay with Marie and Jana. They were my friends, they'd let me shack up. But Ricky was my best friend. I know he doesn't want me to leave. I know he doesn't even think he is doing anything wrong. He is just having a good time. Living his life. Enjoying his success. But, then again, Tiffany was right. I was the one he came home to. I was the one he loved. Am I just being too rigid? Maybe I should start going "out" too. Naw, clubs never did anything for me. I did need to get myself together though. Tomorrow I would call and sign up to take the LSAT.* I had to get my butt in gear.

The house phone rang. "Hello?"

"Is Ricky home?" an unfamiliar female voice asked.

"Who is this?" I asked.

"Is he home?"

"Depends who this is."

"Ask Ricky who this is. He should be getting home any minute now." Click.

I sat up, flicked on the lights, ripped off the covers and got out of bed. I could hear my heart pounding in my eardrums. Adrenaline flew to every imaginable part of my body. I paced up and down the hallway with the portable phone in my hand. I wanted to call whoever it was back, but the caller ID was blocked. I called Ricky's cell. It went straight to voicemail. I dialed again. Then I heard his engine roar as he pulled past the guard.

"Where the hell were you just now?" I asked him before he could even make it inside the apartment.

He stopped in his tracks. He was confused by the sight of me, standing in the middle of the foyer butt naked with a frizzy half-ponytail, half-Afro, the house phone in one hand, my cell phone in the other.

"Where were you, Ricky? Some girl just called here asking for you and telling me she was with you and that you'd be home in a minute." I lied a little bit, but I figured I didn't want to leave any room for him to talk his way out of it.

"I don't even know what you are talking about."

"You know damn well what I'm talking about!"

"Probably just someone playing on the phone. Why you trippin'?"

"Why am *I* trippin'? It's always me that's the one trippin'. I'm so sick and tired of this shit. Where the hell do you go all the time at night? Who were you with? Whoever it was obviously knew you were on your way home."

He walked away and left me standing there in the dark empty hallway. I followed him.

"I'm leaving you if you don't tell me where the hell you were?"

"Stefanie, relax. I was with Jaylin and Kenny." He walked towards the bathroom and headed straight for the shower. "We were eating at Jerry's Deli. You are making something out of nothing once again. Getting all worked up over some girl who has nothing better to do than try to stir up some shit. I swear I was with Ken and Jay. You can call them up at their houses and I bet they are either just getting home or on their way. You wanna call?" He turned on the shower.

I threw both phones on the floor. "Why are you taking a shower?" My hands were on my hips.

"The same reason that you are always accusing me of being with someone else. NO REASON!" He pointed his finger in my face and growled. "Now back up away from me, quit accusing me of shit and we'll be just fine."

Flashbacks of his open hand striking my face threw me back into reality.

I mumbled, "Crazy Dr. Jekyll Mr. Hyde ass." I grabbed my cell phone off the floor and walked into the guest room. I pulled back the covers on the bed and decided it was time to wake up from this nightmare.

When I opened my eyes, I felt like I'd been run over by a steamroller. It was 8:45 in the morning and my cell phone rang loudly in my ear.

"Hello?"

"Stefanie? It's Jimmy. You're late."

"Oh, damn, Jimmy, I forgot I made an appointment."

"That's alright. You wanna come around two instead?"

"Yeah. That'll work. See ya' then." I hung up the phone and shut my eyes.

"You forgot you made an appointment?" Ricky asked. He stood in the doorway in a pair of blue plaid Calvin Klein boxers, his eyes still half shut, with one hand behind his back as if he were hiding something.

"Yeah I'm gonna go at two," I said. He walked over to the bed and carefully got in beside me. He put whatever it was that he was holding beneath the bed.

The sight of him was making me sick. "I'm in the guest room for a reason," I said.

"So am I."

"I'm serious, Ricky."

"So am I," he said reaching under the bed and then placing a red rectangular box wrapped in a white ribbon on my chest. "How's Jimmy doin'?"

"Not good. He's been getting medical treatment for his muscles for six months now and he still can barely lift his left arm. And now it has gone into his right arm."

"*What* has?"

"Whatever it is that is making him lose his strength."

"*What* is it though?"

"The doctors still don't know."

"How could they not know?"

"Medical mystery, I guess. I really don't know." I stared at the tiny box in front of me. Curiosity overwhelmed me, but part of me wanted to throw it against the far wall. Hard. I wanted to break whatever was in it. But the other part of me wanted to rip the ribbon off of to see what was inside.

"You wanna open that, huh?"

"Not really. Guilty gifts don't count."

"Guilty gifts?"

"You did something. You know your ass is guilty. You feel bad. You give me a gift. A guilty gift. And then you feel better about whatever it is that you did."

"How can that be if I bought it yesterday, *before* you started actin' crazy?"

I undid the ribbon.

"It's a thank you gift. You have stuck by me this past year and I feel that I couldn't have made it without you."

It was a tennis bracelet. "Dang Ricky, this is…well, I don't know, I'm speechless."

"Put it on," he said anxiously. He took the box from me. "Here, I'll do it."

As he fastened the string of glimmering diamonds around my wrist, I tried to love it. But I didn't. It just wasn't "me."

"It's perfect," he said.

"Just as perfect as the brand new Porsche you bought and that diamond watch you bought me last month, huh?" I teased him.

"What? What do you mean?"

"No Ricky, it's beautiful, it really is, but don't you think it's a little expensive? I mean do you think we really *need* all these things?"

"I just wanted to say thank you and buy you a present to show you how much I loved you. That's all."

"Well, thank *you*, but next time you know what I'd rather have?"

"Huh?"

"A nice quiet night, just the two of us. Here, at home. Make me a candlelight dinner or something. I just want you, baby, that's all." His face dropped. "That's not what you wanted to hear, huh?"

"No, that's fine, but you do like that bracelet, don't you?"

"Yeah, but it's just not something I *need*. It's *you* that I need. Time. Time with you, okay?"

"Okay," he said, he looked at me both apologetically and intensely. He thought for a moment. "But baby, damn, we *live* together. How much more time do you need?"

"The eight hours we are sleeping together doesn't count, Ricky. I need more."

"Okay when you get back from Kansas City on Monday, everything will be different. I promise." He snuggled his face into my neck and fell asleep.

I lay awake and stared at the row of diamonds that loosely hugged my wrist. Despite my recent protest, they actually did look beautiful and sparkly, almost as if they were smiling at me, yelling to me that Ricky loves me. Suddenly, the nightmare with Ricky the night before slipped behind into a foggy dream. Having him close to me like this was all I needed. Even though he wasn't the perfect man I, as a little girl, had hoped for, he was close.

CHAPTER NINETEEN

Michelle beeped the horn of her silver Mercedes 600 SEL when she saw me walk out of the airport. I threw my weekend bag in the backseat and jumped in the front.

"Well, I'll be damned. Stefanie Pointer finally broke down and ordered that much needed make over."

I laughed lightly. "I don't know whether to say thank you or fuck you."

"Girl, you look good. What the hell happened?"

"The day before I left Ricky came home with enough new clothes to fill five suitcases. He said he couldn't have me going out to K.C. looking all shabby."

Michelle looked down at my shoes. "Those shoes are bad ass. Damn, Ricky has good taste. Keith would rather have me in a pair of old tennis shoes and jeans. Isn't it funny how different they are?" As Michelle pulled away from the curb, she caught a glimpse of my tennis bracelet. "Oh wait a minute! Was *that* in the gift bag?"

I nodded.

"Oh, hell no. You wanna trade brothers?!"

The thought of that was more weird than funny so I changed the subject. "Oh look at the baby!" I leaned over to touch and talk to Michelle's stomach.

"Hi, little baby."

Michelle grinned, "Isn't this somethin'?"

"You look really good for being eight months pregnant. What have you been doing?" I asked.

"Absolutely nothing."

"Figures."

"Well, actually," Michelle said, giggling between each word. "I lied. Keith practically drags me down the stairs by my hair every morning and throws me in the pool. He leans over me while I swim like he's a coach training me for a damn decathlon."

"We should get him a whistle on a string."

"I know... we should! No, for real, I ask him to make me swim everyday. Please Keith wouldn't care if I gained a hundred pounds. Nothing gets in the way of his excitement. He reads to my tummy every night. Sings to it in the shower. And he already opened a trust account for it. In the name of Ryan Powers."

"Ryan? I thought you weren't gonna find out whether it's a boy or a girl."

"We aren't, but its name is gonna be Ryan regardless," Michelle said as she stared back and forth between me and the road. "And what about *you?* You know this means you're next. Mrs. Ricky Powers."

"No, I think you'll be the only Mrs. Powers around here."

"Why? What's up?"

"Nothing. And that's the problem. Ricky just doesn't seem ready. He has been going out a lot with his friends and we just don't seem as close as we were in college. The money and everything seems to be coming between us. I mean it's nice to have, but he just seems like he is changing."

"He's still young, but he'll come around. Or you know you can always *make* him come around?"

"Naw, just 'cause I get pregnant doesn't mean he'll marry me. He's not like Keith," I said putting my foot in my mouth.

"That's not the *only* reason that Keith married me," Michelle protested. *And if he did, so what,* Michelle thought, *you only wish you were in my shoes.*

As they pulled up to the house, Michelle's friend Cindy flew out of the front door and ran toward the car. In her desperate attempt to get to us, she turned her ankle twice. Michelle laughed loudly. "Oh Lord, she must've set the house on fire."

Cindy frantically jumped up and down like a two year old who had to pee, waiting for them to roll down a window so she could deliver the news. Michelle opened her window.

Cindy exclaimed, "I dropped the cake!"

Michelle could only laugh.

"Stop laughing, Michelle. It's not funny. Your baby shower starts in two hours and I dropped the damn cake."

"What happened?"

"Nothing. I was walking out of the house just taking it back to the pool house and it fell out of my hands."

"Let me ask you this. So were you wearing those shoes while you were carrying the cake?" Michelle asked. Then with the quick touch of a button, she rolled up all the windows. I took that as our signal to finally get out of the car. Michelle introduced Cindy and me and we all paraded into the house.

"Cute dress," Cindy said to me.

"Thanks," I smiled.

Michelle spoke up. "Stefanie all fly in her Gucci."

Stefanie, you are slipping. Look at you. You got these girls thinkin' you're comfortable and with their program. Don't lose yourself. Watch it. And don't say I didn't warn you. I hushed the voices inside my head. Maybe I was being too hard on myself. What's wrong with a nice outfit every now and then?

Cindy and I spent the next hour decorating the backyard. Keith and Cindy's Pat had enough time to get across town to a baker and pick up another cake before Michelle shooed them away for an afternoon of golf. The moment they left, the door bell started to ring. Over 35 girls filed through the house and into the backyard for the party. I was surprised that Michelle had made so many friends so quickly, but soon realized that every guest was a girlfriend or wife of one of the teammates. Adorned in, Chanel, Gucci and Donna Karan and armed with Louis Vuitton, Fendi, Marc Jacobs or Prada handbags, the guests might as well have been in Paris at an annual fashion convention. On any other given day in my life, if this were a competition, I would have lost. Before that moment, I wouldn't have been caught dead in such high fashion attire. No Escada for me. No Louis and certainly no objectionably high heels. But it wasn't any other day. It was a new day and my designer dress and heels gave me a ticket to compete. And from the looks, stares and countless comments I received, I think I may have won.

After we played four different games, Michelle spent over two hours opening gifts for little Ryan. "Oohs and aaahs" circulated throughout the yard and sometimes echoed off the green hills that were less than a quarter mile away. The day was perfect and the mood was anxious as it often was when there was a new baby on the way.

That night I woke up on top of the covers. The television was on and so were the lamps on each nightstand. I was momentarily confused, not having the faintest idea where I was. Then the poster-size action photo of Keith catching a game winning touchdown against Ricky's team reminded me that I was still in Kansas City. It was 12:30 am.

Wishing that Ricky had come with me, I pulled my cell phone off the charger beside the bed and dialed our number. I waited. No answer. Instead I got my own voice telling me that we weren't home. I hung up without leaving a message. Then I called his cell phone. Straight to voicemail.

I changed into a homely nightgown my mother bought me for Christmas the year before and carefully tiptoed down the stairs and into the kitchen. Pouring myself a glass of water, I realized that a small lamp had been left on in the family room. I wandered toward the light and was startled by Keith, asleep on the couch with a book laid out across his chest. I gasped and accidentally woke him up.

He focused his half-open eyes on me. "Oh, hi."

"I didn't even see you. I was just about to turn out all the lights."

"Oh," he said, still a bit confused. "I must've fallen asleep reading." I noticed he was reading *What to Expect When You're Expecting* "Where is Michelle?"

"Asleep, I assume. It's after two in the morning."

"Oh, God. I must have been knocked out."

"Yeah, guess so," I said.

"I've been reading this stuff so much lately that I'm starting to have crazy dreams," he said holding the book up. "I mean not because this book is crazy, but I'm ready for her to pop it out already."

"I'm sure all fathers-to-be go through it."

"Yeah, I can't wait to see Ricky when you are expecting."

"Yeah, don't hold your breath," I sighed. I turned off the light and followed Keith up the stairs.

"Be patient. My brother is a rare breed. But if you're patient, it'll happen."

I was too tired to respond.

"Alright, Stef, I'm gonna take it down for the night."

"See you in the morning."

I couldn't fall asleep. The mystery of how Keith and Ricky came from the same parents raced through my mind until the clock turned to 1:49 a.m. I dialed Ricky again. It rang four times before it went to his voicemail.

Ricky stood at the bar in the back room of Club Peanuts and waited for the bartender to take his order. His cell phone vibrated against his leg. He pulled it out of his pocket. "Stefanie is calling" blinked across the neon blue face. He pressed "no answer" and shoved it back into his pocket. He decided not to get a third drink and perched himself on a barstool and watched the grand finale from afar. Jaylin and Kenny were front row and center. They slung a handful of twenties at the naked women who pranced across the stage in nothing but a pair of stiletto pumps, a G-string and a mask. Ricky didn't need to be any closer. His favorite dancer was backstage counting her tips, gathering her belongings. He wished she'd hurry up. After watching nude women gyrate their hips in his face, rub on his penis and swing on the poles all night, he wished he could click the heels of his Timberlands and already be in bed with China.

Finally, she appeared. She held hands with her stage partner, Honey, and searched the club for Ricky. The two of them were dressed in something as skimpy as a summer beach cover up, plastic stilettos and a face full of make-up. Their caramel-colored skin shone in the red lights that lit the club and their long, fake hair bounced with their step as they walked toward Ricky. He rose off the barstool to meet her halfway, waving discreetly.

"Ricky, Honey wants to come with us," China said.

"Okay, but I have the two-seater and last time we did that we got pulled over."

"That's because you were swerving," Honey laughed.

"Honey, will you drive?" asked China. "So that way me and Ricky can sit in the passenger seat?"

Honey nodded and said to Ricky, "Only if you finger her all the way to the hotel."

Ricky corrected Honey, "We're going to my place."

"Where's your girlfriend?" China asked.

"She's out of town."

They walked out into the Los Angeles night air and waited for the valet to deliver the Porsche. Within minutes they stood at the front door of Ricky's apartment and waited anxiously to get inside. Before Ricky unlocked the door, Honey grabbed his hand. "Can I taste?"

Ricky put two fingers in her mouth while China watched.

When they finally got inside the apartment, the girls jumped in a hot shower while Ricky found his way to the kitchen and grabbed two bottles of Cristal he'd picked up earlier that day. Then he thought about it. They were some fine ass broads, but they weren't worth the Cristal. He put the champagne back in the fridge and pulled out one bottle of Moet.

When he heard the shower go off, he met them in the bedroom and dried them off with an extra large black terrycloth towel while the girls slurped from the bottle of champagne. He undressed as the girls made their way underneath the sheets in a matter of seconds. Ricky took a seat on the bedroom couch and watched for a moment while Honey spread her legs and offered herself to China. Ricky tried to maintain himself as he listened to Honey moan, but he couldn't. He put the champagne down and joined them.

"I want some of this," China said grabbing between his legs.

Ricky played between Honey's legs while China sucked Ricky as if she were in a contest. Ricky pushed Honey's head down to join China. "Why don't you taste it, too?"

Honey obliged.

Ricky was beside himself. "Oh shit, ya'all. Damn." He looked around for the box of condoms and clumsily swung around to reach them. With his dangling left foot, he knocked a framed picture to the ground. The sound of shattering glass brought Ricky out of the moment. He peered at the floor. The shattered picture was of him and Stefanie on their last trip to Hawaii. Their happy faces held his stare… but only for a moment.

"Don't worry. We'll clean that up later," China begged.

But Ricky had lost his erection. He got up from the bed and grabbed the bottle of champagne. Ricky took a swig and poured some of it down Honey's chest. China bent over to lick it off. "Stay just like that," he told China as he got hard all over again. Ricky stood behind her, put a condom on, slapped and then grabbed her butt cheeks. As soon as he pushed himself inside her, the phone rang.

"Fuck!" he yelled. He knew it could only be Stefanie.

"Yes, fuck," China said.

"No, I mean fuck this." He pulled himself from China and retreated to the couch. The two girls ignored his retreat and didn't break their stride. Ricky watched from afar, trying desperately to stamp out all thoughts of his fiancée and get back in the mood. He didn't want to waste this moment.

CHAPTER TWENTY

"Honey, grab the baby bottles in the dishwasher," Michelle yelled through the house to Keith. "Hurry, we're gonna miss our flight." She grabbed little Ryan, picked up the smallest of the three suitcases and headed for the garage. They were headed to California for Ricky's first play-off game. Keith's team got bumped out in the first round so they decided to take Ryan out to meet his Uncle Ricky and Auntie Stefanie.

The moment they boarded the plane, the bleach blonde fifty-something year old flight attendant appeared and asked if they would like something to drink. "No thank you," Michelle responded. "We're fine for now."

"My name is Carol if you need anything." Then in a baby voice, Carol added, "What a beautiful baby you are." She extended her index finger for Ryan to grab.

"His name is Ryan," Keith said proudly.

"How old are you?" she asked the baby as if he could answer for himself.

"Come on Ryan, tell the lady you are six months old," Keith said.

Ryan flirtatiously cooed back.

"He's gorgeous, really, he is." Carol offered. "Takes after the both of you I might add. You are such a beautiful family."

Keith returned a sheepish grin while Michelle got settled in the window seat.

"Are you a professional athlete?" Carol asked Keith.

Keith nodded.

"Oh my. For our mighty Kansas City team I hope?"

Keith nodded again. Michelle beamed. She loved it when people noticed her semi-famous husband.

"And you must be his wife?"

"Yep, that would be me."

"Wow! Look at that rock," the meddlesome flight attendant continued.

"Oh yes, my husband has good taste, doesn't he?"

Hours later, Michelle, Keith and Ryan met Malik, Tiffany, Ricky and me in Beverly Hills for a crab feast. At a large round table, we caught up on the recent goings on in our lives. While Ryan clamored for our attention, Ricky teased and taunted the others about whose team was better. Ricky won the debate every single time with, "But *who* is still in the running for the Super Bowl?" Malik and Keith had nothing to say. "Not you," he pointed at Keith. "And definitely not you," he said. "So you both better get down on your ashy knees tonight and pray to the Almighty. You may want to ask him for a place in next year's play-offs."

Tiffany interrupted the constant flow of laughter. Once again, she wanted to make a toast. "I'd like to make a toast to all of you competitive egomaniacs here at this table, including you, Ryan. I see you're already developing into a typical Powers man."

"No wait a minute. I want to make a toast this time," Malik interrupted.

"To *what?*" Tiffany argued.

"To you," he said. He smiled at Tiffany, took a deep breath and pulled a ring box from his pocket.

All of us halted our conversations and stood still with baited breath.

"I want you to marry me."

"You do?"

"Yes."

"Well, okay, I will." Her smile was sweet. He opened the tiny velvet black box and flashed a sparkling princess cut diamond. Again she said, "Yes. Of course I will." Malik placed the ring on her finger as Ricky and Keith smiled and gave a light, quick applause.

It was the simplest proposal any of us had ever witnessed.

Keith raised his glass. "Okay everyone. To Stefanie!"

I looked at Keith, "You mean, to Tiffany!"

"No, I mean to you. The last one standing. A toast to you because you are next. There's no one else left."

Michelle and Tiffany raised their glasses along with Malik and Keith. Ricky was frozen in place, stunned by the pressure of five sets of eyes on him. Even Ryan looked his way.

I saved him by saying, "And I'd like to shift the toast to Malik and Tiffany, congratulations!"

We clinked glasses and quickly forgot about the uncomfortable maneuver Keith had just pulled. Ricky was still wide-eyed and speechless.

Ricky was quiet on the drive home. I didn't want to ask him what was on his mind. But if I had to guess, I would've said that it was the pressure from his family and friends for us to seal the deal.

When we got in bed, he reached in the side drawer of his night stand and fished around. I wondered what he was looking for. He grabbed the pinwheel he bought me at the beach over a year before. He handed it to me. "Here, make a wish."

I handed it back to him. "No, you make one."

Ricky wished that his feelings to venture outside of their relationship would subside.

"What did you wish for?" I asked.

"Nothing. Nosy Parker." He handed it to me.

I blew on it and watched it spin. "I know I asked you this before, but are pinwheels really for making wishes?"

"Remember? That little girl I told you about at the hospital? According to her, they are. Now make a wish."

I blew on the pinwheel and watched it spin around. I didn't know what to wish for. I was all out of wishes. I was empty with hope. Blank.

CHAPTER TWENTY-ONE

itting next to Tiffany at Ricky's play-off game reminded me of old times.
Even though only a few years had passed, driving out to the Rose Bowl
for UCLA games seemed like a foggy dream, an eternity ago. One thing
that remained the same though was Tiffany's ability to talk more than
the sportscasters who sat in the media box above us. She spent more time
checking out the girlfriends and wives in our section than she did on the
game. "Look at that tramp ova' there. Who is that?"

"Don't know. Don't care."

"Look Stef. Ricky is waving to you. Look!"

I waved, smiled and blew a kiss back down to the field.

Tiffany remained engrossed in the patch of women to the left of us.
"Dang, you haven't said a thing to any of those girls, huh? What's up with
that? You just be all over here by your lonesome, an outsider, a clique reject?"

"They talk too much."

"I know. That's how it is in Chicago, too. But you know I be sittin' right
up there talking shit, too."

"The last thing I'm going to do is tell all them my business."

"You don't have any business, Stef. All your business is his business."

"I got business, I just keep it to myself."

"Like what?"

"I found a pair of panties in the drier when I got back from Kansas City?"

Tiffany's mouth fell open. "What did you just say?"

"Ricky tried to say that Jaylin and some of the other guys were over and Jaylin's date took a hot tub and changed in our bathroom."

"And who was *Ricky's* date?"

"Said he didn't have one. He said he was busy cleaning up the place and playing bartender and keepin' the music flowin'."

Tiffany rolled her eyes. "Uh-uh. I hope you didn't believe that bullshit."

"I didn't and I still don't."

"So? What, may I ask, the hell are we doing watching this no-good fool play this dumb-ass game."

"I don't know what to do." I turned away from the field and looked at Tiffany. "What if he really *didn't* do anything? I mean we are always so quick to accuse our men of lying, but what if just once he is really telling the truth? And what if I leave him and we never find out what we could have had because of someone else's shit? I found Jaylin's wallet in the guest room under the bed so it made me think that Ricky could be telling the truth. But I just don't know."

Tiffany shook her head. "Do what you want Stef, but you really have to be careful what you let your man get away with. Because if he starts to act up and you continue to take it, everything will backfire and he will lose respect for you because you are hanging around in a worthless relationship. Even though he is the one creating the mess. And trust me… men will stay around as long as they can when they are getting away with shit."

"Shhh," I warned. Although it seemed they were deep into the action of the game, I didn't want Malik or Michelle to hear our conversation.

Deep down in my heart, I knew Ricky wasn't true to me, but I tried to make myself believe that it would pass. I tried so hard that I lost sight of everything else in my life, including myself. Problem was I knew there wasn't another man on the planet that could make me feel the way Ricky did. I couldn't picture my life without him. If I left him, I might as well be alone for the rest of my life. And the thought of being alone is worse than finding what may have been just an innocent pair of panties in the drier, if there could be such a thing.

"I just can't ever see myself with anyone else."

"And you *could* see yourself with a man who sees *himself* with a bunch of other women?" Tiffany said, in a lower voice, staring at the action on the field.

Keith interrupted from a couple seats down, "Stef, did you see Ricky limping off the field?"

"Uh-uh, what happened?" I asked. I stared ahead trying to spot Ricky to find out whether he was hurt. He sat on the white platform between the offense's bench and the defense's bench. Two team trainers tended to his raised leg. Or maybe, it was his foot.

"Stef, look, he *is* hurt," Keith said.

Michelle gasped.

To the left of us, a small motored cart on wheels emerged from the tunnel. It headed in Ricky's direction. My stomach turned, "Keith, what's wrong?"

"I don't know," he answered. "Sir, can I borrow your binoculars for a minute?" he asked the gentleman seated in the row in front of him. The man smiled and handed them up to Keith. My stomach flip-flopped, somersaulted and then back flipped as I watched them help Ricky into the back of the cart.

I studied him as best I could hoping he'd look up and give me some type of signal that everything was going to be okay, but he didn't.

"Keith, you think they'll let me in the locker room?"

"Yeah, just tell the security guards you're his wife."

"Here." Michelle quickly put the baby in Keith's lap and slid her ring off. She held it in the air for me to grab. "Put this on so they believe you."

Tiffany swatted Michelle's hand away. "Girl, please!" She slammed Michelle with one of her "looks" and pushed me toward the exit row.

The cramps in my arm shot all the way to my fingers and woke me from a not-so-deep-sleep. I raised my head and realized that I'd fallen asleep on the edge of Ricky's hospital bed. The room smelled sterile. Plastic bandages and iodine. I couldn't tell whether Ricky was asleep or still whoozy from the anesthetic.

His surgery had lasted four hours. I had waited patiently in the family waiting room until Dr. Fields burst through the metal doors to let me know Ricky would be okay. Through a barrage of convoluted medical jargon, he explained that Ricky had broken his leg in two places. He went on to explain the procedure of drilling steel pins through Ricky's bones. And then he told me the bad news. Ricky would be out for the remainder of the season, the playoffs and part or all of next season. The doctor's words rang in my ears, "His future in the NFL really depends on his body's capability to heal like new. We don't quite know how resilient Ricky is, but as soon as we know, we'll be able to further estimate how long he'll be out. It could take a few months or up to a year. He may have a 100% recovery. He may never be the same." And then he added, "The therapy will be intense and Ricky will have to be dedicated to work through the pain."

Ricky looked thinner in his pale blue hospital gown. His right leg was hoisted into some kind of complicated contraption that made the injury appear worse than it actually was. I wondered how he would react when he woke up. Would he be angry? Sad? Or scared? Or would he just be happy to be alive?

"Ricky?" I whispered.

He didn't even stir.

I rested my head back on my arms and drifted back to sleep. I dreamed several short dreams, but one stood out in my mind when I woke up. I dreamed of the time Ricky told me I was his Plan "B" and I was all he ever needed.

"Stef?" Ricky whispered. "Stef, wake up."

I couldn't tell if I was still dreaming.

"Stef?" he said again. "Are you awake?"

I lifted my head and tried to figure out where I was. My arms were cramped worse now. The sanitary smell brought me back. I couldn't wait to hear the doctor say that Ricky was discharged so that I could take him home and relieve the nurse of her duties.

"Stefanie? Will you marry me?"

I stared at Ricky. Then I put my head back down on my arms and tried to keep the dream alive. It was a good one.

"Stefanie, wake up. I'm serious."

I was incredulous. "You're serious about what?"

"I'm serious. I want to know if you will marry me." He paused. "Tomorrow."

I couldn't help but laugh. "Ricky, you're on drugs. You aren't thinking clearly. You have just undergone a serious surgical procedure and you…"

"I am serious. I would have a ring for you, but I guess I have a good enough excuse, right?"

We both laughed and tried to gather our thoughts. I gave him a moment to reconsider his proposal. He didn't.

"I promise to have the ring the day I get out of here."

"Yes, I'll marry you. Are you crazy? Of course, I will. But wait, you have to get out of bed and get down on your knee."

He stared at me and laughed at the impossibility.

And for the first time in a very long time, I laughed too.

CHAPTER TWENTY-TWO

T hree weeks later I'd transformed our bedroom into a miniature version of the surgical recovery unit of Centinela Medical hospital. I even had a rolling nurse tray that I kept beside the bed with Ricky's pain medication, a pitcher of lukewarm water and new bandages so I could change his dressing every six to ten hours. He'd watched every movie that Blockbuster Video had on their shelves and sent me to Best Buy several times to buy the movies he wanted to watch that Blockbuster didn't carry. I waited on him hand and foot, only leaving the house to buy groceries, rent movies and fill his prescriptions.

On the twenty-fourth day of his recovery, I finally ventured out farther than the grocery store to Westwood. I desperately needed to get my afro ironed. I left him a refrigerator filled with fresh groceries and a stack of magazines by his bedside. I put the remote control in his hand and like a concerned mother, I said, "Now if the apartment building catches on fire or something crazy like that, your crutches are right there on the floor. But stay in bed as much as you can okay?! I'll cook when I get home."

The moment I walked in Jimmy's salon, I knew I'd be there longer than I'd hoped. Each chair in the waiting room was occupied with an anxious client, hair wrapped in scarves, bandanas or hidden by baseball caps. They

aimlessly flipped through magazines, contributed to the general conversation that hung beneath the jazzy sounds emanating from the corner
speakers, while some just stared out into space waiting to be called. The
somber atmosphere, I thought, could be attributed to Jimmy's announcement that he'd be leaving us for awhile. He was scheduled to leave for
Alabama to undergo a series of comprehensive medical tests to help
determine what the mysterious illness was that had taken the full use of
his arms. I was appalled to find out that his local team of doctors was
baffled by what seemed like a set of symptoms that could be effortlessly
diagnosed. Part of me wondered if maybe Jimmy wasn't telling the truth
and instead was covering up something that he didn't want revealed.

In the mirror, I watched his assistant, Christina, flat iron my hair. On a
scale of 1-10, Christina was a nine. She was one of those girls that would
make you insecure just by being in the same room as her. Dressed in a pastel
green summer dress and a pair of heeled-sandals, she towered over Jimmy
while he stood close by giving orders as if he were training a rookie soldier
for combat. Christina rolled her eyes.

"Yeah, keep it up," Jimmy heckled. He walked to the other side of the
shop and dumped his leather jacket on a chair behind the reception area. "If
you don't listen, I'll be without a clientele when I get back."

"When are you coming back?" I asked.

He yelled from across the room. "In six to twelve months. Hopefully
you'll be married by then," Jimmy teased and decided to tell Christina
and the rest of the waiting clients a few things that weren't their business.
"This girl right here is about to get locked up with the next Jerry Rice. The
greatest receiver to ever play the game."

One of Jimmy's clients took a minute to lift her head from a magazine.
"*Besides* Andre Rison."

Jimmy laughed. "You can not put Andre Rison's name in the same sentence as Jerry Rice. Please."

"You can when you judge by the cuteness factor. Please. What girl cares about number of catches and all that dumb stuff? To me, it's all about how they look in those pants."

"Speak of the man himself. Is that Ricky?" Jimmy asked. He stared out the window at a shiny maroon truck that was parked in the red zone in front of the shop.

I spun my chair around to get a glimpse.

"Oh shoot!" Christina yelped. She held the steaming flat iron in the air. "Warn me please! Or I'm gonna burn your face up."

"Sorry," I said staring through the store's plate glass window. Ricky gingerly stepped down from Malik's truck on his crutches, while Malik patiently stood beside him to make sure he didn't stumble. "What in the world is he doing?" I whispered.

Ricky awkwardly crutched his way to the front door of the shop, stopped and waited for someone to rescue him. One of Jimmy's clients sprung from her seat, dashed to the door and held it open.

"You got an appointment?" Jimmy teased.

I glanced outside again and saw that Malik had jumped back in the driver's side and flipped on the hazards.

"Just droppin' in to say what's up to Jimmy."

"What's up, man?" Jimmy walked toward Ricky and the two exchanged one of those male bravado, machismo-type hugs. They stood beside each other, two wounded brothers, Jimmy in his arm and wrist slings, Ricky on crutches with his leg in a cast.

"Ya'all make a cute couple," I teased.

Ignoring my commentary, the two put a few feet between us and had their own conversation.

Christina resumed her position on the stool beside me. "Umm, Stefanie, could I get one of those?"

"Trust me, he's easy on the eyes, but not on the heart," I warned.

"Oh yeah, I know the type and honey, I don't envy you."

Ricky eagerly re-joined the conversation. "So Stef, I was just telling Jimmy that Malik and I were doing some shopping and ended up over here." Cupped within his hand was a petite navy velveteen box. He placed it on my knee for every person in the shop to see. "And I bought you something."

Ricky handed his crutches over to Jimmy. With a smile that lit up the dreary mood in the salon, he carefully balanced himself, wobbling a bit as he lowered himself down onto his good knee. Hair half-pressed, half-blown, looking just absolutely crazy, I smiled in wonderment from my spot in the black cushy swivel chair. Six sets of eyes tuned in, waiting in anticipation, teary-eyed, surrendering to a female emotion. His simple presence ripped the humdrum air and replaced it with pure entertainment. They were about to witness an old-fashioned marriage proposal, a public tender of eternal love and devotion.

He whispered so only I could hear. "So pick a date so we can plan this thing and go on a honeymoon." He braced himself against my knee, trying to maintain his balance.

"Where do you wanna go?" I asked.

"Wherever you want. Open the box."

Inside was a larger than life princess-cut diamond ring. Christina shrieked and I sucked in a gallon of air.

Ricky lifted himself up, grabbed the crutches from Jimmy and said, "Pick a date by the time you get home." He said to Jimmy, "Good to see you, man."

Ricky raised his hand to shake Jimmy's but when Jimmy tried to lift his arm, it failed him. The jolt of excitement that Ricky's public proposal created disappeared quicker than it came. Tears welled up in my eyes as I stared at Jimmy in the mirror. From what I had just witnessed, it seemed that his condition was headed for permanent paralysis.

I slipped the ring on my finger and waved to Ricky through the window as he pulled himself back up into Malik's truck. Then I blew him a kiss. The waiting clients and Christina surrounded me, all wanting to see the ring up close.

Jimmy blurted, "Just like a Prince riding up on his horse to rescue his Princess. Here and gone in a matter of seconds." He tried to make a flourish gesture with his arm, but again it fell limply to his side.

I tried to hide my concern for Jimmy's failing health with a weak smile. Then I winked at him to stop the tear that threatened to fall at any moment.

CHAPTER TWENTY-THREE

*T*iffany *started her second year of medical school in the fall. Keith and* Malik fell back into the swing of a new season, while Ricky continued rehabilitating his leg. Michelle was busy raising Ryan, who had just started to walk and utter his first word, "Daddy." And me, I began to plan the fairytale wedding that I'd dreamt of since I was a little girl.

I wrote Ricky a note to let him know I'd be back before dinner and attached it to the refrigerator. To kill time, I flipped through the same "Bride" magazine that I'd already gone through a million times. When I neared the end, I was happy the phone rang so I didn't have to scan through it one more time. I tossed it in the garbage and answered the phone.

"Hello?"

"Stef, it's Marie. You ready?"

"Yeah. I'll be right down." I slipped on my shoes and headed for the door.

I jumped in her Explorer and pulled the door shut. "Where's Jana?"

"She had to study."

"She could've studied tonight. It's not everyday that I go shopping for my wedding dress."

"I know. But you know how Jana is. Ms. Overachiever." Marie turned to face me. "So, CONGRATULATIONS! I'm so happy for you! Oh, let me see. Let me see!" She grabbed my hand and fixed her eyes on the diamond. "Dang, Ricky wasn't playing around this time. That's big! That shit doesn't even look real," she laughed.

I said, "So this place we're going is called *Nancy Stross for the Bride*. It's in BH. Tiffany bought her dress there. She said they have a lot to choose from. And she made the appointment, which means we'll get good service."

When we walked in the boutique, I gave my name and Marie and I had a seat. I felt a few stares in the back of my head from the other customers as the owner, Nancy announced, "We can start you right away." Knowing Tiffany, when she called to make the appointment, she told her that I was likely to spend a lot of money.

A woman with a thick Spanish accent offered me something to drink after I told her what style of dress I had in mind. Marie followed Nancy out of the dressing area and left me alone. I sat on a dainty white leather bench and stared at myself in the mirror.

Nancy returned with three dresses. She struggled to hang them on the hook in front of me so I jumped up to help. "These three are close to what you are looking for, my dear," Nancy assured me.

Marie stood by. She held the Vera Wang dress, almost as if she were guarding it. Instead of hanging it up, she began to pull the plastic protector off. "Try this one first."

I took off my clothes and accepted Marie and Nancy's help as I stepped into the dress and put my arms through the thin spaghetti straps. Nancy ran out for two seconds and came back with a veil. "I'm already feelin' like this is the one," Marie said anxiously waiting for me to model it.

Nancy swooped my hair up into a messy French twist, took a bobby pin that was clipped onto her collar and secured the veil on top of my head. Marie zipped up the back. "Okay, come out and look how beautiful you are."

I walked out of the dressing room and stood in front of three wall-to-ceiling mirrors and stared at my reflection. I felt a thousand tears begin to form, but none fell. A vision of Ricky, standing at the end of the long church aisle, passed before me. I smiled at myself, not knowing whether it was how I looked in the dress that finally made me cry or the vision I'd just had of Ricky.

Maxine drove the black Ferrari into the driveway with a burst of acceleration. Before she turned the ignition off, she revved it once. She wanted to warn Dante that she was home and that she was pissed off. She looked at herself in the rearview quickly to make sure her fresh haircut was perfect and in place. She looked down at her skirt and smoothed out the wrinkles. She even patted some powder over her brown, flawless skin. All this to ensure that she looked exceptional when she cussed him out.

Dante heard the door slam loudly. Then he heard her footsteps. Clank. Click. Clank. Click.

Here we go again, he mumbled to himself. He stared at the music video on the television. It was R. Kelly's "Honey Love." He tried to concentrate on the pretty girl that was in the video, but Maxine's voice arrived before she did.

"Dante!? Where are you?"

"In here." He spoke softly, hoping she wouldn't hear him.

Maxine marched into the family room. The first thing she saw was the back of Dante's head. He sat directly in front of a 72-inch projection screen. Dante pressed "play" on the remote control. A soundless football game appeared. Game films. He knew if he pretended to "work" she'd leave him alone.

Not this time. Maxine swiped the remote from the coffee table and turned off the television. "What the hell were you doing at the Wailea resort in Maui last April? And who the hell were you with?"

"Huh?" *Damn,* he thought to himself, *here she go bringin' up some ol' unimportant shit again.*

"What part of my question didn't you understand? Maui! The Wailea! The resort we've gone to every year since we met. The resort we went to when you got drafted THIRTEEN years ago Dante! The resort that we went to for our HONEYMOON."

He snatched the remote from her grasp and hit the power button. He started to watch his films and hoped she would just throw up her hands, give up and tromp out of the room like she usually did.

"Thirteen years Dante and you still haven't learned. I wish you were a fuckin' puppy so I could rub your nose in a pile of shit." Maxine's familiar stare burned a hole in Dante. "So what little tramp did you take there?"

"Maxine, please don't come in here while I'm working and question me," he said calmly.

She picked the remote up off the coffee table, aimed at the television and again, turned it off. "I gave up everything I dreamed about to follow you to Dallas when you got drafted, Dante. I was twenty-one years old and I gave up business school, gave up everything I wanted to do with my life to marry you and start a family. I gave it all up cause I loved your lying, cheating ass." Maxine paced the floor, still holding her purse and keys. She never took her eyes off Dante. "I wish I would've known back then when I was that stupid little girl who was wide open for your no good ass. I wish someone would've told me that the next thirteen years of my life were gonna be a living hell! I wish I had a friend to shake some sense into me and tell me that I shouldn't have married you and let you control me all this time! But no, you drove all my friends away! You conveniently made it so I was completely dependant on you for EVERYTHING!"

Dante spoke slowly and calmly. "Max, stop trippin. You need to calm down. The golf tournament ended up being on Maui. Period. End of conversation."

"Dante," she said shaking her head, "when are you going to stop? Everyday you lie. Every damn DAY!" A tear crept down her cheek as the tone in her voice turned from anger to sadness. "That new dry cleaning place that I started to go to...well the owner there, that Israeli man, just realized I was your wife and he told me that he seen *us* in Maui last year." Her voice cracked as she tried desperately to refrain from breaking down. She was tired of ranting on. She just wanted an explanation. She was tired of being embarrassed. She continued, "He asked me why I couldn't remember him. He said that you and him and I had a drink at the pool together. What the hell was I supposed to say? Oh, no sorry, that wasn't me. C'mon Dante. Why do you do this to me? You embarrass me. You humiliate me. I am supposed to be your wife. What is the definition of a wife to you, Dante? Someone who lets their husband control what they wear every fucking place they go? Someone who lets their husband control the finances, all the decisions in the family, even what they eat every night for DINNER!? Someone who lets their husband do whatever the hell he wants when he's not home? Including screwing other women, even in our OWN bed sometimes!?"

"Max, come on. Don't do that. Don't go there again. You know I've brought you a long way. You weren't shit before I met you. Take a minute to think where you'd be if I didn't marry you."

Maxine ignored his attempt to turn the tide of the argument. "I mean damn, Dante, did she look that much like me that this man thought I was her? Who was she?" The sobs started, and tears streamed down her face. "Do I know her?"

"You know what? Why don't you just get your shit and just go. If you can't take the stresses of dating someone like me, as I've said a million times before, then go."

"Remember Dante? I'm pregnant. I can't leave now."

"Of course you can't leave. You've never left before, so why would you leave now?"

Michelle folded the laundry in the pantry keeping a close ear on the baby walkie-talkie monitor while Ryan played in the family room with his toys. She held up a pair of Ryan's little jeans overalls and stared at them. They were already too small. The nausea she had suffered through the past few days gave her new hope that Ryan would have a little brother or sister soon. She folded them up and put them in a bag. She marked the bag, "Baby #2" and placed it in the cupboard above the washer and dryer.

She heard her portable phone ringing.

"Keith?" she yelled. "Can you get that?"

She glanced out the window and saw him in the pool. She ran down the stairs, two at a time and found the phone near the sliding glass door next to Keith's beach towel. "Hello?"

Keith stopped swimming and peered across the backyard, waiting to see if the call was for him.

"Michelle?" a familiar voice asked.

"Yes?"

"It's Dante. I need to talk to you for a minute. Keith's not home is he?"

"It's for me, baby!" she yelled to Keith. "What the hell are you doing calling here?"

"I *really* have to talk to you about something."

"How did you get this number?"

"A friend of mine that plays with Keith gave it to me."

"Dante you CANNOT call here again. Good bye. I'm hanging up the…" Michelle said adamantly.

"Wait! Michelle," he interrupted, desperation in his voice. "My wife found out that I went to Maui with someone, but she doesn't know who, so I just wanted to give you a heads up in case it comes your way. She's on a rampage to find out who, so just be prepared." His words trampled over each other.

"Since when are you so worried about your wife?"

"I'm not worried about her. I'm worried about you. She gets crazy sometimes and when her little world gets all shook up, she wants to shake everyone else's up too. Plus, I can't let her get away with half my stuff."

Michelle heard the sliding glass door open. She slammed down the phone and ran back upstairs to finish folding the laundry.

CHAPTER TWENTY-FOUR

The engine purred beneath us as we cruised east down Venice Boulevard. Our destination, the Four Seasons Hotel. We had reserved the grand ballroom for the night of April 10th and needed to drop off a deposit and sign the contract. "I have a meeting with the florist to pick the flowers this coming Saturday. You gonna come with me?"

"Uh-uh. I forgot to tell you. I'm going out to Hawaii with some of the guys. We're going out to hang at the Pro-Bowl and support Malik." He yelled to make sure I could hear him over the loud music.

"Who is going to the Pro-Bowl?" I yelled back.

"Well officially only Malik. But me and some of the guys from the team are gonna go out there and chill."

"So just out of curiosity, are you gonna continue to jet set around the globe, go out five nights a week and never invite me to your away games once we get married?"

"Huh?" He used the loud music as an excuse to pretend not to hear me. I knew he did though.

We were on the way to sign the contract for our wedding reception party. I realized it wasn't a good time to start an argument. "Nothing. Forget it."

After we met with the caterers and the hotel manager, they offered us dinner. We accepted and enjoyed selections from the meal they'd be serving at our wedding. Over dinner Ricky said, "Oh, Stef, I forgot to tell you, there is one more couple that you need to add to the guest list." He popped a shrimp into the cocktail sauce and then into his mouth.

"Nope. Can't do it." I took a sip of my wine.

"No, really."

"No, really nothing. We are way over the limit and if everyone on the list accepts their invitations we are in trouble. There is no way we can invite even one more person. I'm sorry. Besides, they can't be that important if you're thinking of them this late in the game. The invitations go out in a few weeks."

"I know, but, Stef, I just want everyone I know to be there. I am so proud of you and I want everyone to see you walk down the aisle to me. I want them all to hear me say 'I do.' I want everyone to know how much I love you."

"Okay. What'd you do now?"

"Nothing. It's not like that. It's true. You've stood by me through some pretty rough times. And I know if you're by my side next year, I'll be okay"

Although Ricky was able to play in the last four games of the season, his gimpy leg still slowed him down and made his coach leery of giving him too much game time.

I stared at Ricky across the table. Traces of maturity had begun to form since we met almost five years before. Instead of waiting for nature to take all of his hair, he shaved off what he had left. He grew out enough hair on his face to cut into a thick, but finely trimmed goatee. I noticed a few faint lines that parenthesized the corners of his mouth and one prominent forehead line that had suddenly appeared over the past year. He was no longer the 20-year-old, backpack-wearing student with the mischievous smile. I smiled and told him that I loved him.

After we finished dinner, the catering director followed us out to the front of the hotel. She was a five-foot nine, Hollywood-thin blonde with a bright smile. She summarized everything for our upcoming wedding and thanked us again for choosing "her" hotel. When Ricky left us momentarily to give the Valet his ticket, she whispered to me, "Stefanie, I'm sorry, but he is just hot." I smiled, even though that wouldn't be something I expected to hear from the catering director of my wedding. Within seconds the classy caterer became just another pesky broad who had eyes for my man.

When Ricky returned she decided to tell him how she felt. She brushed up against him and laughed, "I was just asking Stefanie here how I could find a guy like you." Then she shot him one of those smiles that said—call me and we don't have to tell her anything that happens between us.

On the way back to the apartment I tried not to discuss what I felt about Ms. Lisa Taylor, the woman who was primarily responsible for the success of our wedding reception, but I guess I didn't try hard enough. "So what is it about you that always has women just throwing themselves at your feet? I mean damn, am I invisible? She made a pass at you RIGHT in front of me. What is going on in this world? Don't women have any dignity anymore or respect for one another?"

Ricky laughed. He loved the attention that he'd been getting from women since he was drafted.

I continued, "I mean come on. Would she have been that forward if she didn't know you played ball? Sheesh. I'm so ready for you to get traded. Do they have a team in Alaska?"

"No," Ricky laughed some more. "So that should do it for all the plans for the wedding, right?"

"Besides the flowers. Oh, and do you think I should wear my hair up or down, and do you think I should wear the veil over my face or off my face when I walk down the aisle?"

"On."

"Hair up or down?"

"Down. No up. No wait. Is Jimmy gonna do it?"

"Ya' know, for some reason, Jimmy hasn't even called me. I assumed he wouldn't call for awhile 'cause he was supposed to concentrate on getting better, getting treatments and stuff, but it's been too long."

"Call him."

"Cell phone disconnected. I asked Christina, his assistant, and she hasn't heard from him. All the girls at the gym that used to go to Jimmy, they haven't heard from him either."

"He'll call. Don't worry." We stopped at the light and he did a double take at the car next to him. It was a new model Mercedes Sedan. "Look at that. I'm gonna get you one of those when I sign my next contract."

"Don't Ricky. Just put the money in the bank for a rainy day."

"We're gonna be cool, Stef. We got sunshine comin' way before the rainy days hit. Mr. Schwartz said for me to count on a contract that'll double the size of the one I already signed. Especially if I start by the middle of next season, which, by the way, the Coach said is a strong possibility."

"Really?"

"Yep, he said that he talked to some people, the front office suits, you know the guys who write the checks to the players and they said that I seem to be more of a promising starter than they thought, even though my ankle is still messed up. They are hyped on my speed, I think, especially since I've almost got back to where I was when I got injured."

"Oh that's great." My voice squeaked. My heart sank. The reality was, the more money that was ahead, the more problems we would have.

"So I ordered your license plate. It'll be here around the time we get back from the honeymoon."

"I'm not rollin' around L.A. with REDBONE on my license plate, Ricky. I already told you that."

"Naw it'll be good, just relax."

"I'm calling the DMV and canceling it." I laughed through my protest. The whole thought of it was ridiculous.

"You call to cancel that and I'm calling the wife store and canceling you." He laughed at his own joke and shifted the car into fifth to pick up speed so he could make it through the yellow light ahead.

Five weeks away. It was time to pick up the three hundred ivory ceramic bells that I ordered to be placed at the table settings. They would be hand painted by an elderly woman named Catherine Hanley. She set up her business to combat the loneliness she'd felt since her husband died nine years before. Painting gave her solace. She would paint "Ricky and Stefanie Powers" in gold calligraphy on each bell. And underneath she would paint the date of our wedding. I arranged to pick up the bells at noon that day.

After a brief visit with Catherine, she helped me carry the fragile bells to my car and wished me well with some advice to "make sure you never go to sleep upset with each other." She explained that it was the key to her fifty-one year marriage. And then she said, "And pretend that every day was the first day you met." *Yeah right, Ricky and I are far past that stage!* I thought.

I brought two of the dainty bells inside the apartment and left the rest in the car. "Look Ricky, aren't they cute?" Ricky, wearing a crown of shaving cream, prepared to shave his head as he stood in front of the bathroom mirror.

"Oh yeah, those are cool." He glanced at the ringing phone. "Can you grab that?"

"Hello?"

"Hey. It's me," Tiffany said. "You got a sec?"

My attention stayed with Ricky as he danced naked in front of the mirror. He stopped for a minute and put shaving cream underneath both of his eyes and across his forehead so he'd look like an African Zulu Warrior. Then he continued his attempt at a ritualistic African tribal dance, trying to make me laugh.

"Put some clothes on," I told Ricky, laughing. To Tiffany, I said, "Yeah, what's up?"

"Go where Ricky can't hear you."

I laughed some more and left the room. I walked through the kitchen toward the back patio. "Okay, the coast is clear. What's goin' on?"

"I wish I could be with you to talk to you in person, but since I can't I'm gonna tell you this over the phone."

My stomach tightened up. "Tell me what?"

"Stef, at first I didn't know whether I should tell you, but I feel as a friend I should. I mean, damn, I have been battling with this for over a week now and I know if you knew something like this, you better tell me."

"Tell me what? What is it?"

Tiffany paused. She sighed twice and then finally blurted it out. "Ricky was over in Hawaii during the Pro-Bowl gettin' down with some tramp named Tracy."

Silence.

"Stef, are you there?"

"Yeah, I'm here."

"Ricky needs to stop trippin'. He was probably trying to sew his wild oats before the wedding, but his shit is so sloppy, he just got caught."

"I gotta get out of here. I gotta cancel the wedding. Oh God." My voice trembled. "What am I gonna do?" The initial shock aimed straight for my stomach and then made its way up to my heart. I started to cry.

"Oh, damn. Stef, don't cry. He ain't even worth all those tears."

"He is though. I know he loves me, but why does he do this?"

"Cause, men will be men and you gotta keep a tighter leash on their doggy asses. And it's not just the men. It's those desperate old tramps that go after them, lure them into something that they may not have otherwise gotten into. Ya' know?"

"Yeah." The tears flowed freely now. "But damn, Tiff. We have this big ol' wedding planned. The invites went out just two days ago. Two hundred of them. Two hundred plus a guest. That's almost four hundred people."

"Wait. There's gotta be a solution to this."

"The solution is to cancel it. That's the only solution. I'd be a fool not to."

"No, you wouldn't." Tiffany paused. "Well, maybe you would. Shoot, I dunno. It's up to you. Call your mom. Talk to her about it."

"Oh hell no, she'll tell my father and that will be the end of everything."

Ricky walked into the kitchen. He noticed me on the patio and smiled through the glass. Front and center, he posed, now with nothing on but his jock strap. Still masked in shaving cream, he gyrated his hips and yelled. "Boola boola boola. BOOLA Stefanie! BOOLA!"

I watched him walk to the refrigerator to search for something to eat. He pulled out a pitcher of Tang and poured himself a glass. Then he pulled out a bunch of other random items.

"He's right here. I gotta go."

"Okay Stef, be strong. And don't do anything rash. And don't worry about telling him who told you. I don't care one bit if he knows it was me."

That was the last thing I was worried about.

I wiped my tears and walked back inside the house. Ricky had turned on two burners on the stove. He had spread the necessary items out on the counter to make a ham and egg scramble and some grits.

"Tiffany have some good gossip for you?" he snipped. His back was turned.

I sat on the bar stool and waited for him to look at me. When he did, he said, "What's wrong?"

He reached out to hug me.

"Get away." The tone in my voice made him freeze.

"What happened?"

"You know what happened!" The dam broke and my tears flowed, but the anger in my voice grew with each second. "You know damn well what happened. That's why you came out here before you finished shaving. Trying to make me laugh with your stupid Zulu warrior dances. I know you, Ricky. You knew Tiffany called to tell me some shit. You knew it."

"I have no idea what you're talking about."

"Ricky, I know you were with that girl in Hawaii."

"What girl?"

"Yeah, go on and lie about it." The tears stopped.

"What? Who was that on the phone? I thought that was Tiffany."

"It *was* Tiffany and *Tiffany* told me that you were with some girl in Hawaii when you went out to watch the Pro-Bowl. Some girl named Tracy."

"Well, *Tiffany* is lying. Or somebody is." Ricky's eyes twitched as he glanced at different places around the room. Everywhere but at me. He thought quickly. Then he yawned. And that was when I knew for sure he was lying. He always yawned right before a lie. Every time. It *never* failed.

Through the yawn he said, "I mean, I did meet a girl over there named Tracy, but she and I didn't do whatever it is that you are accusing me of doing."

"Well, why would Tiff come to me with this unless she knew something was up? You and I both know that she is not one to start anything unless it can be backed."

"Right, so call her up and ask her to get whomever on the phone that started all this. I'll prove to you that nothing happened," he said, calming me down a little bit. Tears blocked my vision again. I tried to focus and looked around the kitchen for the phone. It was right beside me.

A few phone calls, and ten minutes later we had Tracy and Tiffany on the phone, three-way. Ricky and I both listened on different phones in the house.

Tiffany spoke first, "Tracy, I am a friend of Jodi's and I am calling because we need to get some stuff that you've been saying cleared up. Ricky Powers is on the phone also. And his fiancée Stefanie."

"Wait a minute, *who* is this?" Her voice was cautious, but unafraid. She sounded like she may have been white.

Tiffany explained, "Apparently, you have been telling people that you and Ricky Powers got it on in Hawaii over Pro-Bowl weekend."

"First of all, I don't appreciate you calling my house accusing me of whatever it is you think you know. And secondly, I don't think I'd be trying to get with Ricky if my man was out there with me," she replied. "I do know Ricky. We partied together out there, but we didn't *'get it on'*...or whatever you said we did."

Partied together? I thought. *Yeah, she is definitely a white girl.*

"Well, apparently, you told Jodi that you and him got busy and if in fact you are going around telling people this," Tiffany cleared her throat, "no wait, I ain't gonna go there with threats, but basically let me just say this. You just really need to keep your loose lips tight and calm your ass down a little bit. And if it is in fact all a big misunderstanding, sorry for interrupting your day."

"Well then, you should be sorry for interrupting my day."

Tracy was lying. I felt it. I felt it all through the phone. I had to say something. "And don't let me find out that you are just another sorry ass groupie tryin' to cover-up for Ricky so you can just keep on doin' whatever you two are doin' cause if I do find that this is all true....." a shot of adrenaline hid behind every single word, "I will beat your white ass until you are black and blue!" The words that came out of my mouth surprised me. I waited for my head to spin around next. I was as frustrated as a detective on the case of a serial killer who'd been trailing his suspect for years. I couldn't seem to catch Ricky. Period.

Tracy tensed up. "Oh my God! You guys are freaking out! I told you *nothing* is going on."

Ricky hung up first. He looked at me from across the kitchen, waiting for me to hang up next. "Was all that necessary?"

"Yeah, it was. And don't come at me like that either. It's those type of bitches that will cover up for a man in a minute."

"And it's those type of bitches that will try to get between us. It could've been anyone of her friends who started that rumor. Stef, do you know how many women out there would like to be where you are?"

"Well in a minute, the position will be open, so why don't you call and let them know they can line up for it?" I handed Ricky the phone.

Coincidentally it rang.

Ricky answered. It was Keith.

I walked into the bedroom and got into the shower to wash off the dirty mess that I'd just sat in. Dirty poison. Smut. Gossip. I needed to figure out the rest of my life. If I canceled the wedding, I had to move out. Find a job. Find a place to live. Find a way to support my way through law school. Find another husband!

I shut my eyes and let the hot water spray directly onto my face. I ran through the list of last minute things I needed to do before the wedding and thought of the money Ricky would lose if I canceled. $28,000, not including the deposit for the Four Seasons. Another $15,000. The rest of the money, approximately $16,000, was refundable. I heard the shower door open and I peeked out of one eye. Ricky climbed in.

I backed up so he'd keep his distance.

"Ryan is sick," said Keith.

"Still?"

"Yep."

"It's been almost three weeks now."

I backed away from the spray of the shower and lathered a handful of shampoo in my hair. Ricky immersed himself under the faucet. I tried to ignore the beauty of his muscular, black body.

"I know. They're worried. The doctors scheduled him for a series of tests and Michelle is freaked out, making Keith even more nervous."

"Tests? Hmmm, that doesn't sound good."

"Don't get all panicky. We need someone in the family to be positive like you always are."

Not this time, I thought. I rinsed the shampoo out of my hair and jumped out of the shower and into my robe.

Ricky asked, "Do you want me to go with you tomorrow?"

"No."

"Don't you have the fitting for your dress?"

"Yeah, but I don't know if I wanna marry you now."

I tied my hair up into a ponytail, threw on my jeans and flip-flops and got out of the apartment before he was through with his shower.

CHAPTER TWENTY-FIVE

The next morning, Ricky tagged along with me on my errands. I knew he was just trying to make up for his near miss, but I didn't mind. Having him along for the ride was in fact comforting. And I liked making him sweat. Making him beg for me to believe him. Making him kiss me every ten minutes, in public, in private, in the car, in the elevator. In the waiting area of the bridal shop.

"Hi, Stefanie," the owner, Nancy, boomed throughout the store when she saw us. She practically ran toward us. "And you must be the fiancé. The football player?" she reached out her hand to Ricky.

"Yes, this is Ricky. And Ricky, this is Ms. Stross."

She shook his hand with a firm, almost masculine grip. She eyed him, gave him a once over and smiled. "Well Stefanie, you certainly are a lucky woman. He is definitely a catch! Where did you find him?"

"We met in college," I said.

Finally she took her eyes off Ricky and put them on me, but only for a moment. "Well, my goodness, you all will be a stunning couple! Come this way." She led us toward the back of her store. "Oh, Ricky, you aren't going to see her in the dress, are you?"

"No, is there somewhere I could wait actually?"

"Sure, honey, come this way. Stefanie, just go upstairs to the right and my alterations department will help you get your dress on and pinned up."

I went upstairs and told the young Latina woman my name and three minutes later she returned with the dress I had ordered. She settled me into a dressing room. "Just yell for me when you are ready to slip it on, you'll need my help," she said in a Spanish accent. "My name is Adriana."

As soon as I was ready, I heard Nancy's voice. "I'm ready," I projected through the dressing room door.

Both of them appeared and helped me into the dress. Nancy zipped up the back and looked at my reflection in the mirror. She couldn't wait to comment. "You are gorgeous! Just gorgeous!"

"Thank you," I responded. Adriana placed a few straight pins in the back of the dress. It was a tad too loose around the waist and it needed to be taken in a couple inches.

"And that future husband of yours. Wow. You are a lucky ducky young lady. Hold on to him now, ya' hear?" she said, shaking her head enthusiastically.

"Please! *He* is the lucky duck," I said.

"Well, you're right about that." Her laugh was phony. "Adriana, you know this young lady is marrying a professional athlete? Isn't that wonderful?" Adriana's already wide eyes got even wider. Nancy kept chattering. "Fairytale life ahead!" Instead of responding to her, I just smiled. "I wish I'd have been as smart as you. I got an old fart, been married to him for thirty-one years. He was an advertising executive. Got fat, and oooh, you should see his stomach. Hangs to the floor. Doesn't it Adriana? He is good for one thing though. Gave me some money to get this place and look how far I've taken it! We started out in a small sweat shop in East L.A. and now look!"

I stared at myself in the mirror and tried to block her voice out.

Nancy continued, "Your husband will never get fat. Did you see the bod on that man? Sheesh! I wish I was thirty years younger!"

I wanted so badly to enjoy this moment by myself, but her obnoxious voice wouldn't let me.

Then she said, "Fairytale life, honey, you remember I said that, okay?"

I had to get off the platform, get out of the dress and get the hell out of there. What did she know about what kind of life I was going to have? I was so tired of everyone thinking I had this perfect little life because Ricky was a pro-athlete. The fairytale had already turned into a horror flick, and still I couldn't seem to walk out of the theatre.

Adriana yanked and pinned a few more times and Nancy finally shut her pie hole.

Adrianna finally spoke, "Eees beautiful on you. I like it."

The antique ivory, almost-white dress was completely backless and sleeveless. It had a tight bustier that lifted my boobs and revealed almost an inch of cleavage. There were two silk micro-spaghetti straps that ran from the top of the bustier over my shoulders and down my back, clear to my waist where a silk bow wrapped around and tied in the back. The skirt was silk, layered by another piece of silk organza.

Nancy started up again, "Your skin color is perfect for this dress. You have that built-in-tan." More phony cocktail laughter flew from her trap. "My pale girls have a hard time with this one because it shows so much skin."

Adrianna finally finished and the three of us took a moment for a final once over. I guess Nancy was right about something... I did look like a princess.

The house was cooler than usual. Keith woke up from an afternoon nap and found his left foot exposed, bare and cold, peeking out from the covers. He aimed the heater remote at the control box and clicked it on. The sounds of the furnace grumbled from beneath the house. Keith scooted toward Michelle, his stomach to her back. He reached over her waist and crawled his fingers underneath her silk lingerie. Even though she was already awake, Michelle pretended she was asleep. Keith worked his way toward her nipples. He knew if he touched them just the way she liked she'd wake up and want to start the afternoon off the same way he wanted. Much to his dismay, she slept through the fondling and continued to lie there breathing heavily, concentrating on being as still as she could. She knew it would only be minutes before he gave up. And she was right. Even sooner than other unsuccessful attempts, Keith got out of bed and walked into the bathroom. When she heard the shower go on, she opened her eyes.

Ever since she caught her ex-boyfriend Michael's voice on the radio, two weeks before, things at home were no longer rosy. Ryan still wasn't feeling well. His flu-like symptoms worsened. His equilibrium was off and he had lost his appetite. The doctors kept telling Michelle that he'd be okay and that they'd be able to give them a diagnosis after the tests. Michelle and Adrienne hadn't spoken to each other in four weeks. Michelle lost whatever remaining respect that she had for her after she received an email requesting a small loan to help her with the mortgage. And she and Keith's arguments had turned from petty to severe.

She looked at the clock. If she knew Keith, he'd been in there exactly fourteen more minutes. Then he would go to the back and work out on his weight machines. She always wondered why he showered before he worked out. But today she was glad. Today she would use the fourteen minutes to surrender to the urge she'd had for the past few days. She grabbed her cell phone off the night stand and dialed Michael Sinclair's phone number. "The number you have dialed has been disconnected," the operator announced into Michelle's ear. She slammed her cell phone closed and shut her eyes again. She couldn't believe he'd finally made it...after all those years. She wanted to congratulate him and tell him she was proud, but how could she find him?

Michelle gasped when the cordless telephone rang, as if she had been caught. She grabbed it off Keith's night stand and picked it up before the second ring. "Hello?"

"Michelle? It's me," Ricky said.

"Hey. What up?"

"Where's my little nephew?"

"He's asleep," she answered.

"So when are these big tests that Keith keeps talking about?"

"Next week."

"It's nothing serious, though, right?"

"We hope not. The doctors said not to worry."

"Oh, okay. Where's the husband?"

"In the shower."

"Have him call me when he gets out."

"How are the wedding plans?"

"Good actually. We're almost done. We just have to figure out who is gonna DJ and some other minor things."

"A friend of mine named Brutus deejays out there. You want his number?"

"Yeah, give it to Stef when you come out here. You are coming out for the shower right?"

"Oh, is that what she's calling it?" Michelle laughed. "You mean the bachelorette party?"

"Yeah, yeah, I'm gonna install some hidden cameras in the suite so ya'all can't get away with nothing. Oh yeah and check this out, think of someone who can sing live. We want to have someone sing something contemporary at the church ceremony. I'm thinking about asking my boy, Robbie Simpson, if he could sing that new one that's out by Michael Sinclair."

At first Michelle thought she hadn't heard him right. "Your boy *who?*"

"Robbie Simpson."

"Sing whose song?"

"Michael Sinclair, you heard of him? He's a little bit new, but he's blowin' up out here." Michelle couldn't believe her ears.

"Uh-uh," Michelle lied. "Never heard of him." There was no way she could tell him that she knew Michael now. She had told Keith that her ex-boyfriend was a doctor. She was too embarrassed to tell him that it was Michael, an unemployed music industry wanna-be. Her mother always told her that men judge the women they meet by whom they dated before them.

"Yeah, his single is already number one on the billboard charts. You haven't heard it? It's called *Love Means.*"

For a minute, Michelle couldn't even speak. Then she heard the shower go off. "Keith's out. Hold on."

CHAPTER TWENTY-SIX

R.S.V.P.s *poured into our mailbox. Ricky came home everyday with new* names to add to the "B" list, hoping for a few invitees to decline, but so far no one had. Ricky's excitement about our approaching nuptials wasn't derived from the fact that he and I would be contractually bound by marriage for the rest of our lives. And I doubted it was true that he couldn't wait to publicly confess his eternal love for me. Basically, I think he was just ready to take me up on my promise that I would get pregnant on our honeymoon.

"Stef? Where you at?" Ricky called as he walked through the front door. I loved the sound of him calling my name when he got home.

"In here. In the tub."

"WhoAAA!" he bellowed. "What happened to your hair?"

"What do you mean what happened to my hair? I was actually thinking I'm gonna wear my hair like this for the wedding."

Half horrified, half laughing, Ricky stared at my wild, crazy frizz. "Sheeeet. You better call Jimmy."

"I'm really starting to worry. His home line has been disconnected for months now. Hasn't even sent his response card to say he is coming to the wedding. Everyone at the shop has called his mom's house and her line is disconnected. I don't even know where to look."

"Damn. I hope he's okay." He let out a heavy sigh. "What if he doesn't end up calling? You got someone else to do your hair just in case?"

"Uh-uh, he'll be able to."

"From the way you're looking right about now, you better find a back-up!" he chuckled.

"Naw, he'll surface. He's got to. We've been talking about him doing my hair for my wedding for six years now...Waaay before I even met you!"

"But baby, you always gotta have a Plan B," he said in a voice trying to imitate mine.

"Shut up."

"Oh, by the way, speaking of Plan B's and football and all that.... my coach is starting me this fall." His smile was almost too big for his face. "I was *ballin'* during mini camp and he's been working with me everyday and says that he never seen someone heal so quickly. I told him it's 'cause he's never worked with a bionic man." He laughed at his own words. "Oh yeah, and he told me him and his wife are coming, but they haven't sent their R.S.V.P. yet."

"Dang, *everybody* is coming. This is gonna be a serious event. I can't believe I agreed to marry your crazy ass," I teased. "You know what you're getting into by marrying me, dont'cha?" He didn't respond. "Marriage is no joke, Ricky. It's share and share alike. What's yours becomes mine and what's mine becomes yours."

He interrupted, "Oh, so what am *I* getting?" he asked sarcastically.

I unplugged the stopper in the tub and got out. "What are *you* getting? A whole lot of good, honest, real, genuine, lovin' every night and everyday for the rest of your life. A good woman. And you know a good woman is hard to find these days, especially in this city. So yeah, back to what I was saying. No secrets, no stray phone numbers on cocktail napkins suddenly showing up around the house, no second phone lines that I don't know about, no secret voice mail numbers, no sneakin' off to the team party house, no lying, no cheating, no nothing." I paused for a minute to curl my towel into a turban around my head.

"Damn! Where did all that come from?"

"From stuff Michelle tells me and Tiffany tells me. I hear all this scandalous activity that goes on and it makes me worry about us. I just want to make sure you are ready for all this. I mean, are you really ready to wake up next to me every single morning for the rest of your life?" He looked at me sheepishly. I raised my eyebrows. "Come on Ricky, marriage is not playing house. For better or for worse, through sickness and health, for richer or for poorer....'til death do us part."

Ricky felt as if he were hit with a stun gun. The part about waking up to the same woman for the rest of his life starting in just a few weeks was what got him. He had this sudden urge to say, *Stef, ummm, maybe that is actually too much of a commitment. Every single day for the rest of my life? When you put it like that, you're right, that may be a bit much.*

But he didn't. Instead he brought up the pre-nuptial agreement hoping maybe she would balk at that and back out once and for all. He took a deep breath and went for it. "Oh yeah, damn, I keep forgetting to bring this up but I have been meaning to bring this up, but I keep forgetting. But I umm..." he stuttered. "Mr. Schwartz needs you to stop by his office to sign a pre-nup. He's already drafted it and everything. You need to just stop by and sign it." He allowed his eyes to meet mine in the reflection of the mirror, but only for a half of second.

My ears must have all of a sudden failed me. *He did not just ask me to sign a prenuptial agreement. This can't be. And the way he asked me... so nonchalantly. Didn't he think I was going to get offended? What, does he think I'm going to leave him and try to take half? Or even better... does*

he think he is going to leave me and leave me with nothing? Yeah, that's
probably what this fool thinks. Whatever. He's lost his mind now. "A
pre-what?"

"A pre-nuptial agreement. I know you, Stefanie. I know you are going
to read into it too much and get all bent out of shape, but it's really not a
big deal."

"Well, aren't you going to ask me how I feel about it? 'Cause to tell you
the truth, I think you have lost your mind. You think if I was the one who
ended up making the money, I'd have asked you?" He tried to interrupt, but
I kept talking. "And if that were the case, do you think I would have married
you if I thought you were planning to take me for everything? I mean really
Ricky, what does that say about what you think about me? Do you really
think I want any of this stupid money in the first place? If you would open
your eyes, you'd see that you are the one who is fiending over all this money,
not me! You're the one buying me all this shit I don't need. Changing my
wardrobe, my clothes, buying me all these expensive ass heels when I don't
even wear heels to begin with, buying me diamonds and jewelry, trying to
change everything about me."

"Stefanie, relax, it's really not that serious. I knew you were gonna get
all upset. I wasn't even the one who thought of it. Mr. Schwartz has all his
clients make their wives sign them."

"Whatever Ricky, I'll sign it, but don't think that I ever want your shit.
If we do get divorced, just know I won't be wanting shit from you. Call
Mr. Schwartz and have him write that in the contract. Have him write it
just like this—Stefanie doesn't want *shit* from Ricky when he leaves her in
the dust."

Ricky continued to egg me on. It was strange because usually he'd have
backed down by now. He knew there was a point of no return for me.
And I'd reached it. He could see it in my eyes and I was surprised he kept

going. "Stef, you know you like all that stuff I buy you. You just pretend that you don't. You think it's cute to pretend you don't want any of it. But I know secretly you're like girrrrl, look what Ricky bought me. I know you can't wait to tell your friends." Now he started mimicking my voice. "Did you see this fat ass tennis bracelet Ricky bought me, girl ain't this the bomb? Look at these fly ass shoes Ricky found for me, aren't I cute? Don't even act like I'm the one trying to change you. You've changed Stefanie, on your own!"

Following too close, Ricky nipped my bare heels with his Jordans as I walked through the bedroom toward the kitchen. He waited for me to respond. But all I could think about was the wedding. If I said what I wanted to say and did what I wanted to do, I knew the end result would be a canceled wedding. So instead I uncorked the last bottle of red wine in our pantry and poured a hearty glass. The first sip added to the already bitter taste in my mouth. "All I have to say to you is I can't believe you have the nerve to blame the pre-nuptial agreement on Mr. Schwartz."

Two days later, I found myself behind the wheel of our truck headed for Mr. Schwartz's office. The law offices of Phillips, Weinstein and Hayes were located on the 26th floor of a high-rise on Olympic Boulevard in West Los Angeles. They represented both entertainers and athletes.

As I sat in the comfortable, beige chair in the lobby and flipped through a magazine that I'd taken off the coffee table in front of me, I noticed the receptionist staring at me. I smiled at her and she looked away. I wondered if she knew why I was there. I wondered how many other women sat there waiting. Waiting to sign on the dotted line. Waiting to agree that marriage is a separate and unequal institution and no longer a lifelong commitment of love. Not anymore. What's yours is yours and what's mine is mine. Ricky had changed. He'd become a different person, someone who allowed money to suck him up into the world where you don't know the difference between what is real and what is not.

"Stefanie!" Mr. Schwartz belted, greeting me in the lobby. I noticed that Mr. Schwartz looked exceptionally handsome that day. Usually when Ricky and I saw him, he was dressed in his Dockers and Topsider shoes, but today he had a chocolate brown suit and tie on. His salt and pepper hair was freshly trimmed and he even smelled good. I wondered if maybe he dressed up for this joyous occasion.

"Hi, how are you?" I stood up and grasped his firm handshake.

"Great, and you?"

Just magnificent, I thought. "Oh you know, as good as I can be with all this craziness. You know with the wedding and all."

I followed Mr. Schwartz down the cold corporate hallways and into his office. We discussed the wedding plans and how they were coming along. He told me that his wife had put their R.S.V.P. in the mail just the day before. I gazed across his desk at him as I sat in one of the two guest chairs. I wondered if he was the genuine, kind-hearted man that I thought he was when Ricky and I first met him. He seemed to be, but you never could be certain with lawyers.

As if he were trying to distract me the way a dentist distracts his patient before a shot of Novocain, he riddled me with small talk while he pulled out several manilla folders. Each document was feathered with yellow "sign here" tags poking out from the pages. He carefully went over the entire agreement so I would understand it in full. As he talked slowly, I drifted in the space between his words wondering how I got to be here in the first place.

"Now I know you are probably a little bit upset about signing this agreement, as most of my client's wives are," Mr. Schwartz said.

What are you a mind reader now? I thought.

"But don't worry, it's really for the benefit of both of you. So that each of you are protected in the unlikely event that the marriage does indeed dissolve. It's nice to have some type of agreement between the two parties just in case."

Parties? So now I was a "party." "No, I'm fine with it. No problem."

"Good. I am sure you and Ricky will be fine, but I have seen some of the craziest things in my days as a sports attorney. Unfortunately, I have seen money destroy many young people, many marriages and many families. Not to scare you, but some of these guys just lose their minds. One of my clients has been playing in the league for four years and he just called me last night at home asking me if he could borrow some money. Can you imagine? He blew fourteen million dollars of his salary. Fancy cars, expensive gifts for his girlfriends, houses for his family members. It's amazing." He cleared his throat and nodded. "But in any case, you got a good one. Ricky has a good head on his shoulders."

I shot Mr. Schwartz a phony smile and signed away on the dotted line.

CHAPTER TWENTY-SEVEN

Little Ryan was with the doctors for over two hours. Michelle stayed close by her son, but Keith ducked in and out of the examination room and paced the hallways anticipating a diagnosis, any diagnosis. Good or bad, he just needed to know something. Finally when the doctor appeared through the double doors and summoned Keith into the hospital room where Michelle held Ryan in her arms, he breathed a loud sigh of relief.

Dr. Tamari rubbed his hands together gently. He had a thin build and a dark complexion. He spoke with confidence as he looked at Ricky through his horn-rimmed glasses. "Mr. Powers, unfortunately it will be another hour or so before we get the final results. From what you and your wife are telling me about his behavior, I can safely assume that he has probably acquired a case of acute anemia. This is very rare in babies this age, especially in boys, but there is always the exception."

"And what exactly does that mean?" Keith's tone was desperate.

"He may need a transfusion. But nevertheless, he'll be fine…that is, if my guess proves to be the proper diagnosis." Dr. Tamari pulled his hands from his pockets and grabbed his metal folder off the counter. "And if this is so, we are going to need some blood. Do you both know your blood types?"

Michelle nodded her head, "O Positive."

"Keith?" the doctor asked.

"Ummm, I wanna say B Positive, but…"

"Come with me. Let's find out for sure." The doctor put his arm around Keith and guided him into the triage area. Dr. Tamari smiled, peering over the top of his glasses, almost scolding him. "As a professional athlete you should know this information as well as you know your drivers license number."

Keith chuckled. "Well to tell you the truth, I haven't the faintest idea what my driver's license number is either."

"Nurse, please help us out here in determining this young man's blood type. I'll be in my office. By the time your blood is sent to the lab, your son should be through with his tests. And then we'll be all set." The doctor left and Keith watched the young nurse tie a long piece of rubber around his arm. He decided to look away as she searched for a vein in his forearm.

Afterwards, he met Michelle in the waiting room. Ryan had fallen asleep in his stroller. Keith told Michelle the doctor asked them to come back in half an hour and suggested they kill some time in the hospital cafeteria.

"I'm not hungry," Michelle said.

"You're never hungry." He put his arm around her. "Come with me anyway."

As Michelle pushed the stroller into the elevator, she stared down at Ryan. "Oh God Keith, I hope my baby is gonna be okay," she whimpered.

Once inside the cafeteria, Keith grabbed a sandwich and a drink and met Michelle at a rickety, fake wood table. Keith set down the tray of food. The Jello and the other mystery dessert Keith had purchased looked repulsive to Michelle. She turned her nose up. "Keith, I'm a little bit scared."

"He'll be fine. I think if it was serious, the doc would have been a little more concerned." He chewed and talked with food in his mouth. After one bite, half the sandwich was already gone. "Be positive. I'm confident Ryan is going to be fine AND that we are going to have another healthy baby soon."

"Let's just wait for awhile before we have another one, Keith. We need to give all our attention to Ryan first."

"Like I said, Ryan is going to be fine. And why do we have to wait? If we start trying now, the new baby won't arrive until nine months from now anyway. And besides, I'm trying to have at least three or four more. Especially since my career is going to be over in a few years so I'll be at home to help you. And I've invested my money so that I don't have to worry about finding a second career. I may coach football at my high school if we move back to Texas, but nothing where I'll be out of the house morning 'til night."

Texas, she thought. *That'll work. Anything, but here.* "Okay, but baby, let's just get through this first."

Exactly twenty-nine minutes later, they walked into Dr. Tamari's office and sat down in the two antique, red-velvet chairs in front of his large maple desk. Framed degrees from Ivy League Universities dotted the wall behind him, bordering the left side of a massive picture window. An entire wall of medical books sat neatly in a dark maple bookcase that matched his desk. Before Michelle could ask what the doctor had discovered, he began, "Well, Mr. and Mrs. Powers, I have some good news for the two of you." Michelle and Keith exchanged quick glances, and then turned back to the doctor. "The good news is that Ryan is going to be just fine. I was right in my initial diagnosis of acute anemia. With a quick transfusion, and lots of tender loving care, he'll be just fine and he'll grow up to be perfectly healthy and perfectly normal. At times, he may develop typical anemic symptoms, but it's nothing that will hinder his lifestyle or interfere with his external or internal development."

Michelle breathed a sigh of relief and exchanged a warm smile with her husband.

Dr. Tamari continued. "So Michelle, we'll need to draw some blood so that we are able to…" Then he interrupted his own sentence, "Oh, Mr. Powers, I'm sorry. I wasn't aware that you weren't the biological father of Ryan. I may not have had to draw blood if I was privy to this information beforehand."

Keith's face became warm. "What do you mean?"

"We'll be fine just using Michelle's blood. Since Ryan is not your biological son, we can't use yours. Your blood type is A Negative by the way." The doctor hesitated, realizing that Keith's expression indicated that he was completely unaware of the facts being presented to him. Dr. Tamari explained further, "It's impossible for you and Michelle to have a child that is Ryan's blood type. And since Ryan is type B Positive…"

Keith sprang from his chair and darted out of the doctor's office. Michelle ran after him, "Wait a minute Keith!" She ran full speed until she caught him half way to the parking lot. She grabbed his arm and said, "Keith I'm sure there's been a mistake." Keith jerked his arm from her grasp and picked up his pace.

Michelle trotted back to Dr. Tamari's office and halted at his door so she could catch her breath. She took three deep breaths and re-entered his office. "I forgot something," Michelle said. She smiled at the stroller and carefully wheeled it out the door.

"I'll give you a call tomorrow, Doctor."

Keith waited in the car with the engine running. Michelle put Ryan in his car seat, and shut the door. Before she opened the passenger door to get in, she stood outside the car for a few seconds. She needed to gather her thoughts. She needed to think of something to tell Keith. Something he would believe.

The cement was cold and hard against her face.

"Wake up! Michelle, wake up! Michelle!" Keith yelled, holding her tightly in his arms. "Michelle!"

Michelle opened her eyes half way and saw Keith's face in hers. His look of concern startled her. "What? What happened?" she asked.

"You just fainted," Keith's voice was stern and his expression turned quickly from concern to anger. He lifted her up and helped her in the car. He walked around the front of the car and slumped into the driver's seat. He restarted the ignition and pulled out of the hospital parking lot.

The awful silence forced Michelle to nervously glance to the back seat and check on Ryan. She needed her gaze to be anywhere but on the veins popping out of Keith's muscular neck. Veins she'd never seen because up until that moment, Keith had never once raised his voice to her. But every time she turned to the backseat to look at her son, she saw Dante. The resemblance made her body shudder and her stomach queasy. *Dante Williams. Maxine. Keith. Condoms. Pin. Holes. Dante. Married.* She squeezed her temples with balled up fists. "Go away!" she screamed.

Startled by her sudden shriek, Keith jumped. He peered at her, only for a second and then looked back at the road. He shook his head slowly. Back and forth. Back and forth... all the way home until they pulled into the garage.

It was dark outside Ryan's bedroom window when the soft sound of Keith's voice drifted from their master bedroom and woke Michelle. Feeling drugged and confused, she realized that she must have slept for hours. She wondered where Ryan was and who Keith was talking to. She walked to the doorway and listened, but was almost afraid to go any farther. From below, she heard the sounds of a Barney video. She also heard Ryan's gurgles and giggles. From their room, she heard Keith quietly mumbling.

Finally, the Barney video playing in the family room ended and she could hear Keith's conversation more clearly. She stood in the center of the hallway. She could see Ryan watching a cartoon that had come on regular TV when Barney ended. Although she couldn't quite make out what Keith was saying or who it was he was speaking with, she could hear him softly crying. Tears streamed down her face. *What am I going to do?* she asked herself for the thousandth time.

Without any idea of what she would say, she found herself standing in front of Keith. He was sitting on the edge of the unmade bed quietly whispering on the phone. "Okay gotta go right now. I'll call you back." He quickly replaced the receiver on the handset.

Michelle hoped that Keith would be able to maintain his gentle nature. "Keith? I don't even know what to say."

"Good. 'Cause there's nothing for you to say." His tone was dry.

"I'm sorry. This is all so terrible. I mean..."

Keith cut her off, "I don't wanna hear no apologies, no excuses, no explanations, no nothing." The sadness slowly leaked out of each word and his voice began to tremble. "I'm totally and completely sickened by this whole thing. By you, by your lies, by ALL OF THIS!" His tone of voice frightened her. Standing, he cut Michelle's tears with a piercing stare. She watched his mouth quiver. She wanted to stop him from shaking, stop him from being angry, stop him from hurting, but she knew there was nothing she could do. She knew that her touch was no longer magic. She knew that in a matter of hours, she had gone from the love of his life to the most horrifying sight he could imagine. His face was crimson, as if his blood were about to boil over. She shut her eyes and hoped that it would all go away, as if it had never happened.

"WHO DO YOU THINK YOU ARE? COMING INTO MY LIFE LIKE THIS AND JUST TURNING SHIT UPSIDE DOWN?!" She kept her eyes shut and tried to remain still. "DO YOU KNOW HOW

MUCH YOU HAVE EMBARRASSED ME AND MY FAMILY? WHO ARE YOU TO THINK YOU CAN KEEP SOMETHING LIKE THIS FROM ME? HOW COULD YOU DO THIS TO ME? HOW MICHELLE? HOW?"

"I swear to you Keith, I didn't know," Michelle whispered. "I swear I didn't." She opened her eyes briefly to look at him, but all she saw was his quivering lips.

"DON'T GIVE ME THAT! HOW ARE YOU GONNA SIT HERE AND TRY TO LIE SOME MORE? HOW THE HELL COULD YOU HAVE NOT KNOWN? WHOSE BABY IS IT, MICHELLE? WHO DID YOU LIE DOWN WITH WHILE YOU WERE WITH ME? HUH? WHO?"

"Please Keith…" she whimpered. "Please stop yelling. The baby…" She opened her eyes quickly and shut them again only enough to see Keith dart towards the bedroom door. The loud slam of the door caused her to open her eyes. She watched him approach her with murder in his haunted eyes.

"OOOOH, YOU DON'T KNOW HOW BAD I HAVE THIS URGE TO SLAP YOUR FACE, MICHELLE!" He raised his hand as she stood in front of him helpless. Hopeless. "I WANNA KNOW WHO THE HELL YOU WERE OPENING YOUR LEGS FOR. DO I KNOW HIM?" His hooded stare backed her up against the wall. "OOOOH, I BETTA NOT KNOW THIS MAN YOU BEEN WITH. I BETTA NOT. YOU HEAR ME?"

Keith's angry words started to run together. Michelle's vision, again, became blurred and disjointed, so she chose to keep her eyes shut. She held her breath and promised herself that she wouldn't tell. *He'll kill me if I tell*, she thought. *I think he will actually kill me.*

Keith continued, but now in a whisper, "You are nothing but a little low life whore. I married a whore. Can you believe this shit is happening to me?" He grabbed his face like he wanted to tear it off and then covered his eyes. The sudden silence opened her eyes as she stared blankly at the colorful Monet she had hung above their bed months before. Frightened to death, she knew it was best to not look in his direction. She had never seen Keith in such an uncontrolled rage. He threw something across the room, but she decided not to look, guessing it was a book. Then, she heard Ryan crying.

"Keith, you're scaring Ryan." She snuck a peek at him while he paced like an animal alongside the floor-to-ceiling window that spanned the entire bedroom. Once again, the silence through the room was still thick with tension. Now was her chance to get out of his path. The baby was crying and she had to go make sure he was okay. She bowed her head as she fled the room. When she slowly closed the door behind her, a loud thump crashed against the door. He'd thrown another book... this time, at her.

CHAPTER TWENTY-EIGHT

"*Stefanie!" Ricky called through the apartment.*

I ignored him as I slapped six chicken breasts and four hot links on the barbecue.

"Stefanie?!"

I ignored him again.

Finally, he found his way into the kitchen and onto the balcony. Frustrated, he said, "What is wrong with you? Didn't you hear me?"

"Just wanted you to know how it would feel if I decided not to show up at the altar," I laughed. I lowered my voice to match the deep tone of his, "Stefanie?! Stefanie, where are you?!" I laughed some more.

He didn't think it was funny.

"What are you gonna do when we move into the house? It is way too big for you to be yellin' from room to room tryin' to find me. You're gonna need a microphone." Ricky had just bought a five thousand square foot home in Marina Del Rey. If escrow closed in time, we'd be set to move the week we returned from our honeymoon in St. Martin.

"Would you just shut up and listen to me for a second?" He teased. "I just got off the phone with Keith. You are not going to believe what I'm about to tell you."

"Huh?" I put the cover on the grill and scooted by him to make my way inside to the kitchen.

Ricky followed close behind. "Oh, my God. This is some shit Stef, you are not gonna believe it!" He put his hand over his forehead.

"What?!"

"Guess."

"They are splitting up?"

"Yeah, but that's not all. It's about Ryan."

"Oh no, is he going be okay?" I asked. I lost count of the cups of water I was dumping into the saucepan so I poured the water back into the sink and started over.

"Yeah, he's going to be fine, but they had to do blood tests and the doctor told Keith that Ryan is not his baby."

"What?" I lost sight of the amount of rice that I was measuring. It went all over the sink and then the floor. A long pause stood between us. "There is no way. What? How? I mean, who's is it then?"

"Don't know. But the crazy thing is, it's not Keith's. Not my nephew and not my parent's grandson."

Un-fucking-believable, I thought.

"I feel so bad for Keith. God, he already had a monster problem trusting women after his last relationship went bad. And now this."

"What is he gonna do?" I asked.

"Don't know. He cried when he told me. He'll probably pack up their stuff and send them on their merry way. I'd kick that bitch in her teeth. That's the difference between me and my brother."

"Yeah, how *did* you two end up so different?"

"I don't know how that happened, *Redbone* of mine." Ricky laughed and dropped a package on the granite countertop. From the size and shape, I knew exactly what it was.

I left the kitchen to check the meat on the grill. Ricky unwrapped the package and met me outside. He held up the license plate. REDBONE. "You know you like being a redbone." Ricky put the plates down and hugged me while I continued to flip the meat.

"I can't believe you actually took the time to order that from the DMV. That is the most ridiculous thing ever."

"What's ridiculous is that you don't want to acknowledge these great attributes you have."

"My light skin is not a great attribute, Ricky. Oh God, Tiffany should hear you." Again, I shoved him aside so I could slide through the screen door.

"Fuck Tiffany."

Fragility. Uncertainty. Hostility. All of it was in the air the next morning when I woke up. I could sense it. Something was coming, but I didn't know what. I felt like a dog that gets antsy moments before an earthquake hits. Maybe it was because of the news about Michelle and Keith that rocked our tight, little circle. Maybe it was because Ricky didn't get home until 5:00am.

I counted down the days until our wedding. Twenty-one. I eased out of bed, careful not to wake Ricky and stood in front the mirror, naked. *Not bad*, I thought. I decided to run to the gym and take a Bootcamp class. I jumped in the shower so I could wake myself up, quietly put on my spandex sports bra and a pair of shorts and got halfway out of the apartment without waking Ricky. Then I realized that a herd of elephants probably couldn't disturb his third hour of sleep, so I purposely let the door slam.

When I got back, two and a half hours later, Ricky was awake, in front of the TV, flipping channels and eating a bucket of Popeye's Fried Chicken and some red beans and rice.

"You went to the gym?" he asked.

"No, I went to a business meeting," I replied, standing in front of him dressed in my Nikes and workout gear.

"You're lookin' good, Stef."

"Obviously not good enough for you to stay your ass at home last night." I walked into the bathroom, slammed the door and ran a bath.

Ricky barged in the bathroom. Every time he stayed out late, he always had a present for me the next morning or an invitation to do something fun. This morning he had both. "You wanna go to the movies today?"

I ignored him and submerged myself in the bubbly, warm water.

"I bought you something."

I ignored him again.

He put it on the edge of the bathtub and left the room.

"Diamonds aren't gonna make it okay for you to come home at 5 am."

He popped his head back in the door. "It's not diamonds Stefanie. And by the way, I ordered it *weeks* ago."

"Whatever it is, I don't want it."

"Okay Stef, what's the problem today? Are you pms-ing again? Or are you still mad about the pre-nup?"

"I wasn't *mad* about the pre-nup, I was just disappointed. But I am *mad* because you got home a few seconds before the sun came up. When during our relationship did you begin to think that coming home that late was okay?"

"Look how insecure you are. Damn, that shit is not cute. Get some confidence. Maybe things will get a little better around here."

He kicked the tiny, rectangular box into the soapy water and left.

"TURN IT AROUND RICKY!" I yelled. "THAT'S ALWAYS YOUR SOLUTION TO EVERYTHING! IT'S ALWAYS MY FAULT. YEAH TURN IT AROUND."

Ricky threw on a pair of jeans and an old USC Football sweatshirt that I bought him one year for a joke, left the apartment and jumped into his Porsche. Before he even got past the guard, he had Malik on the phone. "Leek?"

"Yeah, eight six, what up?" Ricky and all his friends addressed each other by their jersey numbers.

Ricky put in his request, "Call Simone on the three-way for me real quick."

"Dang man, I'm on the phone."

"Just real quick."

"You was just with her all night. You trippin'."

"Man, just dial Simone for me."

"You ain't ready to get married. You better cancel that shit before it's too late."

"You gonna dial it or not?"

"Dial it yourself. Stefanie could open your cell phone bill, see some girl's number on it a hundred times and STILL not leave your dumb ass."

"Yeah, and that's fine. But I'll be married the next time my phone bill comes. And I can't leave her no evidence. Adultery breaches the pre-nuptial I think."

"Rick. Just cancel that shit man. You've been talking to me about how you don't think you are ready. Better now than get a divorce later."

"I can't do that to her. That would break her heart man. She's done everything for me."

"That's no reason to marry her. You got to love her Rick. Love is what people feel when they get married."

"I do love her."

"Not in the way you need to love her to make a marriage work."

"I love her and I respect her, Malik. I do."

"Well, what you're doing with Simone and all them other girls you're messin' with ain't right. That ain't respecting her."

"You know how it is man, come on."

"Man, I haven't stepped out on Tiff like that in a long time. You have to be ready to give that shit up. Stef's good people man, you know what I'm sayin? You gonna drag her through a lot of bad shit if you marry her. Just wait a few more years. Get it out of your system. Stef ain't goin' nowhere."

Ricky was silent. Malik was right. He loved Stefanie and he respected her more than any other girl he'd been with. But he also wasn't ready to resist all of the attention he received since becoming a millionaire, professional athlete.

Malik told Ricky he had another call. He clicked over. While Ricky waited for Malik to come back on the line, he decided that regardless of what happened in the near future, he needed to see Simone just one more time. Malik clicked back on the line.

Ricky admitted, "I'm gonna just see Simone today and that'll be it."

"You got Stef who you know you can trust and you got all these other broads comin' out the woodwork. Why Simone?"

"Simone is cool. She doesn't nag me. Plus she's down to make whatever happen. Threesomes, foursomes, she's up for whatever." Ricky laughed.

"Simone ain't into nothing but your money Rick. Come on."

"And that is why I'm gonna marry Stef. Cause she's the only one I'll be able to trust. But until I say 'I do', Simone can get it a few more times. Come on man. Just do me a favor and get her on the phone. Everything is gonna be cool. It'll all work itself out."

Malik shook his head and gave up. "Damn man, hold on and let me dump this other line."

Ricky had met Simone at the Century City Mall. As a retail clerk in one of the high-end clothing boutiques, she assisted Malik and Ricky in purchasing a couple items for their fiancées. She even modeled a few outfits for them so they could get a better idea of how they would fit. Ricky brought a pair of jeans into the dressing room for his "live" model to try on and Simone asked him to stay while she changed. Ricky obliged and from that moment the two began their secret rendezvous. After each night they spent together, Ricky made a promise to himself that he would end it, especially as it got closer to the wedding. But each time Stefanie bitched and complained about something he didn't do, how late he got home or that she needed more time with him, he ran to Simone. A no-strings-attached relationship. When he was with her, he felt liberated. No checkin' in. No shackles. No tip-toeing in if he was late. No lying to protect her feelings. No pressure.

"Hello?" Simone answered.

"Hey. It's me," Ricky said. "I'm on my way."

"Over here?"

"Yeah."

"Where we going?"

"Back to the hotel."

Simone smiled. "Okay. I'll wait outside," she said and hung up the phone. Simone was only 18 years old. Just months before, she had packed away her homecoming queen crown and her high school diploma and decided that her looks would get her further than a college degree would. Simone's beauty wasn't exceptional when you stood her next to some of L.A.'s finest, but her flawless brown skin, tight size 4 body, and flirtatious smile got Ricky every single time.

Squeezing her boobs into a violet-colored lace bra, she turned to her big sister for approval. "Meera? How do I look?"

"Like a slut." Meera, who was a few years older than Simone, sat on the center of her bed and flipped through a *People* magazine.

"Why does the *smart* sister always hate on the *pretty* sister?"

"Yeah whatever. What is wrong with you anyway? You are still letting this fool have the best of both worlds. He's engaged to the woman that he loves, but he still gets a piece of you ANY time he wants. Don't you have any respect for yourself?"

"Meera, I asked you a simple question. Why you in my business anyway? And since you are, then you may as well know that truthfully he is with me almost as much as he is with her. I mean how often do you see him over here?"

"I *don't* see him over here 'cause I don't look at his sorry ass when he is here."

"The bottom line is that he is with her 'cause he HAS to be. He is with me 'cause he WANTS to be."

"Oh yeah. Sometimes I forget you are only eighteen and a half. But it only takes a minute of conversation with you for me to remember."

"He's got money. And you're just jealous."

"You could have ANY man you want. You are practically perfect and you go and choose this MEATHEAD football player who has no brains, no sense, and no shame."

"*Practically* perfect? Like I said, smart sister," she pointed to Meera. Then she looked in the mirror. "Pretty sister," Simone sang, as she swept herself out of the room.

Ricky was already in front of the house when Simone walked outside. She hopped in the Porsche, lightly touched his face and kissed him on his cheek. They drove up the Pacific Coast highway to The Malibu Beach Inn. Before Ricky was even able to get the key into the keyhole, Simone stood on her tip-toes from behind him and started planting wet kisses along his shoulder. She said, "We should have never left here last night."

"Yeah, and my girl would've beat me down. She's getting meaner by the day."

"Why are you even getting married, Ricky?" Simone asked, as she stepped out of her clothes and got into the bed. Ricky pulled his clothes off and joined her, grabbing the remote control on the way. He flicked on the TV. She cuddled up to him and laid her head on his chest. "Wait, wait, keep it there. The Real World. You seen this yet?" she asked.

"Which one is this?"

"San Francisco. It's good."

Simone ran her tongue over his chest while she watched the TV. "You wanna do it?"

"No," Ricky answered.

"Okay. Neither do I."

"I'm cool just laying here with you."

"Me too."

Ricky and Simone stayed in bed until 8:00 p.m. They caught up on ten episodes of Real World, ordered room service and dozed off and on during commercial breaks.

"Baby?" she looked at him questioningly. "You sleepin'?"

Ricky slowly opened his eyes.

"Baby, please don't do it," she begged. "Don't marry her." She buried her face in his neck. "People don't find this. What we have here, you know what I'm sayin'? They don't find it that often. And you know if you marry her that'll be the end of us." Ricky's eyes fell shut again. He was listening. He hated to think of his life without her. But right then he just wanted to savor the moment and worry about tomorrow when it came. She was right though. He knew she was right. But he'd made a thousand promises to Stefanie that he didn't want to break.

But Simone wouldn't give up. Twenty days left. It was time for her closing argument. "I know you feel you have to be loyal to her since you have been with her for all these years and I know she helped you get through school and all, and that she's been by your side, especially when you got injured, but when people pick loyalty over love, they always end up regretting it. Trust me."

Ricky pretended he was asleep, but her words burrowed deep into his mind as Simone snuggled even closer to him. He knew Simone was just like the rest, but "the rest" seemed to be the choice over Stefanie lately. Especially with Keith's marriage crashing and burning, Ricky found comfort in the thought of regaining his free and independent lifestyle. Life just seemed to be easier for his single friends than it was for his married friends. But with this $50,000 wedding planned and the heart of the faithful Stefanie Pointer in his hand, what was he to do?

CHAPTER TWENTY-NINE

1 *:30 a.m. and still no Ricky. I took off my clothes, crawled in bed and tried to fall asleep. I remembered that I never opened the gift that he kicked* into the bathtub earlier that day. I grabbed it from the bathroom and got back in bed. The faded, soggy paper had dried and although the box looked forlorn, I could still read the inscription on the box top. *XXIV Karats—Beverly Hills.* I undid the wrapping and opened the box. It was a sterling silver charm bracelet. I turned on the light so I could see the charms. There were six in all. One was a tiny bone that was red. One was his football number. One was a heart. One was a football. One was a gavel. And one was a pinwheel.

My cell phone rang as I tried to fasten the charm bracelet on my wrist. "Hello?"

"Stef, it's me."

Silence.

"What are you doing?"

"That's a dumb question."

"Did you open the box that I left?"

"Yeah."

"Do you like it?"

"I guess."

"You didn't think I could be so creative, huh?"

I decided not to respond.

"You're mad still?"

"No, not mad. Just wondering."

"Wondering what?"

"Why I am getting married to you."

"Naw, it's their fault. Listen." I heard Jaylin, Kenny and Malik in the background.

Ricky had left Simone in the room and went to join his friends at a club on Sunset. He wanted to make it look like he'd been with them all day and night. He explained, "They wanted me to have a few drinks with them and then I was gonna come take you to the movies, but it got late."

"Whatever Ricky. I'm sleeping," I lied.

"I love you Stef, damn. Why do you trip off every little thing? Seems like everyday you get mad at me for something," he slurred.

Silence again.

Jaylin spoke into the phone. "Baby girl. You should have weighed the risks when you got with this brotha' here. You get down with a ball player, you gots to brave the crossfire."

Ricky added to Jaylin's disgusting advice. "Yeah baby, no one said this shit was gonna be easy."

Another of his friends spoke from the background, though I couldn't tell who it was, "Why she always trippin' man? You're about to get married, shoot—in a minute, you'll be home with lock n' key!"

Then Jaylin and Kenny started singing, "Shackles on your feet." Ricky laughed.

I hung up the phone. If I didn't, I'd have thrown up.

Ricky called right back. "Why you hang up the phone?"

"Why? Cause' basically you make me sick. You and all your stupid little friends. All of you make me sick. When the hell are you gonna grow up? Huh? When, Ricky?"

"When you gonna stop tryin' to run my life?" He said it loud enough for his friends to hear.

"When you grow up, I'll stop trying to run your life. How bout that?" My tone was condescending.

"Hold on, Stefanie."

I couldn't believe that he put me on hold.

Ricky clicked to his second line. "Hello?"

"You comin' back to the room tonight?" Simone asked.

"Hold on. Don't hang up."

Ricky clicked back to Stefanie. "Stef?"

"What?"

"I can't marry you."

"Oh, you can't marry me now?"

"Naw, there's no way that this is gonna work."

My body temperature rose and it felt like every ounce of blood in my body rushed to my head.

The background music in the club had stopped. His friends had even shut their mouths. No one said a word. And then Ricky spoke again. "I just can't."

"So, it's off?"

"Yep, it's off."

"Whatever Ricky. You are so spontaneous. One minute you are…" Before I could finish, the phone went dead. No static. No bad connection. It just went dead. On purpose. I waited for him to regret hanging up and to call back. Call back so he could apologize and so I could apologize as well. I waited. I lay there and waited, but the phone didn't ring. Dead.

I stared at the television. A repeat of *Saturday Night Live* was on. It wasn't funny. I just sat and stared at the people making fools of themselves.

I begged for sleep to come. I knew that once the sun came up, things would be better. Ricky would come home. I'd wake up and Ricky would be lying next to me. We'd snuggle, apologize, and then off I would go to the gym. But I couldn't fall asleep. I had to keep my ears open. I had to listen. I had to make sure that I could hear Ricky put his key in the door. *Please, come home. Please.*

He didn't come home.

Visions of our wedding ran through my mind, fast forward and back, and then obliterated by the emptiness on his side of the bed. It wasn't going to happen. I felt it in every part of my body. We were over. No wedding. No babies. No home together. No nothing. Dead.

I didn't care that it was after four o'clock in the morning. I dialed his mother's phone number.

"Hello?" Mrs. Powers answered.

"Hi, Mrs. Powers. I'm sorry to be calling so late."

"Oh that's okay, sweetie. Ricky's on the other line."

"Oh God. He is?"

"Yes, don't you worry about a thing. Let me talk some sense into this boy and I'll call you right back."

Before fifteen minutes had passed, the phone rang. I knew it had to be either Ricky or his mother. "Hello?"

"It's me," Ricky said.

"Hi," I said. A breeze of cool relief washed over me.

"I'm sorry, Stefanie. I'm truly sorry. I just can't do it. Right now I'm really going through a lot of things on my mind and there's no way with all this stuff that a marriage would work. We've been fighting and arguing about things that should not be brought into a marriage."

"But..."

The calmness in his voice terrified me. "Please don't try to talk me out of it. My mother just spent over an hour trying to change my mind. I'm sorry. I know this is a horrible thing to do. I know you are going to be hurt. But I just can't go through with it."

"Ricky, it's in three weeks. The invitations are out and I already have..."

"I know all that," he interrupted, his voice now hard. "I know. But I have to make this decision now. Better now than after the fact."

"I love you so much, though." My voice cracked and tears filled my eyes.

"I'm not ready, Stef. You wouldn't wanna marry someone who wasn't ready, would you?"

"I thought you were ready..." I cried. "I thought you loved me and you were proud of me and couldn't wait for everyone to see you..." I cried more, "for everyone to hear you say, I do. I thought..." I couldn't get another word out.

"I'm sorry."

I hung up. I couldn't bear to hear him say it. That he was sorry, one more time.

I picked up the phone and dialed Marie and Jana.

Marie answered, full of sleep. "Hello?"

I tried to say "Hello." But nothing came out.

Marie spoke louder, "Hello?"

Through a river of tears, "You won't believe," I tried to catch my breath mid-sentence, "what Ricky just did?"

"I'm sure I'll believe it. What he do now?" she said not yet understanding how devastated I truly was.

"He called the wedding off." My sobs became uncontrollable.

Marie had knocked on Jana's bedroom door and told her to pick up the phone, and called Tiffany on the three-way. While they talked amongst themselves, I just listened quietly between my pitiful sobs. "Are you *sure* that it's off?" Jana asked.

"Yes. I know Ricky. I know when he's serious."

Tiffany couldn't wait for her turn to speak. "This fool has lost his mind for real this time. And if he comes back and begs for you to forgive him, girl, don't you even think about it. Don't you dare give his raggedy, unfaithful, insecure, gap-toothed, can't-even-write-his-own-paper ass a second chance."

I felt like I was close to dying. Like my heart would stop beating at any moment. But the familiar, honest voices of my closest girlfriends kept me alive. The phone became my IV. My lifeline. I needed them more than I ever did before.

We stayed on the phone until the sun came up, marking a brand new day.

"We'll come get you," Jana offered. "We'll be there in a minute."

"I'm sorry, you guys. Really I am. I know this is a pain for all of you. Keeping you up the whole night and now making you get out of bed at six in the morning."

"Please, we're here for you, girl. Anytime. Anyplace. Don't worry about it. See you in a minute," Marie said.

"Stef, everything is gonna be alright. I promise," Tiffany said softly. "I know I keep saying that, but trust me. I know it doesn't feel like that now, but time will heal your broken heart. He ain't no good anyway. You deserve way better than what he could offer you. You practically gave your life to him and he couldn't give you shit in return but some diamonds, some flowers and a crock full of lies and tears."

"That's not true, Tiff. He loves me. I know he does."

"No, you're right. I do know he loves you. He's just not ready to love you in the way he needs to love you. Just start packing your stuff, girl. I'm sure they'll be there in a minute to get you. And don't look back."

"Okay, I'll call you back when I get out of here."

"And don't think about that stupid wedding. You'll have a better one."

"Okay, I'll call you later."

The wedding, I thought. *The wedding. There wasn't going to be a wedding. There wasn't going to be any pretty flowers or long toasts. There wasn't going to be a church filled with people I loved. There wasn't going to be a chance for my father to walk me down the aisle in my ivory-white dress.*

My dress?

I ran to the closet in the guest room where I had hung it the day before and pulled it out of the protective plastic bag. I knelt down while I continued to hold it. Tears poured down my already swollen face. Tears of sadness. Tears of hopelessness. Tears of pain.

CHAPTER THIRTY

*I*t was seven o'clock in the morning when Michelle parked her car on the side of the road a half block up from Dante's house and turned off the engine. The fog loomed low and the neighborhood stood still and noiseless. She peeked through the rear view mirror and noticed Ryan had fallen asleep in the back seat. Hearing a distant car approach, she turned down the radio. A red BMW flew past her. She turned the radio back up and hummed along with Mary J., bouncing her head back and forth to the beat of the music. Michelle wasn't nervous or fearful of the possible consequences. She remained calm and sure of her decision to wait all damn day, if necessary.

Michelle had been trying to contact Dante since she moved back to Los Angeles. The first step in receiving the child support for Ryan was to inform him that Ryan was his child. But her attempts failed when she discovered he'd changed all his phone numbers. She left numerous messages at his team's office, but received no return call. It was almost as if he was trying to avoid her.

Finally, almost forty-five minutes later, the gates slowly opened. Michelle scooted down in her seat. She peeked over the steering wheel carefully to confirm it was Dante before she pulled away from the curb.

His black Ferrari crept from off the driveway, cautiously at first, but then accelerated past her. Michelle tried to peer into the car, but couldn't see past the black tinted windows. She started the ignition anyway and pulled off.

She followed him down the winding tree-lined road, keeping a bend or two between them so she'd stay unnoticed. Her own laughter filled the car as she deviously shook her head back and forth anticipating his reaction the minute she introduced the son he never knew he had. She laughed louder as she rehearsed exactly what she would say.

The Ferrari bolted onto the freeway faster than she'd expected, losing Michelle for a moment. She frantically searched ahead in the distance for the car. "Dammit!" she exclaimed. Ryan's eyes popped opened as he let out a blood-curdling shriek and then started crying. "Shhhhhh, go back to sleep sweetie. Everything is gonna be okay." When she noticed the Ferrari speeding down the fast lane, she suddenly accelerated trying to gain enough speed to catch up. Dante flicked on his blinker, swept across all four lanes and exited the freeway. Michelle braked and then scooted across, barely making the exit, car horns blaring behind her.

The light at the exit was red. Michelle pulled up behind him and tried desperately to see through the Ferrari's black windows. The early morning sunlight hit at the right place and she finally could see the outline of his blocky head. She wondered if he knew she was following him, but at this point she didn't care. She laughed out loud, glancing back and forth between the red light and the back of Dante's head. Dante seemed to be studying his rearview mirror. Michelle locked her stare in his direction as her laugh turned into a slow, evil giggle. Dante turned his whole body around to look through the back window. The light turned green and he screeched off.

Michelle used her amateur driving skills to stay with him the best she could. But after she chased him down Venice Boulevard for more than a mile, he pulled off into an empty parking lot. She slowed wondering where he could possibly be going. The only store she spotted was a Smart & Final, but it was closed. She watched him ease to the corner of the parking lot and stop his car. She edged towards him not knowing what she should do next. Ryan was still bellowing in the back seat.

"Quiet Ryan, please. You are about to meet daddy, so wipe those tears off your face." Ryan's cries turned into a low whimper as he stared out the window, no doubt wondering who the big man was getting out of his car nearby.

"Hi," Michelle said, as she rolled down her window and smiled. Dante looked at her without expression. "I need to talk to you." Michelle opened her door and got out leaving Ryan in the car. "Sorry to make this a surprise, but obviously I had to track you down somehow because you weren't returning my calls, Dante. Why weren't you?"

Instead of answering her question, he continued to stare at her as if she was some psychotic woman he didn't know. She was ready to show that she was a psychotic woman he did know!

"Dante? What's *wrong* with you?"

"What's wrong with *me*?" he asked, his eyes the size of golf balls. "Are you crazy?"

"Nothing's wrong with me. We need to talk, that's all."

"There's nothing to talk about."

"As a matter of fact there is. Do you want to go somewhere a little more appropriate? Like a park or to a coffee shop or something?"

"*Appropriate* for what? This is fine right here. What is it?"

"No Dante. I really think we should go somewhere else. You should be sitting down." She glanced back at Ryan who was busy trying to get into an old bag of wheat thins he'd found on the seat next to him.

Dante sat down in his car leaving the door wide open and the window down. "Okay, now I'm sitting. What? What do you want?"

Michelle got out of her car and squatted down in front of him. Her heart was pounding, her muscles taut. "I want you to meet somebody."

"Who?"

"Your son."

"My who?"

"Your son, Ryan, Dante. His name is Ryan." Dante's eyes followed hers to the one-year- old strapped in his infant seat.

Dante stood up abruptly. "What!? I knew you were crazy," he mumbled. "What the hell are you talking about? Now I know you are crazy." He slid back into the driver's seat and started the engine.

"Wait Dante. Wait! I made a terrible mistake and I just thought it was time you knew," she begged. He revved the engine loud enough to drown out Michelle's words. She yelled louder. "I'm sorry. I didn't know until recently. Really, I didn't." She put her hand through the window of his car to touch his shoulder. Quickly, he jerked his body away and sped off.

"I'll take you to court, you son of a bitch!" she yelled at the empty space in front of her. "You coward ass little-dicked bastard!" She began to laugh hysterically. "I'm gonna get you."

Ryan watched out of the window as his mommy stood there laughing. He looked around to see if he could find Barney. He didn't. "Mommy laugh," he said as Michelle got back into the car.

"Yeah, my little bumpkin. Mommy laugh." She stood in the opened car door and smiled at Ryan. "Mommy laugh because your daddy is about to get his ass taken to court. Yes he is," she sung. She pinched Ryan's cheek. "You, my son, are my golden paycheck."

Michelle took Ryan home and put him down for a nap in his port-a-crib, next to her bed. Living with Adrienne again wasn't easy, but Michelle didn't have enough money to get her own place yet. She did, however, have a live-in babysitter, which made it easier to start going back to "the Market" on Friday nights. The phone rang just as Ryan was falling off to sleep. "Hello?"

"Michelle?"

"Hey, girl," she said sneaking out of the room trying not to wake Ryan. She walked into the kitchen and perched herself on one of the barstools.

"How ya' doin'?" Kim asked.

Michelle let out a heavy sigh. "Ask me *what* I've been doin', not *how* I've been doin'."

Kim sighed, "Okay Michelle, *what* have you been doing?" Kim braced herself for the drama.

"I talked to Dante. I told him. I told him everything."

"What? Why did you do that? I thought you were gonna leave all that alone?"

"Uh-uh. I need some help. When I start working, I'm gonna have to pay for daycare, not to mention all kinds of other stuff. And I know Adrienne doesn't want me and Ryan staying here forever." She paused, sighed, and continued, "Basically his Daddy is gonna have to dip in his pockets for a little bit of green."

"I don't know Michelle. Dante doesn't seem like the type willing to write a check every first of the month."

"Have you ever heard of the word *garnish*, or how 'bout *arrears?*" she laughed. "You should've seen him today. He didn't even wanna hear nuthin' I had to say. He just got in his stupid little sports car and sped off."

"That's 'cause he probably got spooked when he saw a little miniature version of himself starin' back at him," Kim chuckled. But then she realized that none of it was funny. "Have you talked to Keith?"

"Nope. Not since the day I walked out of his house. Girl, did I tell you he even made me take a cab to the airport? With ALL my stuff."

"*All* your stuff?"

"Well, the other things he is shipping. I'm expecting them to get here in a couple of weeks," Michelle paused, "and I suppose I'll get a set of divorce papers to seal the deal."

"Yeah, you can probably bet on that."

"He was even gonna let me stay with him at first. After he calmed down, he said that he thought maybe he could get over it if I had another one right away. But then he found out it was Dante's and he flipped out all over again."

"How did he find out?"

"I told him."

"Why?"

"Because he kept on asking me, telling me it didn't matter whose it was, but he just had to know. I guess he didn't expect it to be someone he knew. And it's not even like Keith *knows* Dante, he just knows *of* him. It's not like they're best friends or nothing. But you know how brothas trip if you git with another brotha in the league. They can't handle it. He's just mad cause Dante has a bigger contract than he does," Michelle said. "Which actually is better for me in the long run. Kim, do you realize with Dante's salary and his endorsement money, I could get almost twenty thousand a month?"

Kim couldn't muster up a response to what she'd just heard. Instead she just shook her head, listened and wondered why she remained friends with the girl on the other end of the phone.

"Please reset your seatback cushions and replace your trays to their upright position. We will be landing in Los Angeles in less than fifteen minutes." I listened to the flight attendant's warning. Well, to me, it was a warning, a warning that my vacation was coming to an end. I borrowed a thousand bucks from Tiffany and flew to Kauai for a week at the Princeville Hotel. I

needed to be alone, far from L.A., far from the life that I had to put behind me. I had to begin the healing process and spend some time re-evaluating my future without the advice of my friends, without worrying about running into Ricky and without crowding Jana in her own bed. I loved Jana and cherished our friendship more than anything, but waking up next to her every morning instead of Ricky was a hard reality.

As the plane descended, I exhaled. No more Pina Coladas, sleepy mornings by the beach, walks on the fine white sand, and no more room service.

I peered out of the tiny, oval window and scanned the massive jungle below. *Los Angeles... The City of Angels. Ha, what a joke!* I thought. I overheard the two teenagers seated behind me trying to find their house. "I think it's that one over there!" one of them exclaimed. "The one with the pool." Their thrill and enthusiasm over such an unexciting task perversely caused me to try to do the same. Through the thick layer of smog, I searched the homes, homes set in a grid-like pattern. I searched for my house. I searched and searched and searched. And then I realized that I was searching for something that didn't exist. I didn't have a house or a pool. I didn't have an apartment. I didn't even have a car.

An uneasy feeling came over me as I considered all that I had to do within the next couple of months. I had to start from ground zero. I didn't have a job. And when I found one, how would I even get myself there every morning? I didn't have any work experience to put on a resume. So much for me telling Ricky all those years that he needs a Plan B. Where was mine? My week in Kauai was over, it was time to get myself in high gear.

Looking out the window, I wondered where Ricky was at that very moment. If he ended up moving into the house we were supposed to share. If he'd thought about me as much as I did him this past week. I wondered if he was with another girl already. Knowing him, I figured he was. Feelings of rejection began to overwhelm me again but thankfully they were interrupted by the screeching wheels of the airplane as it hit the runway. "Welcome to Los Angeles," the pilot's voice blared from the rickety speakers throughout the plane. He might as well have said, "Welcome to hell. And have a pleasant stay." I pictured two devils in the cockpit laughing. And then I laughed, but it didn't help at all.

You need a shrink.

No, you don't. You'll be just fine.

You are crazy. Seeing devils and hearing things. You're hallucinating. You need a shrink.

No, you don't. You'll be fine.

Get your ass to a doctor. It'll do you some good.

Don't waste your time. Head doctors are crazier than you.

See, you just admitted that you are crazy. You let that asshole, Ricky, make you crazy.

Don't listen to this shit. Get off the plane and go face the world. You have a fresh slate to fill with a beautiful future.

What beautiful future?

The future you will make beautiful by yourself. And you will learn to stop depending on a man to make everything okay. You will learn to be alone and happy.

Yeah, right! People who are alone are never happy. Get real.

Come on, Stef, don't listen to that mess. Being alone is a beautiful thing. It will be a time of self-exploration and independence. You'll see. Just give it some time. You'll be fine.

Quit telling her she'll be fine.

"Stop it!" I said out loud. The young couple sitting next to me turned my way. They stared at me as if I truly were crazy.

By the time I gathered my carry on and walked into the airport terminal, I silenced my inner voices and pulled myself together.

"Hey now!" Marie yelled as I walked into the baggage claim area where a crowd of people stood waiting for their loved ones.

"Hey, girl," Jana said, burying me in a hug. "Look at cha'. All tan n' shit."

"You've turned into a hot little Hawaiian mama. No more yellow banana," Marie added.

"Why I gotta be a banana? Bananas ain't cute," I teased, trying to hide sadness with feistiness. I flashed them a warm smile to let them know it was comforting to see them.

"How are you? How was the trip?" They asked as we headed toward baggage claim.

"Good. Much needed. All I did was lie on the beach and cleanse my soul. There's something about the combination of the sun's rays, a couple of those tropical drinks and no one around, but yourself. That right there is the prescription I would give to anyone who is suffering from heartbreak. It really makes you feel like you just may be all right," I explained. "Not to say I have come back forgetting about the drama that just nearly killed me, but I have to admit, I do feel a little better."

"Good," said Marie. "Cause I will say it once and for all. Ricky is not worthy of you."

It was nice to be in the company of my girlfriends once again.

"How 'bout Killer Shrimp? You hungry?" Jana asked. "We want to take you to dinner. Or wherever you want to go. We could go to the Cheesecake Factory or Fridays. Wherever you want to go... you name it."

"Actually, it doesn't really matter. But let's just try to stay as far from the Marina as possible." The thought of running into Ricky made my legs weak.

"Roscoes!" Jana suggested.

"That's fine, I guess." I shrugged.

"No?" Marie asked.

"Well, it's just Ricky and I used to go there all the time. What if he's there? And what if he's with someone?"

"What if he's *anywhere,* Stef?" Marie asked. "You are gonna have to face him sooner or later. And you are going to do it with a big smile on your face while you look him dead in his eyes. Make him know that even though he broke your heart, he didn't break your spirit."

Jana, noticing the tears in my eyes, put an arm around me, "Let's just stop by the store and get some stuff. I'll cook."

I nodded, happy to remain incognito, still hiding from the prying eyes of too many L.A. friends and reminders of my former life.

CHAPTER THIRTY-ONE

"Hey Pop, it's me, your favorite daughter."

"Hey sweetheart. How you doin'?"

"I'm alright. Hangin' in there I guess."

"You found a job yet?"

"Nope. Not yet. But I got great scores on the G.R.E. and I sent my masters applications off to UC Irvine and a few other schools."

"Well that's good news. So definitely no law school then?"

"I think I'm built more for a career in education than law dad, sorry to burst your bubble."

"No, I support your decision. Education is an admirable profession sweetheart, just not as lucrative."

"At this rate, *any* amount of money would be nice. I need to get an apartment and a bed… and some furniture." I held my breath and continued. "Oh and I need some money for a deposit on my new apartment."

"And for rent every month and for electricity, phone, food, and a car, and car insurance and…."

"I know dad, go on say it. I can hear it in your voice."

"No, I'm not gonna say I told you so if that's what you mean. I am going to say, however, that I hope your next selection when you're out there in the dating world is given a little more thought and that you don't just fall in love on a whim like you did with… the man who shall remain nameless in our family from now on."

"You won't have to worry about me dating for awhile. And when I do, I promise to be a lot more cautious."

"Your mother and I think you should come home and live with us for awhile."

The thought of moving back home to a town with only one stoplight was not a thought I wanted to have. "Thanks, but I think I'm gonna stay around here for awhile. I need to face reality instead of running home to you and Ma."

"That's fine. It'll just be a little more difficult down there in L.A., getting on your feet and what not, but I know you'll be fine. Adversity builds strength and don't you forget that. And don't forget that you are a Pointer either. Pointers never give up."

"Thanks Dad. So…" I took a deep breath, "do you think I could borrow some money until I'm able to get a job? I've been with Jana and Marie for over three months now and I wanted to help them out, you know, give them some money for rent and stuff."

"Has it been that long already?" he asked.

"I can't believe it either."

"All right. I'll have your mother put some money in the bank tomorrow morning. You want to talk with her?"

"Yeah. Thanks a lot. I'll pay you back. I promise." My mother came on the phone.

"Hey, Ma. How are you?"

"Good. Your father and I just got home from dinner. It's our anniversary."

"Oh," I said shamefully. "I'm sorry, Ma. I've never forgotten your anniversary before. Now I feel bad."

"That's okay. I know you are going through a lot right now. We understand. We want you to move back home, though."

"No. I'll be fine down here. I promise."

"But honey, there is no one to take care of you. No one to watch over you. Los Angeles is filled with crazy people and I worry about you. Too much killing." She continued to ramble. "Especially if you get a place by yourself."

"Ma, I'll be fine."

"The two of you still haven't talked?"

"No, I haven't and I don't plan to." My voice choked itself as I tried to hide my tears from my mother. "I gotta go."

"I can't believe he hasn't called."

"He did call. He left a message. He asked for the ring back."

"He did what?"

"Yeah, can you believe that?"

"Stefanie, the little respect that I had for him after what he did to you is now gone. That is the lowest thing I've ever heard. He cancels a wedding that over 300 guests were scheduled to come to and kicks you out of his house and now asks for the engagement ring back?"

I didn't need to be reminded of what a waste of time the past five years of my life was. "Ma, I gotta go."

Feelings of resentment, anger, loneliness, rejection, bitterness and fear crept through me. *My mom was right. That was the lowest thing that anyone could do to anybody. Did he think he could hurt me like that and walk away? That he could just be done with me like that? After all I did for him? After all those years I spent catering to his every need? Making sure he was happy. Making sure he was getting through whatever it was he needed to get through both mentally and physically. Investing all those years into something I thought was going to last forever. And this is my payoff?! What am I supposed to tell potential employers when I start interviewing? That I spent the last four years cooking, cleaning and hopelessly loving this asshole. And then they would ask—well, why did you leave? And I'd say...oh, because he decided to expand his empire and my job got eliminated. Eliminated. Eliminated.*

"Can I borrow your car?" I called from the living room into Jana's bedroom. "I have to run to the store," I lied.

"Sure. But bring me something back to drink. And pick up the new *Ebony* too. The one with Michael Sinclair on the cover."

"Get me a slurpee!" Marie yelled from the loft. "Cherry."

I slipped on my jeans, grabbed Jana's keys and took off. "I'll be back in a minute."

Within twenty minutes, I found myself sitting in front of the house Ricky and I were supposed to live in. The word "eliminated" kept running through my mind. Both his Porsche and truck sat in the driveway so I parked a few houses down to gather my thoughts. An old broken down Toyota Camry sat at the curb, blocking both his cars.

Get the hell out of here. What do you think this is going to solve?

Just relax. Maybe if Ricky sees you, he'll feel something and he'll realize that he misses you. Maybe he'll invite you inside his house.

His house? This was supposed to be your house too. And now it's probably one big bachelor pad.

No, he is probably inside eating his favorite fried chicken watching one of his Laser Discs. He's probably feeling lonely. He'll be glad to see you.

Not likely. Leave while you can. I thought you were waking up and realizing that this fool is no good. You were starting to heal that broken heart of yours while you were in Hawaii. And now look at you. You are asking for more pain. Get out of here now!

I waited and waited and waited. Eight o'clock rolled around and I watched the lights go on in the house. He was home, and it seemed like he was in there alone. He had to be alone. Why couldn't I just knock on the door? *What's the worst that could happen anyway?*

Don't do it! Go to the damn 7-11 and buy yourself something to drink, buy Marie a slurpee and take your ass home. Go now!

Ring the doorbell. Don't you want to see him? Don't you want him to wrap his strong, beautiful body around you? You know he will. He won't be able to help himself. He must miss you as much as you've been missing him. You two were about to be married. Just go. Get out of the car and ring the damn doorbell. Just to say hello.

He ELIMINATED you. You have the right to ask why.

My heart raced as I scurried up the front walk and pressed the doorbell. Only a few seconds later, Ricky swung the door open, almost as if he were expecting someone. From the wad of cash in his hand, I assumed he thought I was a food delivery man.

All the misplaced feelings of love and happiness rushed back into my heart as he stood in front of me. He peered through me as if I were a ghost.

"What are you doing here?" He spoke nervously.

"I missed you. Ricky... I mean I've been missing you really bad."

God, if Tiffany, Marie and Jana knew what I was doing, they would kill me!

I reached out to hug him, but he just stood there. He looked like he was a young child who'd been caught doing something very, very bad. "Sorry for just popping by, but I couldn't take it anymore. I had to see you."

His shame turned to anger. "You just can't come over here like this."

I might as well have been selling encyclopedias. Actually, he would have probably been more cordial to a door-to-door salesperson.

"But..."

"But nothing Stefanie. I'm sorry. I have company right now and I gotta go."

He backed up.

Rage consumed me. *I told you! I told you! I told you!* "Who is she?" I had to see the bimbo that was in my house. I had to see what she looked like. I had to see who was kickin' it at *my* house, sittin' up on *my* couch, with *my* man. Before he had a chance to answer, I ducked under his arm and ran inside the house. I felt him reach out to grab me, but he missed me and grazed the back of my sweatshirt.

When I saw her, I stopped dead in my tracks. He wasn't lying as I'd hoped. He was telling the cold, honest truth. There she sat, embarrassed, scared. The three of us stared at each other wondering who would be the first to speak. I tried. I tried to ask her what the hell she was doing in *my* house. I tried to tell her that he was *mine*. I wanted to scream for her to get the hell out. I opened my mouth, but couldn't speak. I was as still and quiet as a statue.

"Stefanie, come on, please. Let's go."

Ricky reached for my arm to lead me to the front door, but I yanked it away keeping my eyes fixed on the girl sitting on my couch. She appeared young and mildly innocent. She couldn't have been more than twenty years old, with the exact pale yellow skin tone as mine. She wore her hair up in a high ponytail letting the big curls flow down past the middle of her back. Not knowing what to do or say, she shifted her eyes back and forth between the television set and Ricky. She would not look at me at all.

Ricky finally spoke. "Stefanie, this is a friend of mine, Simone. Simone, this is Stefanie."

Simone formed her thin, dainty lips into a nervous smile, but neither of us spoke.

"Stefanie, please, come on," Ricky urged. He gently put his hand on my arm. There was no way I was going to let *him* escort *me* out of *my* house in front of *her*.

A vision of his gun quickly slid into my angry thoughts. *I wonder if he still keeps it in his side drawer by the bed. I could kill all three of us right here. Right now. If I wasn't gonna have him, there was no way this little bitch was.* I started to walk toward the master bedroom. "Where are you going?" Ricky yelled quickly following close behind. "Stefanie!" He caught up with me as we entered the bedroom. I lunged for the night stand drawer, but he cut me off, forcing me down onto the bed. "What the hell is wrong with you?"

"Get off me," I yelled pushing him away from me.

"Are you sick?" His voice was filled with desperation.

"Get off me," I pushed him with all of my strength, but still wasn't able to get him to budge.

"You need to leave," he straddled me using the weight of his body to prevent me from trying to get up. I wondered if he knew that I was after his gun.

"Okay, I'll go. Just let me up," I grunted. "But let me go out the back. 'Cause if I have to walk by that little tramp, I'll..."

"That's fine. Come on." He got up off me.

I forgot about the gun as I focused on his terrified face, speechless.

"Stefanie, you *have* to go. *Now!*" His words were firm. The steel in Ricky's eyes pierced the deepest part of my soul. It was only at that very moment, finally, that I understood that our love was gone forever.

CHAPTER THIRTY-TWO

The next six months were filled with personal revelations, new beginnings and healing. Even though I was suffering a very painful broken heart, I succeeded in walking through each day with a smile on my face. While I mapped out my plan to get into a Masters Program in Education, I interviewed for entry-level jobs, looked for apartments and even joined a new gym. I did all the things that one is "supposed" to do when they get dumped. My feelings of sadness at times turned to anger and hatred. I despised Ricky for leaving me and there were times at night when I wanted to sneak in the back door of his grand house and find that gun so I *could* kill him. Him *and* her. Of course, to avoid any jail time for murder, I would kill myself too. They were revenge fantasies for sure, but the feelings were real.

For days at a time, I'd lie in Jana's bed and shut out the rest of the world. Jana would leave for class early in the morning and I'd pretend I was asleep until I heard her pull out of the driveway. One morning, when the phone rang, Jana had to run back in the house to answer it. I listened through the bedroom wall, wondering who was calling at 6:00 a.m.

"Hello?" she said. "Who is this?" Then she spoke louder, "I can barely hear you. Who is this?" she asked again. "Oh, Jimmy?" She came into the bedroom and nudged me even though I was already awake. "Stefanie, wake up. It's Jimmy."

My eyes flew open and I looked at Jana as she handed me the phone. "Jimmy?"

"Yeah.................. Stefanie it's................. me."

"This is not Jimmy. Who is this?" I asked. Whomever it was, sounded like they were very old and very tired.

"This is...........Jimmy, baby, I'm sorry I.... will.... speak..... slower......." he said. By the way he called me 'baby' I knew it was him, but still, the voice didn't match the one I'd remembered from a short time ago. Not only could I barely hear him, but I couldn't even understand him. He had lost his ability to speak clearly.

"What's wrong, Jimmy? Where are you?"

"I am... in..... San..... Dee.....ego........at my moth.....er's... house. The........ doctors.......... they....................told........me that I..... am gonna............. die............soon."

"WHAT!? What are you talking about?"

"I.............have.......a....disease.............it's....called.......Lou..... Gehrig's.................I wanted....... to..........say.......... good-bye................. to you.................... and to Ricky."

"What? I can't hear you. I'm sorry, I'm trying really hard." I pressed my ear against the phone with all my might. "Just speak a little slower."

"I...............................have.....................Lou Gehrig's disease. I am...............not gonna...................live too much............................longer, prob........ly not until........even.......tomorr...ow............. I wanted ....to say........good-bye." Between each breath and each effort to complete a sentence, I could tell he was trying not cry.

"Jimmy, where are you? I am coming to see you."

"You................are....................gonna see.........me?" He breathed heavily.

"Yes, I want to see you. I've been waiting for you to call. I've been going crazy wondering where you have been all this time. Why didn't you call me?" Then I realized I probably shouldn't be asking him anything that would require a long answer. "You don't have to talk now. I'll talk to you when I see you."

"You....................will.........................really........ ....come here? I.....have been............calling you ov..........er..........there at Ricky's, but...............the number..................... was dis...........connected."

"I'll tell you everything when I see you."

"I...............want   you..............to   talk...............to...my...............mother. Can you call......................back in...........30 min.....utes? She will give.........you the.....directions."

"Okay, thirty minutes."

"I ....love you baby."

"I love you too, Jimmy. I'll talk to you soon." I hung up the phone and quickly dialed my brother's number to ask him about Lou Gehrig's disease. My brother was a medical school resident and I figured he'd give me the answers I needed.

Lou Gehrig's disease attacked all the major muscle groups in one's body. The disease struck the victim's muscles in his arms and legs, slowly disabling them. Then it attacked the central nervous system and, finally, the victim's respiratory tract, making it impossible to draw a breath. After I described to my brother how short of breath Jimmy was and how slow he had to speak, he figured that Jimmy was in the final stages of the disease. And the final stages of his life.

Jimmy, one of the few people in my life who could keep me going when things got rough, was now staring death in the face. I had been waiting anxiously for him to surface so he could lift me out of the hole I'd dug for myself. But now he had called to say good-bye.

I started to cry. I buried my face in the pillow. *Why were all these horrible things happening to me? What have I done in my past that is making my life turn for the worst? Why does Jimmy have to die? He loved life. He loved everyone. Why isn't there a cure for this disease? Why didn't he tell me earlier?*

After I spoke with his mother, Jana suggested I drive her to work so that I could use her car to go to San Diego.

As I zoomed south on the 405, I thought of everything I wanted to say to him. I had never known anyone on their death bed, but I promised myself I'd remain strong. My brother warned me that he may not look the way he did the last time I saw of him. I knew I could get through the visit, but it was the last five minutes that I feared the most. *How was I going to say good-bye with both of us knowing that we'd never see each other again?*

When his mother led me into the room, at first, Jimmy was unaware I had arrived. He lay motionless staring at an NBA game. I stood by his side and watched him. The man who once filled up every room he entered with a jubilant and commanding presence was slumped before me, helpless and unable to breathe without the mechanical contraption that was perched next to him. His face, expressionless. His body, weak and fragile, was literally only skin and bones. A vision of Jimmy walking through the salon hit me like a brick. His laughter, his jokes, his taunting remarks about his clients. I could still hear the life in his voice. And now, as I stared down at him, my eyes filled with tears.

"Hi, Jimmy."

His empty eyes shifted up at me. The delicate smile that emerged from his hollow face was one of relief and happiness. When our eyes met, I felt his pain, his fear and the struggle I knew he had been fighting. I wanted to reach out and hug him and somehow, magically save his life. I didn't want him to die.

"You came," he whispered.

"Of course, I came. And I couldn't wait to come. I couldn't wait to see you, Jimmy. I have missed you so much."

"Hug me," he said. His smile was weak, yet compelling. I reached down to gently hug his frail body.

"I really missed you," I whispered in his ear.

"I am......... so.................... glad you................ came." He talked softly, each word requiring a great amount of effort.

"Me too."

"I am so ....glad." He stared at me as if he couldn't believe I was there. I smiled back. A silent moment passed between us as we continued to appreciate each other's presence. He motioned for me to come closer to him. I leaned down and put my ear near his mouth. "Look at.......... this. Can......................... you............................. believe this?" He glanced down at his bony body.

I shook my head slowly raising my eyebrows trying to keep my eyes dry. "No, I can't. I really can't"

"I'm............. sorry I didn't call........................... but I have....................... been having......................"

"Wait, I can't hear you."

He motioned for me to get the chair in the corner of the room. I grabbed it and brought it next to the bed. As I sat down, I leaned closer so my ear was only inches from his mouth. His lips were dry and chapped and the skin on his face was wrinkled because of the significant amount of weight he lost.

"Sorry........ it's.................... a little............................... hard for me to.............................. talk........................ I'm losing my.................... strength and.................... without....................... this thing I.......................... would not be able........................... to." He glanced at the machine that helped him breathe sitting on the floor next to me.

"It's okay. I'll do the talking."

"How have.................you been do.........ing?" he asked.

"Oh, God, Jimmy, everything has been crazy."

"I............................came to.......................the church."

"What?" I put my ear closer to his mouth.

"I came to.......................the church.................but nobody...................... was.....................there. For your.......wedding."

Again, my eyes felt damp.

"Yes.................................I had....................my mother drive ....me up.................there in…a……van. She.......had to come cause...............................I........................... ....have been......in a wheel ....chair." He breathed deeply. "But, no.................one was .... there."

"Jimmy, I'm so sorry you didn't get a cancellation. My parents sent out cancellations to everyone who received an invitation."

"I didn't know. .... What ....happened?

"He walked out on me three weeks before the wedding."

"When.........................my mother..........wheeled..........me in.......... ....the church...............................and.......it............... was empty......................................something felt................. strange, but....... .... I knew that................... you'd come................... I knew that...................... you'd be there...................... I knew Ricky wouldn't .... do anything............. like that. I............. thought..... .... maybe I................ was early." He started taking a deep breath between every few words. I worried he must be trying to talk too much.

The vision of Jimmy being wheeled by his mother into an *empty* church on my wedding day was just a little too much for me. I felt the tears building, but desperately tried not to cry. I reminded myself that given the situation that I was smack in the middle of, to cry over a stupid wedding that didn't happen would be selfish. I slowly shook my head and looked at Jimmy as I told him the whole story. While he listened, faint expressions of disbelief and anger clouded his gaunt, skinny face. I told him about the fight that sparked it all. I told him about my trip to Hawaii. I told him about Simone, his new teenaged girlfriend. "Since you went away, I haven't had anyone to talk to who would listen without judging me."

He smiled and slowly nodded. "Do.......... you... bee-leeeeeve ....?"

"In what?"

"The after life?"

"Yes, do you?"

"Yes. And.....................I'm… ready.................to.........start.................. my.................. next life. I am................. ready....... to go now........................ and I've................. been............asking Him to................come................. ....and git...................me."

My smile was half-hearted.

"I...................had.......................a...........good...life..Stef.................... but I'm ready.....................for another.............What I.............am ...... going ......through is.......not fun.........you know.................you know how much ....I loved my............life, but.....................it's awful.............to live..........like this." He stared at his body. He tried to reach out to grab my hand, but he didn't have the strength to lift his arm. "Stef, hold.....my.........hand."

I held his warm, but lifeless hand.

"Where's Felicia? Has she been with you through all this?"

"She's...............been gone."

I shook my head without saying a word.

"I......know. She.................was...........bad news................... Stef....

.................I should have listened...........to you. I was..................in love ....with her though. ......that was.......the problem...................... I couldn't........................break myself free.............of her."

"I know the feeling. It's hard to leave someone you love even though you know they aren't right for you. Even if they treat you like dirt, it's so hard to go. Trust me Jimmy, I know."

Two and a half hours had passed when his mother appeared at the doorway. "Time to eat." She was holding a bowl or fruit and some water.

Jimmy looked at me. "Will.................. you....... help me?"

"Of course." I turned to his mother and took the bowl and glass from her. After I helped Jimmy get half way through his lunch, his mother informed us that more of Jimmy's friends had arrived.

"I'll be leaving soon," I told her.

I didn't know how I was going to say good-bye. I didn't want to leave. I wanted to crawl up on the bed next to him and watch television with him for the rest of the day. For the rest of his life.

Fifteen minutes later, I knew I had to get going. A small line was forming in the living room and I began to feel a bit selfish. "Okay Jimmy, I better let the rest of your fan club come in and visit you."

"I......think.......it's some............. more of my old clients that I haven't seen. I felt bad .....at first not ......calling anyone, but....I was very embarrassed................... I didn't................... want........... anyone........... ....to see...................me in a...............wheelchair."

The dam of tears I'd held since I'd first walked in the room broke and streamed down my face as I leaned over to hug Jimmy. "You know my hair is shot to hell now, don't you?"

He smiled.

"I haven't been able to find anyone at all." I took off my baseball cap and pulled the elastic band out of my hair to show Jimmy how awful it looked.

"Cut it. Cut it...................all off."

"Uh-uh Jimmy, no way."

"Well promise me........................one..........thing."

"Okay."

"That you......you'll never........................go back with......Ricky."

I wiped my tears and hugged him again. "Okay, I promise."

"Life........... is too short to............. be taken for granted. Even...........for one day." And then he said, "I love you."

"I love you too, Jimmy."

"No Stefanie, really. I mean it. I really love you. You were always my favorite girl."

"I really love you, too, Jimmy. You are truly one of my most cherished friends."

"Stop..........crying. I'm happy that.........you came to.......see me..................Be happy."

I made a small, failed effort to interrupt my tears with a smile. "Call me tomorrow morning. Have your mother dial the number when you get up, okay?"

"Okay."

We smiled at each other as I walked out of the room.

I cried, non-stop, from the time I left San Diego until I pulled into the parking garage of the apartment in Los Angeles. I knew that was the last time I would ever see Jimmy.

CHAPTER THIRTY-THREE

The phone rang early the next morning. I hoped it was Jimmy. But it was the leasing agent from the Emerald Aisle apartments. She called to inform Jana, Marie and me that our application was accepted and upon execution of the lease, we could move in on or about the 1st of the month. I hung up the phone and breathed a sigh of relief. It was good to start off the day with good news. Marie and Jana had agreed to rent an apartment with me so I wouldn't have to brave the outrageous monthly rents of Los Angeles alone. I was on my way to getting my life back.

The phone rang. Maybe it was Jimmy this time. "Hello?"

"Is Stefanie Pointer there?" I tried to picture a face with the familiar voice, but I couldn't. And then it hit me. It was Michelle.

"Michelle?"

"Hi, Stefanie. I just wanted to call because I've been thinking a lot about you and wondering why we never talk anymore. I mean, come on, we were close there for a *minute.*" She sounded mechanical, almost as if she rehearsed what she was going to say before she called.

I let her ramble on. I needed time to prepare my rebuttal.

"We weren't just friends that meet and hang out for awhile. We were almost like sisters." She chuckled nervously. "As a matter of fact, we almost *were* sisters."

That's when I had to interject. She was going way too far. "Michelle?"

"Huh?"

"First and foremost, I want to say that had I married Ricky and you stayed with Keith, we would never have been sisters. A sister is family. And families are alike... at least *my* family is. You and I...we are different. There are no two likes about us. Our blood is different. Our ideas and beliefs are different. Our values are different."

"I knew you'd be upset with me."

"Upset? Naw, I'm not *upset* with you. I don't think you can truly be *upset* by people who are as malevolent as you are. It's more like I feel sorry for you."

"Stefanie, I didn't know that Ryan wasn't Keith's baby. So don't act like you've never slept with two guys at one time before."

"Come on Michelle. I can see right through women like you. I know your type. And I know them well. I know 'em because I've been having to fight them off my man for the past couple years."

"Stefanie, last time I heard, he wasn't your *man* anymore."

"Like I was saying, women like you don't give a damn about anyone else but yourselves. Tryin' to get paid, trying to get pregnant, wondering how much money you are going to get, how much..."

"Oh God, you're bitter."

"Bitter? I don't think *bitter* is the proper word to be using here. I think it's more like 'through'. I am *through* with people like you. People who come in and wreck other people's relationships without any regard or respect for anyone, even themselves."

She interrupted again, "I didn't wreck anyone's relationship."

"Well give yourself a frickin' award then 'cause you did worse. You wrecked one good man's faith in women. Black women that is. Women like you give women like me a bad name. And what about Keith? Do you think he'll ever be able to have a normal relationship ever again? I'm quite sure he won't."

"Now I'm sorry I spent the morning trying to track down your phone number."

"What did you use Michelle... a turkey baster?"

"Bitter people always like to blame others for their shortcomings. You need to be blaming Ricky. So what would you rather be, Stefanie? Smart and sneaky or dumb and dependent?" Click.

Dial tone.

I hated her.

The phone rang as soon as I put it down. "Hello?"

"Stef? It's Tiff. What up?"

"You don't even wanna know."

"More Ricky shit?"

"No." I didn't even have the energy to tell her about Michelle's call. "He hasn't called since I FedExed him the ring back. I guess the roller coaster ride is over."

Tiffany laughed. "That's a $25,000 dollar tax write off you could've used if you kept it, sold it and given the money to charity."

"Charity? Shoot, I *am* a charity."

"Not for long. You'll get it together. And if you need another reason to justify why it's imperative that you never look back, I'll give you one. You know he had the nerve, the audacity to tell Malik he is coming out to here to visit us after the season."

"So?"

"With some girl."

The air in my lungs collapsed as if I just dropped twenty stories on a ride at Six Flags. Maybe the roller coaster ride wasn't over. For Ricky to have moved on so quickly was one thing, but for him to be mixing his new girlfriends in with my friends was just wrong. "What?! Who? Is her name Simone?"

"No, some girl named May. Some broad he brought out here to a pre-season game when he played Malik's team."

"What? You didn't tell me he brought someone out there?"

"I didn't want to tell you because it was so soon after you guys had broken up. I didn't wanna make you sicker than you already were over his no good ass."

I didn't know whether to be pissed at Tiffany or to be grateful that she was watching out for my feelings.

She continued, "Do you know Ricky forgot to reserve her a ticket? So that heffer had to sit next to me. And girl, she is such a groupie. She thought I was cool, you know, from her camp. She was talkin' all this la la about how she used to mess with Spider Daniels, you know that fool, right? He plays in the NBA."

"Yeah, heard of him."

"Well, apparently Spider dumped her on her ass and she's over here bitchin' to me about how it was hard to start dating Ricky at first because leaving the NBA for the NFL made it so she had to take a pay cut because football players don't make as much as basketball players."

"Please tell me that there is not a woman on this earth that would say something so ridiculous."

"She said it. And then she was telling me that she wasn't worried 'cause Ricky was gonna sign a big ass contract before next season. I told Malik to warn Ricky to get rid of her before he ends up takin' care of someone else's baby thinkin' it's his. Like his big brother."

"No. You need to let his ass get burned." I sighed. "And you know he's also seeing some trick named Simone." I tried to laugh, but couldn't.

"Oh really? Hmmm. I wonder if May and Simone know about each other."

"Please, knowing Ricky...they probably *fuck* each other."

"Apparently Jaylin's woman told me that Ricky had met this May girl even before you and him broke it off."

"I'm sick, Tiffany. I don't want to hear anymore, okay?"

"Well now you have one more reason to burn up all his pictures."

"Yeah, let me go and do that right now."

"Wait. So what else is up? Did you sign up for the G.R.E.?"

"I signed up for the G.R.E., did good, got into UC Irvine Masters in Education program and start in four months."

"Shut up! When did you do all that?"

"Long time ago, I just never told you. I was tired of your mouth," I teased. "So I decided to just do my thing without having you and Marie and Jana on my back all the time."

"Stef! That is so good. I'm so happy for you. Forget Ricky. See, you got your stuff together just in the nick of time. How have you been getting around L.A.? Did you get a car?"

"No. I'm using public transportation. Every time I ride that damn bus I think about Ricky and how he just threw me away and moved on. Now I keep hearing from people about how he's doing really well and how he may make the Pro-Bowl in the next couple of years and how he is about to sign a fat contract and all this stuff. And here I am riding the damn bus."

"Stef. Mark my words. He will never make the Pro-Bowl."

"How do you know?"

"Don't forget that's all Ricky ever talked about. That was his ultimate goal in life."

"So how do you know he'll never make it?"

"Because he thought he could slap you around Stefanie and get away with it. That is just wrong. Nigro thinkin' he's Ike and you're Tina. He can't get away with that. Is he crazy? And also because he *still* is not living an authentic life. He has multiple girlfriends with no regard for anyone's feelings. He's having threesomes, he's going to strip clubs, leaving random nasty ass panties in his dryer, watching porn… Stefanie, come on, there has GOT to be a price that's associated with being a fool."

I couldn't help but laugh. "Tiffany, you really hate Ricky, huh?"

"Ever since I heard that he hit you, yes, I do."

"Well, not to defend him, but he only hit me one time and I'm sure it was an isolated incident."

"I still hate him."

I laughed some more. "I hate him too."

CHAPTER THIRTY-FOUR

Maxine lifted Dante Jr. out of the tub and wrapped a baby blue hooded towel around him. "Mommy loves you so much," she whispered in his ear.

"Ba-ba," he gurgled.

"Okay, I'll get you a bottle as soon as we put on your pajamas. It's almost dinner time and daddy will be home any minute." After Maxine had dried him off, he took off running across the floor. "Get over here, you little naked boy," she said, laughing at the sight of his cute tiny body and noticing how much he was already a mini replica of her husband.

When little Dante was born, the three of them became inseparable. "I knew one day you'd come around. I just didn't know it would take a baby to settle your fast ass down," Maxine had told him. Dante's love for his wife had finally emerged to the point where he was able to recognize the value of a woman who loved him unreservedly. No more getting home late because he was supposedly watching films at the practice facility. No more week-long golf trips. No more hiding his credit card statements. No more mysterious women calling the house claiming they're calling on a business related issue. Although it was a rough and rocky road, and although she knew anything could happen especially because Dante was still in the league, Maxine hoped that the worst was over.

"Git your little booty over here, Dante," Maxine demanded playfully as she watched her son hurry around like a miniature half-back.

"Ma-ma."

The doorbell rang.

"Come on, Dante. That's probably daddy. He probably forgot the gate clicker again. Come. Hurry up. We have to go let daddy in the gate." Quicker than usual, she slapped a diaper on him, wrapped him in a blanket and walked down the wide spiral staircase.

"Honey?" she said as she pushed the talk button on the intercom wired to the front iron gate. "Honey?" she yelled loudly. She pressed the "listen" button, but didn't hear anything. "Dante? Is that you?"

No answer.

"No, actually it's Michelle, an old friend of your sister-in-law."

"Huh?" Maxine wasn't sure she heard right.

"It's Michelle DeVeaux," Michelle, speaking up, said clearly into the box that sat atop a metal post at the gate. "I'm a close friend of Cindy, your sister-in-law."

"And?" Maxine's voice soured.

"I'm new here in California and she thought I should call you. But I happened to be in your neighborhood so I wanted to stop by and introduce myself."

Maxine looked at the intercom box as if it were actually a person. She arched her right eyebrow, not trusting the unseen visitor.

"Now *who* exactly are you?"

"I met you before at a football game last year. My husband is Keith Powers, well, my ex-husband. He plays for Kansas City. He walked out on me so I moved out here to California to start fresh. I don't have any friends here and Cindy suggested I call you." Her voice was filled with desperation.

"Oh okay, I see."

Michelle was relieved that Maxine's response was suddenly filled with sympathy. "I know it's strange for me to be just popping up and I'll understand if you don't want to open the door. I guess I should've called."

"No. No, I'm sorry. It's just that there are a lot of crazy people around here. That's all. You just have to be careful these days. Hold on a second." Maxine pressed the open button, walked out the front door and watched Michelle pull up the driveway. While she stood on the porch with Dante on her hip, she shot Michelle a fake, uncomfortable smile. She pointed to the basketball hoop, directing Michelle to park beneath it. That way Dante would have enough room to park in his preferred space, especially since he would be home any minute.

When Michelle opened the back door to unbuckle Ryan from his car seat, Maxine realized that she had met Michelle and her son at one of Dante's games. She fixed her eyes on Ryan. *That beautiful baby,* Maxine thought. *How could I have forgotten? This girl was with Ricky Power's girlfriend. She's probably desperate for friends or needs help finding a new man. I'll offer her a glass of wine and then send her on her way.*

Maxine was used to other women trying to gain her friendship. She knew their efforts weren't genuine, only hoping to weasel an introduction to one of Dante's teammates.

"Actually, I do remember meeting you. You came to a game with Ricky Power's fiancée."

"Ex-fiancée."

"Fiancée, ex-fiancée whatever. People break up and get back together all the time in our world. You never know. We may see her sittin' in the stands at the next game," Maxine laughed. "I've counted out girls before and years later, I mean years later, they pop up like nothin' ever happened."

Michelle surveyed the front yard. It seemed like centuries ago that she'd pulled up with Dante in this very driveway on their first night out together. She wondered where Maxine was that night.

Maxine reached over and gently pinched Ryan's cheek. "And how could I forget this cute little face? Wow! Aren't you gonna be the lady killer when you grow up. You handsome little devil you." The women exchanged a phony laugh as Michelle and Ryan followed Maxine and little Dante into the house.

"This is Dante. Say hi, Dante." Maxine put him on the floor and watched him run ahead into the family room and head straight for his giant toy box. Ryan struggled to get out of Michelle's arms so he could follow Dante. "So, what brings you here? Actually, what I want to know is how did you find this place? I know Cindy may have given you the address and the phone number... but wow... most of our close friends can't even find us up in this forest."

Michelle maintained eye contact with Maxine, but her thoughts drifted from the conversation as she starting to regret her purpose for being there. She was about to throw a bombshell right in the middle of Maxine's happy little day. Michelle thought maybe she better just leave Maxine out of it. But when little Dante ran back in the room to grab the viewfinder he'd left on the floor, she decided to stick to her original plan. It wasn't fair that Maxine and her baby got to live in such a palatial estate while she had to live at home with her mother. *Mrs. Williams and her perfect little life. I deserve this, too,* Michelle thought.

"Would you like something to drink?"

"No thanks."

Maxine grabbed a bottle of water from the refrigerator and Michelle sat at the table in the kitchen nook in front of a floor-to-ceiling glass wall overlooking a black-bottom pool with a full-sized tennis court behind.

Maxine joined Michelle at the table. "The boys must be in there playing nicely, I haven't heard a peep."

"Yeah, I'm sure they're in there having a good ol' time," Michelle replied. *After all, Ryan is his half-brother,* she thought.

"Little Dante is learning to share and let others play with his toys. He has a playgroup twice a week. I stay with him of course, but……."

Michelle wanted to stop this woman before there was any possibility of a friendship developing. "Uh Maxine, I don't mean to interrupt, but there is something we need to talk about."

Maxine wrinkled her brow. Her happy-go-lucky Friday afternoon mood shifted to one of caution. "And what exactly would that *something* be?"

"Well, it's very difficult for me to say what I'm about to say and part of me has been hesitant to even say anything at all. But...it's the only thing left for me to do."

"What? What is it?" Maxine's eyes became desperate.

"Oh God, Maxine, I feel terrible telling you something that may shock the hell out of you, but then again, it may not. You know with Dante's extracurricular activities and all, you may not even be surprised."

Now Maxine's eyes grew hard. She knew. She knew that whatever it was that this stranger was about to tell her, it was going to be horrifying. She continued her ice, cold stare into Michelle's eyes.

"Maxine, my son Ryan, he..." she hesitated. "He is... his father is... Dante is his father." Michelle took a deep breath.

Maxine was paralyzed.

"Wait. Before you go into a panic, you have to realize that I didn't even know Dante was married and I didn't even...I went to Dante first and asked him...to help me support...I asked him to..." The anger in Maxine's eyes forced Michelle to stop trying to explain herself. There was no need to go on.

Maxine jumped out of her chair and ran into the family room. Dante was pushing Ryan in a monster buggy around the massive play area. Both boys smiled up at Maxine when she entered the room. She leaned down and pulled Ryan out of the toy car. She lifted him up and brought him close. His legs dangled in the air as he stared back. "Oh my God," she whispered. She put him down and slowly walked back into the kitchen.

"GET OUT OF MY HOUSE! YOU AND YOUR BABY. GET OUT! ALL OF YOU JUST GET OUT!" Maxine was hysterical. Her lips were trembling and she felt faint. "GET OUT!"

Michelle jumped at her sharp words.

As Maxine continued to yell for Michelle to leave, they both heard a key in the front door. Then Dante appeared. "Max? What the hell is going on?" He could see that his wife was the color of death. And then he saw Michelle. His eyes shifted between his wife and his nightmare. "What is going on here?" he asked calmly, trying to maintain his composure. Before he could ask again, Michelle quickly disappeared, grabbed Ryan and hurriedly walked toward the front door. Dante used his body to block her exit.

Nervously, Michelle spoke, "Hi Dante. I thought I would bring your son over to play with his brother. But Maxine, excuse me *Max, as you call her*, wasn't too thrilled that Dante junior has a brother."

Dante raised his hand. He gritted his teeth, his raised arm shaking and then stopped in mid-swing. "YOU ARE ONE CRAZY BITCH!"

"My check better be in the mail, Dante. Oh, let me give you my address," Michelle said. "Do you have a pen?" Her grin was wide and evil.

"THAT'S IT. I'M CALLING THE COPS! I'll get your ass for trespassing." Dante turned to Maxine who stood in the background, still in shock. "Why did you let this looney tune in the house?"

Before Dante could reach the phone, Michelle scooped up Ryan and slipped out the door.

CHAPTER THIRTY-FIVE

As Marie and I patiently waited in the airport for Tiffany to arrive, I realized how long it had been since we had spent any time together. She was in her final year of medical school and traveling to Los Angeles for a residency interview at Cedars Sinai Medical Hospital. I had missed her terribly and tried to keep our friendship close through telephone calls and emails, but it just wasn't the same. I missed her discordant opinions, her often happy-go-lucky attitude and her confident and sometimes cocky temperament.

Marie and Jana waited with me, but had found a seat on a bench near the baggage claim carousel. I watched them from a short distance talk on their cell phones, probably to their boyfriends, and wondered if they ever grew tired of my unpredictable mood swings and sometimes depressing presence. But something told me that they weren't. And that, I believed, was the true meaning of friendship.

Impatient and wondering if Tiffany's plane had even landed yet, they trekked toward me and stood in the path of on comers.

"Thanks," I said to them.

"Thanks for what? Marie asked.

"Thanks for always listening to me and for always being there for me.

I couldn't have got through all this without you two. If I didn't have you as my friends, I'd have ended up at home having to live with my father's I-told-you-so smirk for the rest of my life."

"Hey now!" Tiffany yelled as she rode down the escalator toward us.

After Tiffany practically dog-piled us, we hugged and complimented each other on our clothes and hair styles. We walked to baggage claim and waited for her luggage to appear on the carousel.

"So," Tiffany said to Marie and Jana. "Has it been hell living with this pitiful soul?" Tiffany looked at me teasingly.

"No, she's actually been strong given the circumstances," said Jana. "If my boyfriend did that to me, I'd have been somewhere in a padded cell in a psych ward with a straight jacket on talking to the voices in my head."

I laughed at the vision, knowing that it wasn't too far from the truth of where I'd been only a few months ago.

"You hungry?" Tiffany asked.

All three of us nodded.

"It's been over a year since I've got to eat some of Roscoe's chicken and waffles so if I get to choose where we eat, that's where *I'm* going," Tiffany said, still searching for her luggage.

Jana and Marie glanced at me to see if I would object. "Yeah, that's cool with me," I said.

Tiffany grabbed her suitcase off the carousel and smiled my way.

We piled into Marie's car and headed straight down La Cienega until we got to Pico where Marie made a quick right. When we pulled into the parking lot, I noticed an old white Benz that resembled the one Michelle used to borrow from her mother. To prevent Tiffany from getting all wound up for nothing, I didn't say anything. If she was inside, I'd deal with it then.

The moment I walked into the restaurant, I spotted her. Michelle was sitting in a booth cuddled next to a man whose face was familiar, but that

I couldn't place. Since I wasn't in the mood for any drama, I decided not to point her out. I made it half way through our meal before I broke down and surrendered to the natural female urge to stir things up. "Okay now don't get all crazy, but guess who is sitting in front at one of the tables?"

"Who?" Marie asked.

"Michelle."

"Michelle-the-skeezer-DeVeaux?" Tiffany said.

"Yep."

"And you are just *now* saying something?" Tiffany said.

"I see her." Jana added. "And she is with some foine ass somethin' somethin'."

"I have *got* to say something to that bimbo," Tiffany decided.

"Like what?" Marie asked, laughing at the impending drama.

Tiffany got up. "I'm just gonna walk up there and start talking like I'm glad to see her, I guess."

As Tiffany walked through the restaurant, her eyes darted around the front seating section searching for Michelle. She quickly noticed a girl from the back with a cascade of honey brown ringlets that flowed to the middle of her back. She edged around to get a better view.

Loudly, Tiffany exclaimed, "Hey Michelle. Fancy meeting you here! How are you?!"

Marie, Jana and I heard her from the other side of the restaurant. We laughed but didn't let the priceless entertainment keep us from eating our waffles.

Without even a "hello" from Michelle or an invitation to sit down, Tiffany scooted into the empty side of the booth. She glanced at the strikingly handsome man sharing the table with her.

"Whoa, what a surprise," Michelle finally said.

"Yeah, Stefanie said she saw you as we walked in so I wanted to come over and say hello. See what new things you got going in your life." Tiffany turned dramatically to Michelle's male companion.

"Oh," Michelle's voice quivered. "Well nothing really, nothing at all."

"And you must be 'nothing'," Tiffany said keeping her attention on Michelle's date.

"Oh, I'm sorry. This is Michael. Michael Sinclair. Michael, this is Tiffany."

"Oh, hi, Michael. Nice to meet you."

"Likewise," he muttered.

"And who is it that you play for?" Tiffany asked matter-of-factly.

Shoving what seemed like half of a waffle into his mouth, Michael spoke, "Excuse me?"

"Which team do you play for? I mean surely you play for someone. The NFL. NBA. I don't know, shoot, at the rate Michelle moves, you probably play Major League Baseball." Tiffany laughed at her own joke.

"He *doesn't* play anything, actually!" Michelle answered, embarrassed. Her anger simmered in her eyes.

"Oh, how unusual for you."

Michelle hadn't yet told Michael she had a one year old son. Before Michelle could think of something clever enough to get Tiffany to excuse herself, Tiffany said, "So, how do you like being back in California? I bet you missed it, didn't you?"

"Yeah, I did. I missed the weather the most."

"Where are you living now?"

"Back with Adrienne."

"Adrienne?"

"My mother." Michelle summoned their waiter as he flew by. "Excuse me. Can we get the check, please?"

The waiter nodded.

Michael interjected, "Wait baby, they never brought me my greens."

"It's okay. I'll make you some greens."

"So where do you live?" Tiffany asked Michael.

"On Wilshire," he replied.

"He lives on the corridor," Michelle crowed, hoping that the conversation would stay on Michael until the waiter brought the bill.

"Oh, the corridor. Well, well, well. And what might you do for a living?"

Again, Michelle answered, "You ever heard of Michael Sinclair?"

Tiffany nodded.

"Voila!" Michelle exclaimed.

Tiffany's eyes widened "Oh, you're him?"

Michael nodded.

"That's him," Michelle said, proudly.

"Oh," Tiffany said. Then she paused, nodding her head slowly. She looked back and forth between them. "I see."

Michelle continued to grin, hoping Tiffany would disappear.

"How's Ryan?" Tiffany asked.

Michelle gasped "He's fine." She *had* to change the subject. "How's Stefanie?"

Tiffany had never seen the color seep out of anyone's face so quickly. She noticed Michelle's reluctance to talk about her son. "Stefanie's good. She's right over there. So, Michael, have you met her son, Ryan? He's adorable. Looks *just like* his daddy…"

Michael was perplexed. He dropped his fork and turned to Michelle. "Who's Ryan?" he asked.

Tiffany smiled brightly and said, "Oh goodness, my food is probably cold by now. Gotta go. Kiss the baby for me. Ciao. Oh, nice meeting you, Michael. Good luck with your career."

Before Michelle could even think of a credible excuse for not telling

Michael about her son, Tiffany was gone. Just like that. Came in and left like a damn hurricane obliterating everything in its path.

"What son?" Michael asked, his brow deeply creased.

"My son. His name is Ryan."

The waiter placed the check on the table. "You can pay at the front."

"Why didn't you tell me?"

"I don't know."

"You lie so damn much, Michelle. I thought you'd have outgrown that by now."

"I wasn't lying, Michael. I just was scared to tell you right away."

"Right away? Please. That's not something you hide from anyone for *any* amount of time. And how did Keith let you just leave Kansas City with his son. Does he ever see him?"

"Well, most of the time Adrienne has him but Keith sends for him sometimes. He's too young to get on the plane by himself so he hasn't sent for him yet," Michelle said realizing that she was talking in circles.

"I thought you just said that Keith sends for him sometimes. Does he or doesn't he?"

Michelle decided she better not tell anymore lies. She better not jeopardize her relationship with Michael any further. If she told him the truth, he'd respect that. No matter how ridiculous it was going to sound. She held her breath. "Ryan's not Keith's son."

Michael took a deep breath and leaned his body all the way back in the booth.

Her face begged for empathy. "It's someone else's." *Oh God, that sounded awful,* she thought. She tried to cover her tracks. "Before I was with Keith I met someone and thought I was in love. And accidentally, I came up pregnant."

"So Keith was willing to accept your son?"

Tell the truth, she told herself. "Well, no. It wasn't quite like that. You see, Keith thought it was his son. Actually, so did I." Michelle hung her head in embarrassment. "Keith married me because he thought he was the one who got me pregnant."

Michael stared at Michelle and asked himself what on earth he was doing at the same table with this woman. Her beauty was dissolving with every word. As she continued, Michael saw her transform into all the other women he had been dealing with since Michelle had left. Just like all the rest. Another pretty face with a hidden agenda. His immediate reaction was to get up from the table and leave her with the tab, but first he had to hear her pathetic story. He wanted to hear about the other suckers who'd fallen to her charm.

"We didn't find out it wasn't Keith's baby until the baby got sick and needed blood for an operation. At first Keith was going to forgive me, but when he found out it was Dante's baby he asked me to leave. None of this matters anyway Michael. You're the one I have always loved. Really, Michael, that's the truth."

"Who's Dante?" Michael wanted to know more. He was becoming amused by her sheer gall and stupidity.

"Dante Williams."

"Dante Williams? The Dante Williams?"

Michelle nodded. "He's really not all that, though."

"Apparently you thought he was."

"Whatever. What are you gonna do, kick me out of your life too, just because I have a son?"

"No, not because you have a son, but because you are just like all the rest, Michelle. Just looking to git paid 'cause you're too damn sorry to take care of yourself."

Michael pulled out his wallet, pulled out two twenties, then changed his mind. He stuffed the cash in his pocket and squeezed his way over her and out of the booth. "I'm outta here."

"Michael wait! Why are you trippin?" Michelle pleaded.

And that's when we passed her table on our way out, just in time to see her fumbling through her purse to find enough money to settle the bill. Tiffany stopped by her table and stared down at her. "You need to borrow a few dollars?" Tiffany asked.

"Fuck you Tiffany," was all Michelle could say.

The three of us couldn't help but let go of an electrifying bolt of laughter that echoed throughout the restaurant and straight into Michelle's ears.

CHAPTER THIRTY-SIX

I stretched out on the chaise-lounge next to the pool at my apartment and realized that a whole year already passed since the day I was supposed to marry Ricky. I wondered what we would've been doing to celebrate our first year anniversary. I waited for the waves of nausea to hit my stomach as they often did when I thought about him. I waited for the thoughts about how wonderful my life would've been if we stayed together to hit me hard in the heart. But surprisingly, this time, I was thankful that we weren't together. I was free from the world he'd pulled me in to. My brain finally took charge of my emotions and allowed me to reconcile all that was lost. The five years I spent with Ricky were becoming a part of my past that I was ready to leave behind.

The mailman walked through the front gate and grumbled a quick, "How are you today?"

"I'm doing good, you?"

He smiled and nodded.

I heard the window above my head slide open. "Hey girl," Jana said, sticking her head out from our kitchen. "Come on, get up. Roll with us to Home Depot. Marie and I are gonna get some flowers to plant and put out on the balcony."

"No thanks. I have to catch the bus up to campus. I've gotta study."

Marie popped her head out of the window. "You can study when we get back."

"No, I think I'm just gonna go up to campus and get it over with. Plus I'm gonna see a career counselor so that they can help me make some sense out of my life."

"How is a *career* counselor gonna help you make sense out of your *life?*"

"Part of the Masters program requires that we tour some of the schools in South Central before we start student teaching and after a few of those episodes, now I'm wondering if I picked the right career. Those kids out there are no joke."

Marie jumped off the kitchen counter and appeared by my side a minute later. "Okay listen. I've got it all figured out for you. I think you should stay in the program at Irvine, but you should also take some time and write a novel."

"About what?"

"The last five years of your life. You're a good writer Stef. All those love letters you wrote to Ricky. And all the letters we asked you to write for us to our boyfriends! You could do it. I know you could."

"Writing a simple love letter is a little bit different than writing a book."

"Think about it. Think about it while you ride that stinky ass bus up to campus."

I sat in the first row of seats on West L.A.'s Big Blue Bus and stared out of the window as it crept up Westwood Boulevard. I didn't think about writing a book. Instead I thought about the fact that I hadn't stepped foot on UCLA's campus since I graduated and how it may be a bit awkward. The bus trailed past Jimmy's old salon as we entered Westwood Village. I thought how great it would be if I was able to just pop in and see his smiling face.

I walked through the cement pathways of the college and admired the European-influenced architecture trying to push away the memories. Memories of Ricky and me holding hands, walking to class, chillin' on the freshly manicured green grass together, talking, kissing. Memories of this place we met. The campus where we built our dreams together. It was an eerie feeling to be there again.

My time with the career counselor was short. She didn't do much but shove a bunch of Teach America, Inc. brochures in my hand and send me on my way. Afterwards, I went to the University Research Library to study for a few hours.

I wanted to get on the bus before the sun went down to avoid the crazies, so I made my way to the intersection of Westwood and Weyburn. *Where's the damn bus?* I asked myself, trying to pretend it wasn't cold outside. I looked down and noticed that my arms were covered with goose bumps and realized that I should've worn a pair of shoes instead of flip-flops. Then I thought about all the pairs of heels that Ricky bought me over the years and thought maybe I should sell them. I could probably make enough money to buy a car! I thought maybe I should sell the diamond watch and earrings, and the tennis bracelet too. Something about walking around dripping in diamonds while I had a negative balance in my checking account didn't seem quite right.

Even though there were a few times when I almost slipped into believing that material items such as luxury cars, precious gems and designer clothes brought happiness to my life, after Ricky and I broke up, I stepped back into myself and realized I'm just a simple person who just needs the basics in life. I looked at what I'd thrown on my body before I left home that day. A t-shirt from Urban Outfitters, a pair of Abercrombie and Fitch jeans, an Oakley backpack and my flip-flops, courtesy of Roxy. I smiled at the comfort my old rags provided me.

I looked up the boulevard. Still no bus.

Then I saw it.

No, not the bus. But instead, a brand new black Mercedes Benz station wagon sitting at the light. It purred like a black panther ready to pounce. Waiting for the light to turn green, the woman driving sat high in her seat. She glanced over at me, looked right through me and into the shoe store behind me. Her long curly hair flowed between the leather headrest of her seat and her back. Her skin was flawless. She stared into space as if she didn't have too much on her mind. Her hands rested on the steering wheel, decorated in rings and bracelets, an exorbitant diamond sparkled in the sunlight. I wondered who her husband was. Where she was going or coming from. If she even worked and how she managed to be so comfortable in life at such a young age. I wondered if it was she or her husband that wanted those ridiculously flashy rims that glistened in the evening light, rims that you'd see in a hip-hop music video.

I stared at her and kept wondering. She was anxious for the light to turn as she fidgeted with her hair. She looked around inside her car and started playing with a pinwheel she found on the seat beside her. She blew it and watched it spin. She blew it again. I watched her and wondered if she was making a wish.

And then as the light turned green, the shiny black car pulled across the intersection in slow motion. The personalized license plate brought me off the bench. R E D B O N E.

And then it all made sense.

No wonder Ricky's name had mysteriously dropped from all conversations between me and my girlfriends. Even though I had urged them to stop discussing his business with me, they had continued… until recently.

They probably feared what I would do if I found out he married another.

As I watched Simone zoom off, I realized I didn't hate her. I didn't envy her. I was actually glad that it was her navigating the shiny Mercedes with the loud rims and that I was nothing but a passenger on public transportation. I hated that he had replaced me in such a short time, when I had waited for what had seemed like forever, but I knew what was in her future. I knew that although her life appeared to be so glamorous and mine so cheerless, that in actuality, my simple life would suit me fine.

I thought about the fact that she got to crawl in bed with him every night and that I crawled into bed alone. But I decided that being alone in bed with a pint of Ben and Jerry's would be better than being in bed with Ricky begging me for a threesome. I thought about her sitting in *my seat* at the games from now on and me watching Sunday football on my ancient Zenith nineteenth inch television set and smiled. But that was okay because I didn't have to get my hair done and dress the part anymore. I could put on my sweats and enjoy the game in the privacy of my own home without wondering if Ricky had one of his "girlfriends" up in the stands nearby.

I felt as if I was free. Free from the concealed pain and unhappiness I endured for all those years. From the emptiness. From my insecurities that had limited my personal growth. It was as if someone else had stepped out of my body at that very moment and let me go back to me. I was free. Free to be me.

It was her turn now, and I wished her all the luck in the world. She certainly was going to need it.

Printed in the United States
92973LV00003B/100-315/A